H.M.S. Hannibal at Palermo and Naples

During the Italian Revolution, 1859-1861

SALZWASSER
VERLAG

Rodney Mundy

H.M.S. Hannibal at Palermo and Naples

During the Italian Revolution, 1859-1861

Reprint of the original, first published in 1863.

1st Edition 2022 | ISBN: 978-3-37500-702-7

Verlag (Publisher): Salzwasser Verlag GmbH, Zeilweg 44, 60439 Frankfurt, Deutschland
Vertretungsberechtigt (Authorized to represent): E. Roepke, Zeilweg 44, 60439 Frankfurt, Deutschland
Druck (Print): Books on Demand GmbH, In de Tarpen 42, 22848 Norderstedt, Deutschland

H.M.S. "HANNIBAL"

AT

PALERMO AND NAPLES,

DURING THE

ITALIAN REVOLUTION, 1859—1861.

WITH NOTICES OF

GARIBALDI, FRANCIS II., AND VICTOR EMANUEL.

LONDON

1863.

CONTENTS.

CHAPTER I.

1859.

PAGE

Introductory Historical Sketch.—Appointment to the Mediterranean Station.—Arrival at Malta.—Mission to Egypt.—Cruise on the Coast of Sicily 1

CHAPTER II.

Messina.—Unfriendly Officials.—Syracuse.—Prince Castelcicala.—Imposing Force of the Squadron.—Visit to Marshal Rodriguez.—Panic among Officials.—Great Delight of Visitors to the Ships.—Return Visit of the Governor 10

CHAPTER III.

Catania.—Visit of Prince Fitalia.—Mr. Jeans, the Vice-Consul.—Reception of the Nobility on Board.—Sudden Storm, and Abrupt Termination of the Fête.—The *Victor Emanuel*.—Unfounded Charge of enticing away the principal Band from the City 23

CHAPTER IV.

Return to Syracuse for Supplies.—Reggio.—Man Overboard.—Stromboli.—Terrific Squalls 38

CHAPTER V.

The Gulf of Spezia.—Site for first-class Arsenal.—Description of the Fortifications.—Cavaliere Tholozano.—Mr. Charles Lever.—Organization of the Police 46

CHAPTER VI.

PAGE

Malta.—Signor Carafa.—Corfu.—Visit of Sir Henry Storks.—Austrian Merchant Ship saved from Fire.—Procession of Saint Spiridione.—Visit of the Archbishop.—Prince Alfred.—Paper Hunt.—Opening of the Parliament.—Sporting Excursion in Albania.—Good Feeling of the Gentry 57

CHAPTER VII.

1860.

Departure from Corfu.—Gibraltar.—Termination of the Spanish-Morocco War.—Mr. Drummond Hay.—Return to Malta.—Impending Disturbances in Southern Italy . 68

CHAPTER VIII.

Landing of Garibaldi at Marsala.—Departure for Palermo.—My Instructions.—General Salzano's Letter to Mr. Goodwin.—Measures for the Protection of Foreigners.—Visit to General Lanza.—Austrian Squadron.—Authentic Account of Garibaldi's Movements.—Interview with the Principal Merchants 73

CHAPTER IX.

Palermo.—Restoration of Arms to British Subjects.—General Lanza's Proposal of Intervention.—Garibaldi's Approach.—Celebration of Her Majesty's Birthday.—Endeavours to Prevent a Bombardment 92

CHAPTER X.

Palermo.—Excursion in the Neighbourhood.—Narrow Escape.—Misilmeri.—Impending Attack on the City.—Insurrection.—Bombardment.—Entry of Garibaldi.—Mr. Goodwin's Courage.—Refugees on Board.—Bombardment resumed 104

CHAPTER XI.

PAGE

Palermo.—Escape of Political Prisoners.—Captain Cossovich. — My Intervention solicited. — Visit from Commanders of French and American Ships. — Lieut. Wilmot's Interview with Garibaldi. — Effects of the Bombardment on the City 116

CHAPTER XII.

Palermo.—Reinforcement of the Royal Troops.—Proposal for my acting as Mediator renewed.—The Bombardment resumed. — Narrow Escape of the British Consul. — Humiliating Position of the Royal Commissioner.—Preparations for the Conference 133

CHAPTER XIII.

Palermo. — Arrival of Generals Garibaldi, Letizia, and Chretien on Board.—Violent Conduct of General Letizia. — Articles of the Proposed Convention. — Armistice agreed to 147

CHAPTER XIV.

Palermo.—Preparation for Renewal of Hostilities.—Extension of the Armistice.—Departure of General Letizia for Naples. — Visit to the City. — Frightful Results of the Bombardment. — Captain Vacca. — Murder of Police. — Interview between Generals Letizia and Garibaldi. — Battle at Catania 160

CHAPTER XV.

Palermo.—Evacuation of the City by the Royal Troops.—Return of Refugees to the Shore. — Excursion to the Camps.—Animating Scene in the Bay.—Narrow Escape of the Austrian Commodore.—Farewell Visit of General Lanza.—Celebration of Her Majesty's Accession.—Garibaldi's Visit to the Ships 170

CHAPTER XVI.

PAGE

Palermo.—Interview with Garibaldi.—Royalist Refugees on Board.—Proclamation of a Constitution.—Arrival of French Volunteers. — The Dictator and La Farina. — Unsatisfactory State of the Island.—Visit to Garibaldi.— His Farewell Letter.—My Answer.—Sail for Naples . 185

CHAPTER XVII.

Naples.—The Prince of Syracuse.—Admiral de Tinan.— Overtures from Neapolitan Naval Officers.—Audience of the King. — Riot in the City. — Insult to the French Admiral and British Consul. — Prince Luigi and the British Sailors on Shore.—Captain Flores in a New Character.—The National Guard 198

CHAPTER XVIII.

Naples. — Battle of Melazzo. — Visit of the Lord High Admiral.—Admiral Persano.—Arrest of Prince Luigi.— Naples in a State of Siège.—Celebration of the Fête-Days of the Emperor Napoleon and the Emperor of Austria.— The French and English Squadrons. — The Marquis Villamarina.—Foreign Refugees on Board.—Landing of Garibaldi at Melito.—Visit of Alexandre Dumas . . 212

CHAPTER XIX.

Naples. — Fête-Day of His Royal Highness the Prince Consort. — Magnificent Naval Spectacle. — Seizure of the *Orwell*. — Advance of Garibaldi. — The French Minister.—Signors Pilotti and Settembrini . . . 220

CHAPTER XX.

Evacuation of Salerno.—Preparations for the King's Departure.—His Proclamation.—Flight of the King to Gaeta. —Deputation to Garibaldi.—Measures for the Protection of the British and French Legations 230

CHAPTER XXI.

PAGE

Naples.—Entry of Garibaldi.—His further Projects.—Great Rejoicings of the Populace.—Interview with the Dictator.—Arrival of Piedmontese Reinforcements.—Garibaldi's Departure for Sicily.—Invasion of the Roman States by General Cialdini.—Saint Januarius . . . 237

CHAPTER XXII.

Naples.—Address of the Dictator.—Great Battle on the Volturno.—Visit to Mr. Elliot at Castellamare.—Fall of Ancona.—Proclamation of King Victor Emanuel.—Arrival of English Volunteers.—Departure of Admiral de Tinan for Gaeta.—Decree on Annexation.—Meeting of Victor Emanuel and Garibaldi.—The *Orwell* again.—The *Sylphide*.—Father Gavazzi 250

CHAPTER XXIII.

Naples.—Boat-Race.—Annexation to Sardinia.—Capitulation of Capua.—Distribution of Medals by Garibaldi.—Interference of the French Admiral at Gaeta.—Entry of Victor Emanuel into Naples.—His Devotions at the Shrine of St. Januarius.—Decorations of the City.—The King's Visit to the Theatre.—His Reception of Garibaldi.—Major Missori.—The Dictator's Farewell Address to his Army 266

CHAPTER XXIV.

Naples.—Farewell Interview with General Garibaldi.—Sketch of his Person and Character.—Visit from Admiral Persano.—Audience of King Victor Emanuel . . 280

CHAPTER XXV.

Naples.—Sir William Codrington.—Decree respecting the Garibaldian Army.—Small-Pox.—Reported Participation of Seamen in the Revolution.—Attacked with Small-pox.—Departure of the King for Palermo.—Excursion to

PAGE

Pompeii.—Dissolution of the English Legion.—Review of the National Guard.—Adventures of a British Seaman in the Royal Palace 295

CHAPTER XXVI.

1860–61.

Naples.—Dine with the King.—Sardinian and Danish Etiquette.—Grand Ball of the National Guard.—Departure of the King for Turin.—Reactionary Plots.—The Archbishop Sforza.—The Burgher Militia.—Prince Carignano.—Signor Nigra.—Armistice at Gaeta.—Departure of the French Fleet.—Dine with Prince Carignano.—Capitulation of Gaeta 315

CHAPTER XXVII.

1861.

Naples.—Suppression of Monasteries.—Farewell Dinner of Prince Carignano.—The English Protestant Church.—Refusal of the Grand Cordon of St. Maurice and St. Lazarus.—Departure from Naples.—Arrival at Malta.—Capitulation of Messina.—Termination of the Italian Civil War.—Departure for the Coast of Syria 331

CHAPTER XXVIII.

Arrival at Beyrout.—Lord Dufferin.—Visit to Jerusalem.—Sureya Pacha.—Excursion to the Lebanon.—Accident on the Journey.—Fuad Pacha.—Departure of the French Army.—Death of the Sultan.—Great Augmentation of the Fleets of France, Russia, and England.—Leave of Absence from Ill-Health.—The Syrian Question Settled . . . . 3[illegible]

CHAPTER XXIX.

Efficiency of the French Navy.—Comparison with English Ships and Seamen.—Serious Illness.—Return to England 354

H.M.S. "HANNIBAL"

AT

PALERMO AND NAPLES.

CHAPTER I.

1859.

Introductory Historical Sketch.—Appointment to the Mediterranean Station.—Arrival at Malta.—Mission to Egypt.—Cruise on the Coast of Sicily.

EARLY in the month of January, in the year 1859, after the memorable words which had been addressed by the Emperor of the French, on New Year's Day, to the Austrian Ambassador, Baron Hubner, a general impression gained ground that hostilities would shortly take place between the Austrian and Sardinian armies, which were massed in formidable numbers on their respective frontiers, in Lombardy and Piedmont.

The general tenor of the language held by His Imperial Majesty to the various members of the by many competent judges; and it may be a question whether, under all the circumstances of the case, a simple resignation would not have been the more independent and proper course.

Overtures were made to me at this time, to ascertain if I was willing, at the forthcoming elections, to stand for the Southern Division of the county of Derby, as it was determined by the Conservative Committee to endeavour to regain the seat which had been lost at the two last elections, and which had been held for more than fifty years by a member of my family; but, being anxious for active service afloat, I refused to allow myself to be put in nomination. Mr. Mundy, of Markeaton Hall, however, with true public spirit, consented to come forward, and, after the hardest contest ever known in the county, defeated his opponent by a majority of *one*, the numbers respectively being, for Mr. Mundy 3185, and for the Hon. A. Vernon 3184.

For the same reason, namely, that of an anxious desire to continue in the active line of my profession, I refused requisitions which had been made to me to allow myself to be put in nomination for the boroughs of Devonport and Dover, a decision at which I had very shortly special reason to rejoice, as I not only learnt during the following week that our naval force, both at Corfu and Malta, was to be immediately augmented, but I had, at the same time, the agreeable surprise of receiving a communication from the First

Lord of the Admiralty, in which he stated that it was his intention to appoint a Rear-Admiral to act as second in command of the Mediterranean Fleet, and that if I was disposed to accept that position, he would confer it upon me.

This offer was accompanied by a proposal that I should hoist my flag in the screw 91-gun ship of the line *Hannibal*, and proceed to Malta so soon as the ship could be got ready. I immediately accepted this advantageous offer, and on the following day proceeded to Portsmouth and hoisted my flag.

On the same evening a telegraphic message arrived, bringing intelligence that the Austrian forces had crossed the Ticino on the 28th of April, and that the French army, which had descended into the plains of Piedmont, had marched to Novi.

On the 10th of May, the French Emperor left Paris, and, reaching Genoa on the 15th, took command of the allied armies, one hundred and thirty thousand strong, inclusive of eighty thousand Sardinians: the Austrian army mustering at this date nearly one hundred and fifty thousand men, in the plains of Lombardy and on the banks of the Sesia and Ticino.

On the 21st of May, I sailed from England in Her Majesty's ship *Hannibal*, and, as may well be imagined, at a moment of such interest to Europe, made the best of my way to Malta, in full expectation that I must hear, on reaching that island, of the commencement of one of the most momentous campaigns of modern history.

Carrying strong westerly winds from Gibraltar, I anchored in the grand harbour of Valetta on the 11th of June, and found it deserted by the shipping, Vice-Admiral Fanshawe being absent on the coasts of Italy and Sicily, with the ships of the line, *Marlborough*, 131; *Conqueror*, 91; *Renown*, 91; *Victor Emanuel*, 91; *Orion*, 91; *St. Jean d'Acre*, 101; *Princess Royal*, 91; *Brunswick*, 80; and the frigate *Euryalus*, in which ship was embarked His Royal Highness Prince Alfred, as naval cadet.

At the same time, I heard of the defeat of the Austrians at Magenta, of the astonishing exploits of the great independent chieftain, Giuseppe Garibaldi, with his gallant volunteers, in the vicinity of Como; and, a few days subsequently, of the entry of the Emperor Napoleon and of King Victor Emanuel into the city of Milan.

In the course of the same month a large French fleet had passed along the shores of Sicily, and, avoiding the coasts of the Ionian Islands, had entered the waters of the Adriatic, without a vessel being seen either from Malta or from Corfu; a movement which was highly creditable to the tactics of the French admiral in command, and which proved that the above-named insular dependencies, however impregnable they might be as fortresses, are not indispensable as outposts of observation.

On the 22nd of June, it became known at Malta that a new Government had been formed, of which Lord Palmerston was Prime Minister, Lord John Russell Secretary of State for Foreign Affairs, the Duke of Newcastle Secretary of State for the Colonies, and the Duke of Somerset First Lord of the Admiralty. The Derby Ministry had fallen on a direct vote of want of confidence, 323 voting in favour of the motion, and 310 voting against it. This majority of 13 was certainly small, but it was decisive; and the Conservative ministers had no other alternative than to place their resignation in the hands of Her Majesty.

News of the decisive battle of Solferino, and of the retreat of the Austrians to the left bank of the Mincio, followed up by the personal interview of the two Emperors at Villafranca, which terminated in the cessation of hostilities and the surrender of Lombardy to France, reached Malta as I was on the eve of sailing with a squadron of six sail of the line for Egypt.

The mission with which I was charged in that country having been satisfactorily arranged, at an audience granted me by His Highness the Viceroy on the banks of the Nile, I left the roadstead of Alexandria on the 1st day of August, and, after working against constant westerly winds, sighted Cape Passaro on the 19th of the month.

On the same afternoon, I received despatches from

the Commander-in-Chief, directing me to cruise until further orders off the eastern coast of Sicily, thus giving me a latitude of action which would admit of my visiting the ports comprised within the limits of my station, and afford me opportunity of acquiring useful information.

Having now brought down the extracts from my journal to the period in which I first came into official relations with the Neapolitan authorities, I think it will be desirable I should at once state that in giving publicity to what I had originally written entirely for private reference, I am actuated by the desire that a true account should appear of the principal transactions in which I was engaged whilst in command of a large division of the Mediterranean fleet, during the great crisis of the Italian Revolution, and through which I shall be able to show that in no instance was any departure made from the line of strict neutrality and non-interference which had been peremptorily enjoined by stringent instructions from Lord John Russell, Her Majesty's Principal Secretary of State for Foreign Affairs.

I may here also mention that I have given the foregoing short history of the leading features of this remarkable year, in order that the reader may be enabled more readily to connect the chain of events from the commencement of the misunderstanding between Austria and Piedmont to the time when the British naval force first appeared on the coast for the protection of British subjects, and thus keep in his mind the successive changes which have occurred, and which, in spite of adverse circumstances and of innumerable difficulties, terminated in the establishment of the kingdom of Italy.

CHAPTER II.

1859.

Messina. — Unfriendly Officials. — Syracuse. — Prince Castelcicala.—Imposing Force of the Squadron.—Visit to Marshal Rodriguez.—Panic among Officials.—Great Delight of Visitors to the Ships.—Return Visit of the Governor.

I HAD long been aware that, for many years past, the Sicilian authorities, acting probably under dictation from the Supreme Government at Naples, had greeted with indifference the arrival of the few ships of war which occasionally visited their maritime cities; and I was therefore prepared, whenever communication took place, to be received with a punctilious decorum, instead of that cordial welcome to which I was fairly entitled; moreover, I specially bore in mind that as, on the present occasion, the ships under my command had recently returned direct from the coast of Egypt, an excuse for denying *pratique* would easily be manufactured by unfriendly officials. Any obsolete document connected with quarantine might be moulded into form by the Board of Health servants, and then produced as a warrant to justify prohibition against our having intercourse with the shore.

With these impressions on my mind, I despatched the *Assurance* gunboat to Messina, giving Commander Aynsley directions to endeavour, in the first instance, to communicate as a matter of course with Mr. Richards, the Vice-Consul, but in the event of objection being made to his landing in the city, he was to place before the authorities the clean bill of health with which the ships had been furnished at Alexandria, representing to them at the same time that had I proceeded with the squadron either to the Ionian Islands, to Malta, or to any friendly port on the Continent of Europe, I should have been admitted to *pratique* without question or comment.

At the expiration of forty-eight hours, Commander Aynsley rejoined my flag, bringing me confirmation of the sinister impressions which I had only too correctly entertained. He had been received by the governing powers with that minimum amount of civility which almost bordered on rudeness; and to all remonstrances on the part of the Vice-Consul the reply was the same, that the squadron under Admiral Mundy could not have entrance into any port in the Sicilian dominions, unless under the rigour of lengthened quarantine. Perhaps had these misguided officials known that the sentiments entertained by the British Admiral at this time towards the youthful sovereign of the Kingdom of the Two Sicilies were those of true sympathy for the difficult position in which His Majesty had been placed by the questionable proceedings in Northern Italy, they would have acted in a manner more in accordance with the dictates of prudence and common sense.

Discomfited at Messina, I now turned my attention to the city of Syracuse, which, containing within its radius one of the finest harbours in the world, lay invitingly at hand, and to carry the squadron within the shelter of its circuit was evidently the right direction for the next effort to be made. The happy thought had struck me that, should there be a line of telegraphic communication either by semaphore or by electricity between this ancient emporium and the capital of Sicily, the semaphoric arms or electric wires might be usefully employed in furtherance of my design. I knew that the present Lord-Lieutenant or Viceroy of the Island, the Prince Castelcicala, who had long resided in London as Neapolitan Minister, was favourably disposed to the English in general: I therefore determined to appeal to His Excellency should the Governor of Syracuse prove equally obdurate as his colleague at Messina, and refuse the admission of my ships to the harbour.

To Captain the Hon. Charles Elliot, in command of the *Cressy*, brother of Her Majesty's Minister Plenipotentiary at Naples, and an officer on whose tact I could fully rely, I entrusted the conduct of this delicate mission; he was instructed to proceed forthwith into the harbour of Syracuse, to endeavour, in the first instance, to effect a landing as a matter of right, but if prohibited from so doing by competent authority, he was then to place himself in communication with the Governor of the province; and failing to obtain from that functionary a favourable result, he was, as a last resource, to address himself by telegraphic message to the Viceroy at Palermo, using such arguments in maintenance of his case as his judgment considered best.

At noon the *Cressy* dropped anchor in the centre of the harbour, and about an hour before sunset the yellow flag hoisted at the fore royal mast-head gave evidence that the persuasive efforts of her captain had not been successful. A signal, however, apprized me that a message by semaphore had gone forward to the Viceroy, and that an answer might be expected in the course of the evening. On the following morning at daylight the *Cressy* was observed, under full power of steam, standing out from the harbour, with the signal flying at the main that the Viceroy had acceded to the requisition of the Admiral, and that the squadron was at liberty to enter the port, and would be immediately admitted to free communication.

A great diplomatic victory had been won, and Captain Elliot was complimented on the success he had obtained.

I must here mention that, owing to the extreme jealousy and unreasonable suspicion of the Government of the late King Ferdinand, a stringent order had been promulgated that not more than four foreign ships of war should remain at anchor at the same time in any Neapolitan port. Interpreting, however, the permission now granted by Prince Castelcicala in a liberal sense, I conceived that, if judiciously worked, a favourable opening was presented for the abrogation of an order so senseless and unusual.

The squadron under my command was the largest that had appeared off the coast of Sicily on a friendly mission since the close of the great war of the French Revolution, and consisted of the following ships, all fitted with the screw:—*Hannibal,* 91, Capt. Connolly, bearing my flag; *St. Jean d'Acre,* 101, Capt. Thompson; *Victor Emanuel,* 91, Capt. Wilcox, C.B.; *London,* 91, Capt. Chads; *Cressy,* 80, Capt. The Hon. C. Elliot, C.B.; *Brunswick,* 80, Capt. Ommaney; *Doris,* 32, Capt. Heathcote; *Assurance,* 4, Commander Aynsley; the whole of which force showed itself at anchor in the harbour, between the 21st and 25th of the month, to the astonishment of the authorities and to the great delight of the population.

On the day following our arrival I landed in full uniform, and, accompanied by my flag captain and the whole of my staff, paid an official visit to Marshal Rodriguez, the Governor of the district. The reception he gave me was both formal and distant, and though I told him at once that I had brought in the squadron with the hope that he would honour me with a visit on board the *Hannibal*, and also inspect the ships of the great naval Power which had always been so friendly to his nation, he did not respond to my invitation with the good-will I had expected. When, however, I mentioned that two of the line-of-battle ships would put to sea so soon as their water should be completed, his countenance brightened up, and on my quitting the palace he announced his intention of returning my visit on the morrow.

Meanwhile, the greatest excitement was observable throughout the city. Additional troops were marched in from the detached posts in the interior, sentries were doubled, and the fortifications manned day and night by extra artillerymen, though not a gun could have been fired without danger of explosion. Whilst this unmeaning panic reigned in the breasts of the officials, our ships were thrown open from morning till sunset to every class of the people, and thousands of both sexes daily crowded the decks, and seemed delighted with the really hearty welcome they received from all on board. The great majority of our visitors were of the ecclesiastical profession, young and old, orders of every denomination, lay and clerical, Jesuits in numbers, monks and friars, the latter principally of the mendicant class, Franciscans and Capucins. The dress of the regular clergy, I remarked, was exactly similar to that worn by the

Roman Catholic priesthood at Malta. They all conducted themselves with perfect decorum, yet it was a melancholy spectacle to behold so vast a multitude of able-bodied youths, who, in total disproportion to the spiritual requirements of the community, were destined to be abstracted from wholesome labour, and either to be transplanted to the cells of monastic institutions, or to be forced by the discipline of the Church to compulsory celibacy.

One elderly gentleman, who perhaps in earlier days had derived some material advantage from the presence of the English forces, expressed himself in terms of great delight at the presence of the squadron. He was positive in his assertion that so large a number of vessels of war had not been anchored in the harbour since the close of the last century, when Admiral Nelson brought in the British fleet for a supply of water and provisions.

On hearing this remark, I looked back to the pages of our Naval History, and found that Rear-Admiral Nelson, having failed to discover the enemy's fleet on his first arrival off Alexandria, returned direct to Syracuse, into which port he was admitted through the influence of the Queen of Naples, on the 18th day of July, in the year 1798. At Arethusa's fountain his ships were completed with water, and ten days subsequently he fought and gained the glorious battle of the Nile.

I read also that Nelson was nineteen days beating back from the coast of Egypt against constant westerly winds, and that during this period only one of his vessels, the *Orion*, was missing for twenty-four hours, proving the great attention paid by the captains in keeping their position in the order of sailing.

Let me, then, be allowed the satisfaction of stating that during the passage of the squadron I had the honour of commanding, which traversed exactly the same ground, from Alexandria to Syracuse, at the same season of the year, occupied the same number of days, and met the same constant contrary winds, each one of the ships was at all times in sight, and that not a spar was carried away, nor did any collision take place, though moving in two columns, often in close order of sailing; a result highly creditable to the able officers in command.

On the forenoon of August 23, the Governor returned my visit, and was received on board my flag-ship, under a salute of seventeen guns, and with the customary honours due to his exalted rank. The day was magnificent, and the calm surface of the harbour covered with boats of every size and form, conveying their delighted occupants to the different ships, whilst the decks of the *Hannibal* were already so crowded that the Marshal could with difficulty find space to move round our quarters. I soon perceived that His Excellency was still uneasy in his mind as he gazed on the numerous vessels which continued at anchor within the waters under his jurisdiction, and on my addressing to him a remark which touched the subject of his reflections, he at once frankly confessed that he had, early in the morning, telegraphed to Palermo, asking the Viceroy's instructions as to the propriety of requesting me to order some of the ships into the offing.

At this part of my history I may mention an incident which is worthy of notice, as giving proof amongst others of the nature of the Government under which the Sicilian people were at this period living. When it became known to the fraternity of butchers, who were resident in the city, that fresh meat to a large amount would be immediately required for the consumption of the British fleet, they called a meeting of their body, and after a lengthened discussion came to the unfriendly resolution of raising the price of beef to a fabulous figure. Now, it so happened that our Vice-Consular agent, a Maltese by birth, a septuagenarian in age, long resident in the country, and totally unacquainted with any one single duty of his office, had received instructions from me to place himself in communication with Mr. Morgan, paymaster of the *Hannibal*, and in conjunction with that officer to endeavour to make arrangements for a supply of fresh provisions and vegetables for the squadron under my command. One thousand English sovereigns were in the strong-box of the paymaster, in readiness to be laid out, so soon as any reasonable contract should be concluded, a sum of money in gold coin which probably had not been seen at Syracuse since the day when the Spaniards yielded the island to the Bourbons.

Gratified beyond measure at the magnitude of his mission, the Vice-Consular agent landed to enter upon his work, when, to his astonishment, tidings reached him of the resolutions of the butchers. Enraged at a proceeding so destructive to his hopes, and so offensive to his dignity as England's representative, he hastened to the Palace, and, pouring forth his griefs into the ears of the Field-Marshal, was on the point of obtaining an order for the arrest and imprisonment of the offending monopolists, when I suddenly entered the apartment and joined in the conference. I instantly notified my intention of withdrawing the order for the purchase of provisions, if it in the slightest degree interfered with the price or supply of food for the city, or drew down upon any class of tradesmen the displeasure of the Government.

The settlement of this vexed question was finally solved by a declaration on the part of the Governor of his intention of abstaining from interference in the matter, and by the issue on my part of fresh instructions to the agent, empowering him to proceed at once into the country districts, where he was, if possible, to enter into direct negotiation with the farmers, and so endeavour to open a market for the supply of our wants.

Measures to this effect were accordingly taken, and resulted in the completion of a contract which gave satisfaction to all parties. Fresh beef and vegetables, of good quality and of fair price, were to be brought down daily to the beach in readiness to be conveyed on board by the boats of the ships, and live bullocks in stated numbers were also to be furnished as required for sea stock. Thus harmony was restored, and the townspeople were relieved from the fears they had entertained of an increase in the price of the necessities of life.

Late in the evening of this day, an aide-de-camp came on board and delivered to me a polite message from Marshal Rodriguez to the effect that he hoped I would not carry out my proposition of sending two of the ships of the line to sea, as there was no longer any objection to the whole of the vessels remaining at anchor in the harbour. Nothing was said by the staff officer of a telegram from Palermo, but the message was clearly an indication that orders had been transmitted to the Governor not to interfere with my movements.

The ships having now been completed with water, and supplied with as many bullocks as they could conveniently stow, I sailed from the harbour at dawn of the 25th of August, followed by numerous bumboats, which accompanied us many miles to sea.

How different was the scene which had presented itself only a few days before, when these little skiffs, laden with fruit and other edibles, on the near approach of the squadron hovered timidly in the distance, and, though anxious for traffic, were fearful to venture alongside the strangers until better acquainted! A perfect confidence between us had since been fairly established; indeed, during the whole of our stay in the port, an excellent feeling had existed between the ships and the shore. I had given permission on a Sunday for the chief and first-class petty officers to land from each ship, and I was pleased to observe the kind attention which was shown by the inhabitants to a few of the number who, having miscalculated the strength of the beverage placed before them, were not so capable of taking care of themselves as when mustered on the quarter-deck in preparation for their leave.

In the course of the day, I received despatches from Malta, and amongst them a letter from Rear-Admiral Codrington, the Superintendent of Her Majesty's Dockyard, in which he informed me that, should I require a stock of bullocks, he should shortly have the opportunity of forwarding them to me. Great, then, was my satisfaction at being able to acquaint him that not only was the port of Syracuse open to British ships of war, irrespective of numbers, but that a contract had been signed with one of the principal merchants of the place, by which fresh meat and vegetables, of excellent quality and reasonable in price, would henceforth be in readiness when demands should be made.

CHAPTER III.

1859.

Catania.—Visit of Prince Fitalia.—Mr. Jeans, the Vice-Consul.—Reception of the Nobility on Board.—Sudden Storm, and Abrupt Termination of the Fête.—The *Victor Emanuel*.—Unfounded Charge of enticing away the principal Band from the City.

After remaining three days at sea, for the purpose of exercise in evolutions and gunnery practice, I bore up with the squadron for the roadstead of Catania, and anchored before the city at sunset on the 27th, in order of sailing in two columns, in thirteen fathoms, about half a mile distant from the shore. File upon file of really beautiful equipages of the nobility and gentry, and crowds of the population, seemed massed together on the beach in eager gaze at a sight which had never before been witnessed by the oldest inhabitant. The wind was moderate from the sea, the surface of the water smooth as on a lake, and the vessels in compact order, under a heavy press of canvas, appeared almost touching the line of cliff as they rounded-to in succession, and then brought-up by signal with their broadsides to the shore.

Catania is a handsome city, disclosing to view a

larger number of palaces, and possessing a finer range of streets, than either Palermo or Messina. It is situated on the very brink of the water, and is built on a plain, which in a gradual slope rises to the cultivated ground at the foot of Mount Etna, and, when looked upon from the sea, has a beautiful effect. It is the great seat of the Sicilian aristocracy, with a population physically more robust and in spirit more independent, than in any other province of the insular portion of the kingdom.

During the great Revolution, now eleven years ago, the people fought heroically for the attainment of a rational freedom, and though unsuccessful in the struggle, have borne their misfortune with resignation, and still look forward, with a buoyancy of hope, to the dawn of a brighter day.

Sunday, August 28.—At daylight, an officer in full military uniform came on board and announced himself as an aide-de-camp of Prince Fitalia, the Civil Governor of the province, who had charged him to make a request that I would not continue at the anchorage with more than three ships of the line, any excess of that number being in direct contravention of the regulations of the port.

In answer to a message of so unpalatable a nature, and which I was called upon to digest at so very early an hour, I directed my flag-captain to repair immediately to the Palace, and to give assurance in my name to the Prince of the pacific character of my visit, and of my intention of waiting officially on His Excellency whenever it should be convenient to him to give me a reception. A few hours subsequent to this incident, we were all assembled on the main-deck, engaged in the service of the Church, as became our duty on the Sabbath, when the officer of the watch came below and whispered into the ear of Captain Connolly that the Governor and his suite, with the general commanding the troops and his staff, had suddenly come alongside, and were now in the after-cabin waiting to pay their respects to the Admiral. I sent the captain to keep these high authorities company till the religious service was concluded; and when I joined them on the poop found their Excellencies in a most affable frame of mind, and loud in their praises of the singing of the boys, who were chaunting the "Te Deum" as the party stepped on the deck.

Prince Fitalia then informed me that he had hastened on board the *Hannibal* in order that he might personally acquaint me of his having received, only an hour ago, a telegraphic message from the Viceroy, instructing him to make no objection to my anchoring in the Bay of Catania, with any number of ships I might think proper to bring; and to afford me every civility and assistance in his power.

It was clear from this intelligence that a favourable report had been made of our proceedings at Syracuse, and that Prince Castelcicala had no inclination whatever to prohibit communication between the ships of a friendly Power and the populations under his rule. In the afternoon I received a note from Mr. Jeans, the Vice-Consul, in which he informed me that several members of the aristocracy and gentry had expressed to him their desire to pay their respects to me on board my flag-ship; and, at the same time, that they were anxious to take their wives and families afloat and give them the opportunity of visiting some of the ships. I conveyed a reply to them immediately that the *Hannibal* and the other vessels of war in the roadstead were open at stated periods to all classes of the people, and that I should personally be happy to see as many of the nobility and gentry as would honour me with a visit. I notified, at the same time, that an hour after noon on the day but one following would be agreeable to me, if convenient to them; that a *déjeûné* would be provided, and that I should be greatly disappointed if the young ladies should be too timid to present themselves on board, as the band would be in readiness and the decks prepared for dancing: great, then, was my surprise at receiving notice, late in the same evening, that after mature deliberation these representatives of upper Catanese society, who had made the proposal in the morning, were suddenly under apprehension that their visit to an English ship of war might compromise them with the authorities, as the idea had gained ground that I was charged with a mission unfavourable to the Government. In return to this communication I made known to the Vice-Consul that I should make no change in my plans, that the boats of the squadron would be at the landing-place according to previous arrangement, and that I should still hope at least a few of the Sicilian gentry would show sufficient moral courage to dismiss these unworthy fears and to come on board the *Hannibal,* as originally settled.

August 29.—At 11 A.M. I landed with the flag-captain and my staff, and, accompanied by Mr. Jeans, paid an official visit to the Governor. Prince Fitalia has the character of a liberal-minded man, whose individual opinions are favourable to a more enlightened form of government than that which is at present in the ascendant at Naples. He greeted me with a cordiality which, whether sincere or assumed, was at any rate agreeable, and I left the Palace under the belief that our relations with the shore would henceforth be amicable.

On my return to the mole to re-embark, I found a large number of the inhabitants drawn up on each side of the street, who testified their satisfaction at seeing a British Admiral amongst them by respectfully moving their hats and by other tokens of good-will; but scarcely a word was spoken till I was stepping into the barge, when a few of the people close at hand, exclaimed in under-tone, "*Benedetto*

Ammiraglio Inglese, benedetto Ammiraglio Inglese! benvenuto, benvenuto!" "Blessing and welcome to the English Admiral!" Possibly, these individuals were under the conviction that the advent of so imposing a naval force must necessarily have been linked with some political object, and that an amelioration of their condition would be the result of our visit. How great, then, would have been their disappointment had they known that my object in bringing the squadron to their waters was solely to make myself acquainted with the capabilities of the roadstead, to give practice to the ships' companies in the useful exercise of up and down anchors, and perhaps to afford opportunity to the younger officers to scale the snowy peak of Mount Etna.

The *Argus*, 6, Commander Ingram, joined this evening, from Messina, making with the *Hannibal*, *St. Jean d'Acre*, *Victor Emanuel*, *London*, *Cressy*, *Brunswick*, *Doris*, and *Assurance*, the ninth pennant that had appeared on the coast.

August 30th.—The weather, from light variable winds and a clear transparent sky, became early this morning overcast; and the summit of Etna, which since our arrival had been pencilled in distinct outline on the blue vault above, was now covered with clouds. The distant shore of the Southern Calabria was also enveloped in a sheet of mist. The barometer began to fall, and atmospheric phenomena gave warning to the seaman that he must prepare to get an offing from so exposed an anchorage. This change was inopportune. It was the day fixed for the reception of the Sicilian nobility and gentry; and after the pithy correspondence which had taken place, I was very anxious the boats should be on shore according to promise, and that the self-invited guests should at any rate have no other excuse than their own want of pluck if they failed to come on board.

The sea proved calm at the hour appointed, and the barges, pinnaces, and cutters of the line-of-battle ships proceeded to the mole. I had a sort of presentiment that some few of the feminine portion of the community, either through a natural curiosity, or an earnest desire to see an English man-of-war would overcome the dismal scruples of their relatives of the masculine sex, and that some of the boats would not return on board tenantless.

In this view I was correct. Half-an-hour after midday the whole of the boats were seen rounding the pier-head, and pulling at racing pace towards the squadron. They were crowded with sitters, the sexes apparently equally divided; and I had shortly the pleasure of receiving between fifty and sixty of the *élite* of Catania on the deck of the *Hannibal.* Neither the rank nor the name of any individual of the party was known to myself or to any one on board, and of the number only two were acquainted with the English language, and not many more could speak a little French. Fortunately, I had some knowledge of the Italian idiom, so was enabled to give them a welcome in a few words of their own tongue.

After going round the armament and exploring the intricate wonders of the engine-room, attended by Captain Connolly and a few of the officers, they adjourned to my cabin ; and I have no other remark to make on their appreciation of an English luncheon, beyond the unmistakeable fact of the great preference shown by the men for Allsop's bitter ale over every other beverage.

I was congratulating myself on the good-humour and apparent satisfaction of my guests at the reception we had given them, and also upon the good taste which they had shown in avoiding all allusion to political matters, when I suddenly overheard a conversation in the starboard side cabin, between a few of the elders who had congregated there, which shadowed forth an intention, before they quitted the ship, of proposing my health, and at the same time of coupling this most legitimate toast with the less orthodox supplement of a reference to their present deplorable social condition, and of their hope that the presence of the English squadron would bring about beneficial results. With this key to their programme I thought no time was to be lost, so immediately rose from the table, and, giving notice to the ladies that the band was on the poop, moved at once to the quarter-deck, when dancing was commenced, and the scheme of the committee of action completely overthrown. The enjoyment of this exhilarating pastime was however speedily brought to a close, for the weather had now assumed so threatening an aspect that it became necessary to man the boats and hurry away our visitors with all possible despatch.

Before leaving, they bade me farewell in my cabin, and were eloquent in their expressions of delight at the novelties they had witnessed. Twenty years had passed away since a ship of the line had appeared off the city, and none of the party had ever before seen one of the leviathan screws. It may, then, easily be conceived that there was no exaggeration in the sentiments of pleasure to which they gave vent.

One of the ladies, both young and good-looking, to my great dismay and astonishment, insisted on kissing my hand with evident signs of emotion; and on my inquiring into the object of this most unusual compliment, I ascertained it arose from a persuasion in her mind that, by some process or other, the British Admiral was destined to bring about an amelioration of their present despotic form of government. She belonged to that class of young Italian females who may be termed political enthusiasts, holding in abhorrence the Bourbon dynasty, and clinging to the belief that the fleet on which she looked was the harbinger of brighter days for her long-afflicted country.

Great exertions were now made by the young officers in charge of the boats to get the party safely on shore before the impending storm should burst forth, but their efforts were in vain; the rain descended with tropical intensity, and in spite of mackintosh and umbrella, every individual was drenched to the skin; and I fear I must add that the beautiful dresses of the ladies, which possibly were displayed for the first time on this festive occasion, were either irretrievably damaged or totally destroyed.

Meanwhile, the breeze continued steadily to increase, and set in directly upon the shore. Fires were lighted throughout the squadron, and shortly after dusk all the ships excepting the *Hannibal* and *Victor Emanuel*, weighed, and steamed out to a rendezvous twenty miles east of the city.

About twenty officers of the squadron had made the attempt at different times to ascend Mount Etna, but I believe Captain Ommaney, of the *Brunswick*, Captain Chads, of the *London*, and three officers of the *Hannibal*, Captain Pickard, R.M., Lieutenant Welch, and Mr. Hodges (engineer), alone succeeded in gaining the summit.

August 31.—During the whole of last night and the early part of this morning, the weather continued squally, with heavy thunderstorms and lightning; but clearing up at 9 A.M., I went on board the *Victor Emanuel* for muster and inspection. The excellent practice made by Captain Wilcox with shot and shell at a target, greatly delighted the natives who, happening to be afloat, had this good opportunity of witnessing the astonishing precision of modern gunnery. The *Victor Emanuel*, named after the gallant soldier-king of Sardinia, with her cutwater surmounted by a colossal figure of His Majesty, became the great object of attraction to crowds of admiring people, who either went on board her in hundreds, or hovered in boats beneath her bows, thus testifying their admiration of the crowned hero of Palestro and San Martino.

In the evening I received a letter from the Vice-Consul, informing me that he had been requested by the nobility and gentry, who had visited the *Hannibal* on the day previous, to transmit to me their cards, and to express to me at the same time their thanks and best acknowledgments of the kindness and courtesy which they had met with from all on board.

In contrast to this pleasing epistle, a second despatch, also from Mr. Jeames, was placed in my hands, enclosing a communication from the Governor, expressive of his regret at having to make a complaint against the Captain of one of the ships under my command, who had enticed away from their duties the whole company of musicians, forming the principal band of the city, and had carried them out to sea, in contravention of the laws of the Island; and furthermore that, not content with this outrage, three gentlemen, who had trusted themselves on board, had been forcibly detained, causing the greatest anxiety to their relatives and friends.

The alleged delinquent ship I understood to be the

London, commanded by Captain Chads, a correct and experienced officer; and though I felt convinced the history of the carrying off against their will of any of the inhabitants of the city was nothing more or less than a gross fabrication, and that the entry of any number of musicians on the books of the ship could only have taken place by voluntary enlistment, the whole proceeding was nevertheless annoying and provoking. It would necessarily entail explanations and probably a long correspondence, and would neutralize the effect of that good understanding, which, with so much trouble, I had succeeded at length in establishing. The *London* was at this time cruising to the southward, within compass of recall by distant signal. As soon, therefore, as possible, she was brought within range of communication, when I learnt that, amongst a large number of Sicilians who thronged on board the ship on the eve of her departure, three individuals, after being warned that the hour had arrived for returning to their homes, requested to be allowed to go to sea in the vessel, it being known that she was only bound outward for a few miles, and that there would be an opportunity of landing the next morning in one of the beach-boats that accompanied the ship. The request of these gentlemen had been, perhaps, too easily granted, and not very long before I had telegraphed to Captain Chads for information respecting them, they had warmly thanked the officers for the novel treat of a short sea excursion, and had betaken themselves to the bumboat, and returned to their dwellings. Probably, whilst detailing to envious friends anecdotes of their interesting trip, and expatiating on the pleasure derived from the expedition, they learnt, for the first time, that the Admiral had been seriously called to account by the paternal authorities for the atrocities which had been perpetrated against their personal liberty.

Thus was the first and principal accusation disposed of; but unfortunately it pointed out too strongly the animus of the Governor, and modified considerably the favourable opinion which I had formed of the character of Prince Fitalia.

September 1*st.*—Thick squally weather, and wind blowing fresh upon the shore—the *Hannibal* and *Victor Emanuel* got up steam—the rest of the squadron under easy sail in the offing. I had now received in full from Captain Chads the account of the entry of the musicians on the ship's books. Out of thirty performers, comprising the principal band of Catania, twenty-two of the best men, including the bandmaster, had been engaged; but the transaction, so far as the Captain of the *London* was concerned, had been completed in regular form. The men had volunteered, and the officer who had arranged the terms of the enlistment, after an appeal to the Vice-Consul for an opinion as to the legality of the agreement, had learnt from him that no regulations existed which could prohibit the musicians from disposing of their talents to the best advantage. They accordingly went on board the *London* in open day, taking their music-books and instruments with them. It was only when it became known to the police that they had not been provided with passports, and that by such omission certain fees had been evaded appertaining to their force, that the ire of the Government was brought down upon my head.

In order to satisfy myself thoroughly that there could be no mistake relative to the opinion which the three gentlemen had formed of their excursion to sea in the *London*, I sent Commander Aynsley and my flag-lieutenant, Mr. Wilmot, to the Vice-Consul, with a request that he would endeavour to obtain from the individuals themselves some account of their expedition, and if possible elicit a confirmation of the official report I had received from Captain Chads. The Vice Consul was also to give me a statement in writing relative to the transaction of the entry of the bandsmen, so that, if called upon by superior authority, I might have such papers in my possession as would refute any complaints that might hereafter be brought against me. The documents required were furnished in the course of the afternoon, together with a statement from the three gentlemen, corroborative of the kind reception they had experienced whilst embarked in the *London*; and the weather having now become decidedly bad, I steamed out from the roadstead in company with the *Victor Emanuel*.

CHAPTER IV.

1859.

Return to Syracuse for Supplies.—Reggio.—Man Overboard.—Stromboli.—Terrific Squalls.

I HAD, late in the preceding evening, received despatches from the Commander-in-chief, enclosing instructions for me to proceed to the Gulf of Spezia, with four sail of the line and smaller vessels, in order that a naval force might be in a central position to watch the progress of events in Northern Italy, which, since the cessation of hostilities, had assumed a character so unexpectedly complex, that the ablest diplomatist might have been puzzled if called upon to determine how regularity of government could be maintained.

Whether democracy was to triumph, under the dangerous ascendancy of Mazzini, backed by the well-known republican opinions of Garibaldi, or moderate liberal institutions, by annexation to Piedmont, or despotic rule by the restoration of the exiled princes, was the great question to be solved in the Æmilian Provinces, and in the neighbouring territories of the Grand Duke of Tuscany.

The French Emperor had returned to Paris, followed by the greater part of his invincible legions. The King of Sardinia had made his triumphal entry into Milan, and had ample work to perform in the organization of his new kingdom of Lombardy. Garibaldi had been stopped in his career of victory in the mountainous region of Como and Lake Garda, by the armistice of Villafranca; and Cavour, the great master mind of the peninsula, had retired into private life, mistrustful of the future intentions of the mysterious monarch of France, who, having announced that Italy should be free from the Alps to the Adriatic, now drew off his forces and declared the war to be at an end.

I little imagined, when I first entertained the project of opening the port of Syracuse to any number of our ships, that in less than ten days from the birth of this idea I should find in its accomplishment the greatest public utility; yet so it happened.

Before proceeding to carry into execution the new mission with which I was intrusted, it became necessary that the ships of the line which were to form the naval force destined for the bay of Spezia should be completed with water and filled up with coal; and unless I had been able to seek the shelter of a friendly harbour, where I might in smooth water tranship the fuel from the vessels ordered to Malta, I should have been obliged to return to that island, and thus lose several days and much valuable time. Now, I had

Syracuse under my lee, and, favoured by a strong north-easterly wind, the *Hannibal* and six of her consorts bore up for that port, and passing safely through the narrow channel between the fort and outer rocks, anchored close off the city as darkness set in.

I will now take up my narrative by extracts from my journal without keeping strictly to day-by-day details or consecutive dates.

I remained forty-eight hours at Syracuse, and after filling up our bunkers with coal, our tanks and casks with water, and taking on board a large stock of fresh provisions and bullocks, we sailed from the harbour at daylight on the 4th of September, my reduced squadron consisting of the *Hannibal*, *St. Jean d'Acre*, *London*, *Brunswick*, and *Assurance*.

In taking a final leave of this once famous stronghold, so interesting from its undoubted antiquity and historical associations, I must mention that our old friends received us on our second visit with every demonstration of joy and good-will. The mosquitoe fleet of shore boats, with their cargoes of sight-seers, were active as ever in pursuit of their avocations, and the vendors of curiosities annoyingly clamorous to obtain entrance to the ships. By some inexplicable freemasonry they had ascertained before our arrival that monthly money and savings had been paid down to the crews, and they doubtlessly calculated on a rich harvest of gain. They were permitted in limited numbers to have their run on the lower deck, and probably soon learned by experience that the English seamen of the present day are as capable of taking care of their money and of appreciating its value, as any other class of men in the same relations of life.

Her Majesty's Vice-Consular Agent was found at his post, and was again put in requisition for many little services; but, as on a former occasion he could not be restrained within the limits of official etiquette, when the affair of the butchers excited his indignation, so, in the present instance, after he had been good enough to hire a public vehicle to convey the Captain of the *Brunswick* and a few of his young cadets to the cave of Dionysius, he managed to concoct a quarrel with the unfortunate driver, and from a warfare of words proceeded to demonstrations more hostile in character.

I chanced at the moment to be walking in the main street adjoining, and, hearing the altercation, turned down upon the Marina, when I observed, to my astonishment, the irate Consular Agent engaged in pugilistic combat with the guide or cicerone perched on the box, who, although defending himself with some agility, had just been knocked down on the footboard, and was crying for help.

On asking an explanation of the cause of the conflict, Captain Ommaney could only assure me that there was no just reason for so discreditable a disturbance, which he attributed entirely to Signor Azzopardo's impetuosity, and to his anger at observing the cicerone had dared to adorn his head-covering with a piece of gold lace in imitation of the Vice-Consular cap. I had intended to address a few words of advice to the above-named gentleman, but there was something so truly ridiculous in the whole nature of the scuffle that I was unable to restrain the risible faculties, so passed on to my galley without offering a remark. Let me, however, add, that men of this stamp should not be allowed to hold appointments in the consular department. They bring discredit upon the office, and lower the nation they represent in the eyes of the Government to which they are accredited.

As we approached the old town of Reggio, on the Calabrian coast, the current and wind being both against us, the ships were put under steam, and were proceeding in close order at rapid speed, when I suddenly heard the cry of "a man overboard." I sprung into the stern walk, to seize the circular life-preserver, which always hung suspended for instant use, when I observed the big drum floating in the ship's wake, and a young seaman, only a few yards from it, striking out, evidently with the action of an indifferent swimmer, and endeavouring, with desperate energy, to grasp this beacon of safety. A few more feet would save him, but the effort was ineffectual. There was a struggle of despair, an uplifting of hands, a splashing of water,—and he was gone.

As soon as the cutter had been lowered and despatched in the hope of rescue, I sent to inquire how it happened that the drum was astern of the swimmer, which fact had not at first been perceived, as reversing the usual position of the article thrown overboard for the life-buoy. No satisfactory explanation of this singular coincidence could be given until the return of the boat; when it was found, on examining the drum, that the small holes in the wooden frame had been stopped up by oakum and pieces of canvas, so as to insure flotation when immersed in the water. It was then suspected that the man must have dropped the musical instrument into the sea from the port, and then jumped after it. Such was probably the case. He had been confined during the morning watch as a prisoner between two guns on the main deck, on the charge of thieving from his messmates, and observing that the ship was steaming at a very short distance from the land, he made this desperate attempt to reach the beach, and thus save himself from trial and punishment.

We were nine days on our passage from Syracuse to Spezia, having anchored for twelve hours in the vicinity of Messina; but as the authorities of that town had thought proper on our first arrival from Egypt to show us much discourtesy, I would hold no communication with the place.

Near the burning mountain of Stromboli we met squally weather with thunder-storms and heavy rains, and during the night, being close off the island, the view of the flames issuing in continuous flashes of great brilliancy from the crater, had a fine effect.

From this latitude to the entrance of the Straits of Bonifacio, we had light contrary winds, against which the squadron proceeded under easy steam. Here the wind became favourable, and we had every prospect of being carried under canvas to the Italian coast, when one of those changes, so prevalent at this season, came suddenly upon us. I had remarked, during the evening of the 12th, that the sun had gone down behind a bank of massive clouds, tinging them with that blood-red hue which is so often the forerunner of tempestuous weather; and though the mercury in the barometer remained steady, above thirty degrees with a convex bulb, and the breeze moderate on the quarter, I thought it advisable to telegraph to the squadron to furl sails and proceed under steam. We were at this time approaching the narrowest part of the channel between the eastern coast of Corsica and the dangerous shoals of Formica, from which we were only a few miles distant, and to keep steam ships of the line under sail alone, when in the vicinity of an intricate navigation I have always considered proof of want of judgment on the part of the officer on whom the responsibility rests. It was well that the precaution had been taken in time. The ships had scarcely been made snug, and under steam command, when the breeze suddenly fell; and after a short interval of calm, a furious gale sprung up from the northward, the course on which we were steering to pass between Elba and the extreme point of Corsica being N. ½ E. At 1 o' clock on the morning of the 13th the squalls were terrific, with torrents of rain, thunder and lightning; and the *Hannibal*, at the height of the tempest, with her weak auxiliary power, was unable to keep her head to the sea.

At intervals by the lightning flashes, I could perceive the *Brunswick*, which was the leading vessel of the lee column, also unable to keep steerage way, whilst the *St. Jean d'Acre* and *London*, with their excellent machinery, steadily held their course, and appeared to bid defiance to the elements.

Daylight relieved my suspense, and the cares of a most anxious night by a sudden shift of wind to the eastward, accompanied by a gradual dispersion of the clouds, which, as they lifted from the surface of the water, showed us the land broad on both beams, apparently from its rugged and lofty character disagreeably near, although in reality at a distance sufficiently great to preclude all danger of being driven upon it, had the gale again recommenced.

CHAPTER V.

1859.

The Gulf of Spezia.—Site for first-class Arsenal.—Description of the Fortifications.—Cavaliere Tholozano.—Mr. Charles Lever.—Organization of the Police.

At sunset on the same evening the squadron anchored in the Gulf of Spezia, half a mile distant from the entrance of the dockyard creek, causing equal astonishment to the Sardinian authorities on land, and to the Commodore commanding a division of the Sardinian fleet moored off the town, as did our sudden appearance at Syracuse three weeks before.

At this anchorage I remained ten days, during six of which the equinoctial gales blew fiercely, but, even with the wind directly in from the S. E., there was not much sea, and from every other quarter there was perfect shelter.

On the 15th, during the height of one of those tremendous squalls which sweep down occasionally between the ridges of this mountainous district, carrying destruction to all neighbouring vegetation, the boatkeeper of the barge moored astern was blown into the water. The ship's awnings were sloped from the forecastle to the taffrail, the rain descending in volumes from the confines of a waterspout, and, joining the white sheets of spray from the sea, was driven horizontally athwart the vessel, and though the time was midday there was a darkness around, as if the sun had been obscured by a total eclipse.

I happened to be in the stern gallery at the moment, watching the effect of the storm, and, seeing the man fall overboard, threw my cork life-buoy to his aid; but, caught up by the whirlwind, it was carried towards the land, and fell into the water at a hundred yards distant. Fortunately, the ship's bum-boat, containing three rowers, had taken shelter under the quarter, and was moored to the rudder-chains. They had not observed the accident, nor was it perceived by those on deck, but on my calling out to them in Italian that one of the seamen was drowning, they cast off the painter with much smartness, and by strenuous efforts at the oars succeeded in reaching the boatkeeper at the moment when, borne down by the weight of the pea-jacket, he had sunk two feet below the surface of the water. He was dragged insensible into the boat, but his life was saved.

On the following day my steward gave me a letter from the man, in which he thanked me for rescuing him from a watery grave. Now, a seaman writing to his Admiral was certainly not quite in accordance with the rules of naval etiquette; however, under the circumstances of the case, at my next muster of the crew, I did not think it necessary to do more than recommend him to show his gratitude by conducting himself well during the rest of the ship's commission. He made me a promise to this effect, and we must hope he will endeavour to keep his word.

Spezia is a small town situated at the north-western extremity of the deep gulf of that name, and the ground in its immediate vicinity is probably destined at some future day to be transformed into the principal naval *entrepôt* of the enlarged Sardinian Kingdom. It had been found that the small artificial port of Genoa was too confined to contain the vessels of war as well as the merchant shipping, and it therefore became necessary to examine the various inlets on the coast for the purpose of selecting a site eligible for the construction of a first-class arsenal, with basins and dry docks attached.

The remarkable natural harbour of Spezia, which the great Napoleon, during the zenith of his power, had contemplated rendering a naval station, equal in efficiency to those of Brest and Toulon, had been fixed upon by the Piedmontese Committee of Selection as the spot embracing every requisite qualification; and some years ago large sums of money had been voted by the Parliament at Turin for the construction of fortifications on both sides of the entrance of the bay. These had not been commenced when the late Admiral Lord Lyons visited the harbour in the summer of the year 1857, in his flag-ship the *Royal Albert*. However, at the time I now write, in September, 1859, considerable progress had been made in the formation of several extensive works, which are evidently under the supervision of competent officers, and promise, when finished, to do credit to the Sardinian engineers.

I was enabled, during my stay in the roads, to visit personally most of the principal points where the workmen were actively engaged, and I give the following extracts as the result of my observations:—

"On the southern side of the Island of Palmaria, which commands the western approach, three batteries are in course of erection at a distance of one hundred yards from each other, each battery capable of mounting four or five heavy guns. They are placed at an elevation of four or five hundred feet above the level of the sea, from which the land rises nearly perpendicular. From the formation of the ground these batteries will probably, at some future period, be connected together, and so form an extensive range of works in communication with the principal fortress or citadel on the height above. They will command the Bocca de Tino, or passage between the Islands of Tino and Palmaria.

"A semicircular fort, capable of mounting from fifty to sixty guns, in two tiers, is now building on the extremity of Palma Point. The sea-face is nearly vertical, and the lower tier forty feet from the water. There is no ditch in front, but a small one between the tiers. A ditch in the rear, close to the fort, about twenty feet deep and fifteen feet wide, is one-third cut through, and when finished will extend across the peninsula, which at this point has a breadth of about one hundred and fifty yards.

"A substantial road, fifteen feet broad, winds with an easy ascent from this fort to the summit of the island. The road is capable of bearing the heaviest artillery, and is almost completed. It is from two to three miles in extent, and at its termination at the highest gorge, a space half a mile long by fifty yards wide, has been levelled. On this flat the foundations for an extensive citadel are now in progress, the guns of which will command both the Bocca de Tino and the anchorage off the northern shores of the island. A large tank has also been excavated close at hand.

"A branch road for artillery from the fort on Palma Point to the bay on the north side of Palmaria, where a new mole is being built, will shortly be finished; and all the works probably completed in two years from this date.

"Fort Scola is built on a small rock, in the centre of which is a spring of fresh water, and is only a cable's length, two hundred yards, from Palma Point. The fort is now a ruin, and will be replaced by a tower, on which one heavy pivot-gun is to be mounted.

"On the extremity of Castagna Point a large fort is building, intended to hold from sixty to one hundred heavy guns on two tiers, with five faces. These faces are steep towards the beach, with a ditch round them twenty feet wide; the height of the lower tier from the water's edge being forty or fifty feet. A narrow ditch in the rear, stretching across the peninsula, which at this part is about four hundred yards wide, has just been commenced, and a space is being cleared away behind it, on which barracks are to be erected for two thousand men. The Fort of Castagna is well placed to protect the approaches to the western shores of the gulf, and a good road for artillery connects it with the highway to Port Venere.

"Fort Santa Maria is an ancient and well-built fort; the embrasures have lately been repaired, but there are no guns mounted. A small battery, *à fleur d'eau,* is to be made on the sea-face on the southern side, where the ground is rocky.

"The great hospital, and adjacent buildings on the Varignano Point,* are now unoccupied, and workmen are engaged in converting them into an Admiralty house, barracks for seamen and marines, and store-

* I little imagined, when I examined and noted so minutely the extensive works in progress on this point and in its vicinity, that it would, in three years from that date, receive Garibaldi as a prisoner, and become a marked place in history.

houses for the proposed dockyard. Behind these buildings is a bagno, where four hundred and fifty convicts are now lodged. They are working at a deep cutting, which will extend across the peninsula, and is intended, when finished, for bomb-proof magazines.

"The fort on the extreme edge of Pezzino Point is in ruins, but new works are contemplated.

"On the loftiest peak of Mount Castellana, sixteen hundred feet above the level of the sea, a fort, called 'Fort Napoleon' is in course of construction; but, from its immense height and distance from the anchorage, it can never be really effective in preventing the approach of an enemy's fleet. A new road to this fort, in communication with the highway between Spezia and Port Venere, is half completed, and winds with a gradual ascent up the steep slope of the mountain.

"On the eastern shore of the gulf none of the projected works are yet commenced, but plans for three detached forts have been approved of. One is to be placed on Point Sta. Teresa, a second on the point of Maralonga convent, and the third near the village of Telaro.

"The distance across the gulf, between the forts on the eastern and western shores, varies from two to three and a half miles, the latter being the space between the fortifications on the island of Palmaria and the intended work at Telaro."

I have given the above statement at length, exactly as noted in my remark book, from the belief that great public interest will eventually be attached to this remarkable spot, and if the proposed gigantic works should really be carried out, Spezia may, in twenty years from this date, be a second Toulon.

On the 19th, Cavaliere Tholosano, the Intendente, or Civil Governor, came on board the *Hannibal* to return an official visit which I had paid to him on my arrival, and was saluted with seventeen guns. He was discreet, and diplomatic in his observations relative to the present condition of Northern Italy—briefly informing me that Ricasoli ruled at Florence, and Farini at Parma, whilst the national representative assemblies had decreed the perpetual banishment of their former Sovereigns, and voted unanimously for annexation to the constitutional kingdom of Sardinia, under the sceptre of Victor Emmanuel. General Garibaldi had the command in chief of the Tuscan, Modenese, and Parmesan troops; and Fanti those in Romagna.

I also received a visit from Mr. Charles Lever, the Vice-Consul, well known as the talented author of "Harry Lorrequer" and "Charles O'Malley;" and I may mention that during our stay in the port the consular house was always open to the captains and officers of the squadron, and that his hospitality was unbounded. He seemed to think that the stipulations of the treaty of Villafranca for the restoration of the former rulers could never be carried into effect without foreign coercion; though, on the other hand, he feared there would be difficulty in preserving order under the system of fusion of provinces so dissimilar in habit and feeling as those of Tuscany, Modena, Parma, and Romagna.

Every one with whom I conversed seemed strong in the belief that the hatred of the people for the Princes of the House of Austro-Este, who had ruled in Modena, of the Bourbons of Parma, and of the priestly government in Romagna, was so inveterate that to reinstate them in power without bloodshed would be impossible. The dynasty of the House of Austro-Lorraine, which had governed Tuscany, was not so unpopular.

The feeling at this time apparently uppermost in the minds of the Italians was a deep-seated apprehension that Prince Napoleon would be forced upon them as Sovereign of the central provinces, which, it was rumoured, would be erected into an intermediate kingdom between Piedmont and the States of the Church. This arrangement, however, was only to take place in the event of the original plan of the Emperor for a general confederation under the honorary presidency of the Pope not being satisfactory to the people.

On the other hand, there was one bright beam of light which cheered them in the midst of the political chaos around. The great principle of non-intervention had been propounded by Napoleon himself, who had declared that if he should not suceced in uniting the Princes and people in mutual accord, it was not his intention to force either the one or the other; adding, that as Italy owed her liberties to him, he would not take them away from her.

It was also well known that, several weeks previously, Lord John Russell had announced in his place in Parliament that the British Government was favourable to the Italians being left to choose their own form of government, even as Sweden, Belgium, Holland, France, and England had done under similar tribulation. In the same speech the Minister for Foreign Affairs also informed the House that he had received a despatch from the Austrian Minister, in which His Excellency expressed his belief that the people of Modena and Tuscany would eventually be glad, of their own free will, to receive their former Sovereigns. A bold prophecy, indeed! the fulfilment of which, up to the present moment, has in no way advanced.

I had given permission to such of the officers of the squadron as were inclined to make an inland excursion to proceed as far as Turin, Milan, or Florence, and I need hardly add that several gladly availed themselves of the boon. Some few visited the battle-fields of Magenta and Solferino, and all returned delighted with their expedition, and reported perfect order reigning everywhere.

To give an idea of the organization of the general police throughout the country, I may relate that three seamen belonging to the *St. Jean d'Acre* having deserted from one of the boats on duty at the watering-place, managed, by travelling during the night, to get safely to the frontier near Piacenza, and whilst endeavouring to cross the river were captured, and on the fourth day brought back and delivered to our custody. The usual reward of nine pounds sterling had been offered, but the Governor, both verbally and in writing, informed me that no sum of money could be delivered over to the police for the performance of an action in the strict line of their office.

CHAPTER VI.

1859.

Malta.—Signor Carafa.—Corfu.—Visit of Sir Henry Storks.—Austrian Merchant Ship saved from Fire.—Procession of Saint Spiridione.—Visit of the Archbishop.—Prince Alfred.—Paper Hunt.—Opening of the Parliament.—Sporting Excursion in Albania.—Good Feeling of the Gentry.

I TOOK my departure, with the squadron under my command, from the Gulf of Spezia on the 24th of September, and, passing along the western shores of Corsica and Sardinia, anchored in Malta Harbour on the 5th of October. Here I found the *Renown* 91, Captain Forbes, and *Exmouth* 91, Captain Stopford, which vessels were placed under my orders, thus completing my division to six sail of the line.

The first document which I received was a despatch from Vice-Admiral Fanshawe, enclosing an official complaint from Signor Carafa, Minister for Foreign Affairs of His Majesty the King of the Two Sicilies, to the Hon. Henry Elliot, Her Majesty's Minister Plenipotentiary at Naples, relative to the conduct of the officers of Her Majesty's ships which had recently visited Palermo, Messina, Syracuse, and Catania, and calling upon me to furnish such explanation as I deemed necessary. I give the complaint verbatim, as it is unique of its kind.

"Certain officers belonging to English ships stationed at Palermo, Messina, Syracuse, and Catania, have spoke in a very indiscreet manner of designs attributed by them to their Government, and have asserted that the various English fleets were in Sicily to protect the interests of British subjects in an impending insurrection.

"Finally, on the departure of four English ships of war from Catania on the night of the 30th of August last, they took away with them a portion of the musical band of that town, without the permission of the authorities, as well as three inhabitants of Catania, who happened to be on board out of curiosity.

"The Royal Government is the more displeased and surprised at the above-mentioned events (of the serious nature of which Mr. Elliot can well judge) in that the officers and crews of the English navy have at no time been ever guilty of such breaches of discipline, preserving, on the contrary, that behaviour and regular conduct which is an adjunct to the influences of the forces of a great nation."

To this extraordinary accusation I was enabled to

give a satisfactory reply, having, as already mentioned, provided myself with the materials before leaving Catania. The letter of Captain Chads, the declaration of the Vice-Consul, and the statement of the three gentlemen visitors on board the *London*, were conclusive evidence that nothing had been done but what was strictly courteous and defensible. I concluded my justification with the following paragraphs.

"Nearly the whole of the principal noble families of Catania visited the *Hannibal*, where they were received with that good feeling and hospitality which I hope I shall always offer to distinguished visitors in foreign ports. I believe they were moved to visit my flag-ship from respect for the British character, and from the natural desire of seeing a large screw ship of war, no ship of the line having anchored at Catania during the last twenty years.

"Not one of my guests made any observations on politics, nor were they alluded to either by myself or the officers; and I am really at a loss to account for this gratuitous and unfriendly accusation, brought forward by the Neapolitan Government against English naval officers, who, I must do them the justice to say, exerted themselves to the utmost to show civility to the Sicilians of every condition in life, who, in numbers amounting to between twenty and thirty thousand, crowded our ships during the short stay at Syracuse and Catania."

At this date the ships under my immediate disposal had not visited the ports of Palermo and Messina, but I learnt that the allusion to those places arose from an officer of the Royal Marine Light Infantry belonging to the *Orion* having presented to a young lady of the former city an ornamental cake, on the white sugared exterior of which was unfortunately planted two pasteboard standards, one representing the union-jack of Great Britain and the other the tricoloured national flag of Italy; but as these emblems were intertwined with numerous other figures and devices, as on twelfth day and wedding cakes in England, the unsuspecting officer had not noticed the objectionable banner. He imagined himself to be performing an act of ordinary politeness or of gallantry, and found himself denounced as a conspirator and revolutionist.

On the 20th of October, I received a telegram from the Admiralty as follows:—"Be in readiness to put to sea with the ships under your orders at very short notice." And as war between Spain and Morocco was imminent, I thought Gibraltar would be the probable rendezvous.

The doubt was cleared up at the end of the month. Corfu was my destination.

I left Malta on the 31st, and on the 3rd of November cast anchor off the Citadel, having with me the *St. Jean d'Acre, London, Racoon,* and *Osprey.*

On the following day I paid an official visit to His Excellency Sir Henry Storks, the Lord High Commissioner of the Ionian Islands, who immediately took me over the north wing of the Palace apartments, which in the kindest manner he placed at my disposal, inviting me at the same time to be his guest so long as I should remain on the Adriatic station.

On the 5th, His Excellency returned my visit on board the *Hannibal*, and was received with manned yards and a salute of seventeen guns. Major-general Sir George Buller, K.C.B., commanding the troops, also came on board with his staff, and was saluted on leaving the ship with thirteen guns.

On the 9th, an Austrian merchant vessel took fire in the middle of the night, and was saved from destruction by the prompt action of the fire brigade of the squadron, under the orders of Captain Connolly, for which service the Lord High Commissioner and the Austrian Consul transmitted to me a letter of thanks.

On Sunday the 13th, the celebrated religious procession of Saint Spiridione took place. In former days it was the custom both of the Lord High Commissioner and the heads of the civil and military departments to walk a certain distance in company with the ecclesiastical authorities, thus showing what was considered a praiseworthy deference to the moral feelings of the community. This has now been altogether discontinued. Sir Henry Storks, his aide-de-camps, Major Peel and Lieutenant Strahan, and myself, took up a position in the front balcony of the palace, and as the archbishop, with a phalanx of priests, passed round by the broad road, abreast of the portico, our hats were raised as a mark of respect to this national festival.

The archbishop, a handsome and venerable prelate, who wore upon his head the magnificent crown of the orthodox Greek Church, and was attired in splendid sacerdotal robes, stopped for a few minutes beneath the balcony, as an acknowledgment of this courteous act on the part of the Lord High Commissioner, and certainly the bearers of the saint, who were groaning under the weight of the massive case in which the body was carried, appeared gladly to avail themselves of this momentary rest.

The remains of the martyred dignitary of Cyprus were plainly visible through the glass window of his receptacle, which, constructed in the form of a common sedan chair, exposes the upper part of the figure to the gaze of the multitude; and, considering that the mummy has undoubtedly been entombed for the space of four hundred years in the Cathedral Church of Corfu, and had previously reposed more than double that period in a Christian sanctuary at Constantinople, it is wonderfully preserved.

On the 17th, the Archbishop honoured me with a visit on board the *Hannibal*, attended by a numerous retinue of the regular clergy; and having the honorary title of an Ionian Senator, His Eminence was received by a guard of honour, and a salute of thirteen guns. He spoke to me of the Archbishop of Canterbury, and the bishops of the Church of England, as if he considered them brothers in the faith, and alluded with gratitude to a prompt service which had been rendered to him lately by Commander Blomfield, son of the late Bishop of London, and in command of the gunboat *Osprey*, who had gone to the Archbishop's assistance when stranded on one of the small islands at the entrance of the Adriatic.

On the 2nd of December, the *Euryalus* frigate, Captain Tarlton, arrived from the Piræus, having on board His Royal Highness Prince Alfred. By express commands of the Queen, the royal midshipman was received with the honours due to him as a member of Her Majesty's family. The ships were dressed with flags, royal salutes were fired, and when the youth landed at the pier, he was received by the major-general commanding the troops and myself, and conducted to the Palace; at the head of the grand staircase, Sir Henry Storks, the Archbishop, the Senators, and Members of the Lower House, met His Royal Highness in state, and conveyed him to the throne room, where the presentation of the authorities in due form took place. The Prince wore the uniform of a midshipman, and was attended by Major

Cowell, the friend and governor, who has watched over and carefully instructed him for so many anxious years.

His Royal Highness remained four days at Corfu, two out of which I may pronounce as having been passed in a manner more than usually agreeable. On the first he attended a paper hunt, arranged for his amusement by Captain Ponsonby, which brought twenty sportsmen into the field, and produced a capital run of thirty-seven minutes; and on the second he steamed over to the Albanian coast, and enjoyed the laborious pastime of woodcock-shooting in thick cover, and, I believe, on this occasion brought his first long-bill to the ground. The other two days were occupied by a visit to the shrine of the patron saint, and by excursions into the country.

His reception everywhere by the inhabitants was cordial and respectful; but with the exception of his visit to the opera, where he met with a welcome unmistakeably loyal, there was no symptom of enthusiasm.

His Royal Highness re-embarked under the same ceremonies as on landing.

On taking leave he presented me with a full-length portrait of himself, admirably lithographed, which found a place in my after cabin by the side of Her Most Gracious Majesty, His Royal Highness the Prince Consort, and his brother the Prince of Wales.

On the day after the departure of the Prince, the Lord High Commissioner opened the Parliament in State, and his reception by the people as he passed from the Palace to the House of Assembly was courteous and deferential. Rumours had been current that opposition would be offered, by members of the extreme left, to the entrance of the Queen's representative into the body of the House, and that the mob who on these occasions had access to the galleries, would show their desire for union with Greece by acts of riot and disorder. If such hostile demonstrations were ever seriously entertained, they were completely overthrown by the firm attitude and composed demeanour of the Lord High Commissioner.

I now close my remarks for the year 1859 by an account of a second expedition to the coast of Albania, in search of the feathered game which, at this inclement season, forsakes the mountain's side and seeks shelter and sustenance in the watered coverts of the vast plains of Butrinto.

Embarking on board the *Assurance* at early dawn with three-and-twenty officers of the United Service whom I had invited to accompany me, and taking with us the same number of seamen to act as beaters, and fifteen dogs, we steamed to the opposite shores, and anchored at the entrance of the river as a gale of wind sprung up which threatened in a few hours to render the bar impassable. Dividing ourselves into four parties, we spread across the whole area of the district, and scientifically began our work as the sun gained the meridian. The morass was in many places knee-deep, and the wooded brakes difficult of access; but game was abundant, and the spirit of the sportsmen equal to the occasion.

At the conclusion of the day's amusement, the general bag amounted to ninety-nine woodcocks, nineteen snipe, and a teal, killed by eleven men of the party, who, accustomed as old hands to the peculiar nature of the ground, managed to bring down a small percentage of the birds at which they fired, whilst the younger and less-experienced gunners were no less astonished than annoyed to find every woodcock escape. Sixteen woodcocks were drawn forth by my coxswain at the final muster on the beach, a number which he evidently considered most satisfactory as the product of the admiral's fowling-piece. Colonel Elmhirst, of the 9th Regiment, and Lieutenant-Colonel the Hon. Edward Gage, of the Royal Artillery, were equally successful in making a good bag.

During the first watch, the *Assurance* regained the anchorage at Corfu, amidst torrents of rain and a gale from south-west.

On New Year's Day, 1860, *two hundred and seventy-one* gentlemen, principally Ionian Greeks, wrote their names in my visiting-book, a number almost incredible for so small a community. I willingly accepted the compliment as a proof of the good feeling of the native gentry towards the Royal Navy of that country against which, in its capacity of protector of the Septinsular Republic, so much unmerited abuse has been lavished by agitators.

CHAPTER VII.

1860.

Departure from Corfu.—Gibraltar.—Termination of the Spanish-Morocco War.—Mr. Drummond Hay.—Return to Malta.—Impending Disturbances in Southern Italy.

In the middle of February, in consequence of the serious complications which were brought about in Western Europe by the continuance of the war between Spain and Morocco, I received orders to proceed with all despatch to the Straits of Gibraltar, and on the 18th of the month I finally quitted Corfu.

During the three months and a half which I had passed in the roadstead, I was the guest of Sir Henry Storks, the Lord High Commissioner, and our relations with each other, both public and private, were uniformly friendly. With a form of Government theoretically unexceptionable, but practically unworkable, and with a mixed people, under any conditions most difficult to rule, His Excellency had succeeded in gaining the esteem and affection both of the city and rural population, and it is to be hoped he may eventually bring within reasonable bounds the revolutionary tendencies of the members of the Lower House. In this, and in every other good work, he is ably assisted by the Government Secretary, Mr. Drummond Wolff.

On the day before my departure I took my farewell ride with my friends of the "Royal Paper Hunt," whose bi-weekly meetings I had frequently attended, and from which exhilarating sport I had derived so much healthy exercise and rational amusement. I have to thank Colonel the Hon. Leicester Curzon for a first-rate mount on his thorough-bred Arab "Marengo," which carried me without a fault, and which he had kindly placed at my disposal during the whole of my stay at Corfu.

On the passage from Corfu to Gibraltar we met constant gales from the westward, and the *Hannibal* sprung a leak. This was repaired during a short stay at Malta, but burst forth again in a heavy sea off the coast of Tunis, obliging us to keep the pumps at work, and causing some apprehension.

On the 19th of March, thirty days after leaving the Ionian Islands, we anchored in the Bay of Gibraltar, the squadron then under my orders being,—the *Renown*, 91, Captain Forbes; *James Watt*, 91, Captain Codd; *Agamemnon*, 91, Captain Hope; *Doris*, *Scylla*, and *Vulture*, frigates; and *Mohawk*, *Quail*, and *Redpole*, gunboats.

From Captain Warden, in charge of the dockyard, I ascertained that I had arrived at a moment when a decisive battle between the Spaniards and the Moors might be hourly expected. The Spanish army, twenty-five thousand strong, under Field-Marshal O'Donnell, had quitted Tetuan and commenced the march upon Tangier; whilst the army of the Moors, nearly double that number, counting the levy of irregulars, under the command of the Viceroy, a younger brother of the Emperor, was in position to guard the approach to the mountain passes which intervened between those cities.

Four days after my arrival the Christian and Mahomedan forces came into collision. The battle, as expected, was decisive. The Moors fought bravely, and their losses were enormous, but the Spaniards were victorious in every part of the field.

On the 25th of March, preliminaries of peace were signed between the Viceroy and the Marshal, and it was well that the Don had hurried forward this settlement, for on the following day seven thousand of the warlike tribe of Shebaur possessed themselves of the country on the south-east side of Tetuan, in rear of the Spanish army, and, on the 28th, twelve thousand Relfians also reached the scene of combat. The Viceroy had long expected these auxiliaries, and bitterly upbraided their chiefs for their tardy appearance.

Thus terminated the Spanish-Morocco war, after a duration of less than six months. It was conducted in a manner highly creditable to the Spanish army, which exhibited during the campaign, under heavy trials from the severity of the winter and difficult nature of the country, many soldierlike qualities, good discipline, order, and sobriety.

The terms of the treaty were onerous to the vanquished. The Emperor agreed to pay, as an indemnity for the expenses of the war, four hundred millions of reals, equal to four million pounds sterling, besides rectification of the frontier by the cession of land round the fortress of Centa and other advantages on the coast of Mogador.

At this crisis in the history of the only remaining independent Mahomedan empire in Northern Africa, I had been in daily communication, by a relay of despatch vessels, with Mr. Drummond Hay, Her Majesty's agent and *chargé d'affaires* at Tangier, who, continuing to reside at his post in the city, was enabled to do good service to all parties engaged, and to uphold at the same time the great interests of our country.

On the 8th, my flag-captain, Captain Connolly, invalided and left the ship for England, much regretted by all on board.

The presence of a large naval force being no longer necessary in these waters, I left the bay of Gibraltar with the squadron under my command for Malta on the 10th of April, and after a boisterous passage reached the Island on the 21st, where I found the Commander-in-Chief, with five sail of the line and several smaller vessels.

Intelligence from Southern Italy and from Sicily had just been received, giving evidence of impending disturbances. Naples was unquiet, and at Palermo a partial insurrection had broken out on the 4th of the month, but was immediately suppressed by the storming of the rebel head-quarters at the Convent of La Guancia by the Neapolitan troops.

In Central Italy marvellous changes had taken place. The Æmilian Confederation had been, by an almost unanimous vote under universal suffrage, annexed to the Kingdom of Sardinia, and King Victor Emanuel found his dominions augmented by the additional provinces of Tuscany, Modena, Parma, and the Romagna. The cession, however, of Savoy and Nice to France, after the solemn declaration of Count Cavour to Lord John Russell that no such sacrifice would be made, was a blot in the grand scheme of Italian regeneration which no subsequent arrangement can ever obliterate.

CHAPTER VIII.

1860.

Landing of Garibaldi at Marsala.—Departure for Palermo.—My Instructions.—General Salzano's Letter to Mr. Goodwin.—Measures for the Protection of Foreigners.—Visit to General Lanza.—Austrian Squadron.—Authentic Account of Garibaldi's Movements.—Interview with the Principal Merchants.

On the 5th of May I sailed from Malta with four sail of the line, to cruize off the east coast of Sicily; and on the following day I had the good fortune to save the life of another seaman by throwing my ring life-buoy into the arms of the struggler, as, in the trough of a bubbling sea, he was sinking beneath the counter. I may here, I think, venture strongly to recommend every officer in command of a ship in possession of a stern cabin, to have this life-preserver at hand, which, at a moment when least expected, may prove essentially useful.

On the 15th of May I returned to port to replenish water, and then learnt from the sanatory authorities that Garibaldi had landed at Marsala with twelve hundred men, only four days previously.

It so happened that at this period ten sail of the line were at their moorings in the grand harbour of Valetta, and the four flag-officers, including Rear-Admiral Dacres the captain of the fleet, on service in the Mediterranean, were also on the spot. It had been the intention of the Commander-in-Chief to take the whole force to sea, for practice in steam evolutions and gunnery, but the sudden and unexpected landing of Garibaldi effected a change in his plans. It was evident that, whether the great adventurer succeeded or not in his desperate enterprise, the lives of British subjects would be endangered and their property compromised by the revolutionary movement, and that the officer in command on the coast of Sicily at such a crisis, would be placed in a situation of unusual interest.

Under this impression I waited on the Commander-in-Chief, and requested that I might be sent forthwith to the Bay of Palermo, on which city, by the latest intelligence, Garibaldi was marching. After mature deliberation, Admiral Fanshawe acquiesced in my proposal; and on the evening of Sunday, the 18th of May, by means of torches at the fair way buoys, I steamed out of the harbour, and by midnight was rapidly passing Gozo Lighthouse, with a moderate breeze in our favour, and with a sea as smooth as could be desired.

The following simple instructions were furnished

as a guide to my proceedings, and were the first and last which I received during the lengthened period of my employment on the coasts of Sicily and Italy.

"*By Arthur Fanshawe, Esq., Companion of the most Honorable Order of the Bath, Vice-Admiral and Commander-in-Chief, &c., &c.*

"The insurrection in Sicily against the Neapolitan Government having spread throughout the Island since the landing of General Garibaldi with an armed force of Italians, it has become necessary to provide additional means of protection to British persons and property.

"You are therefore hereby required and directed to proceed in Her Majesty's ship *Hannibal*, bearing your flag, to Palermo for that object, taking under your orders the *Amphion*, *Argus*, and *Intrepid*.

"Your chief duty will be to afford every assistance and protection to British persons and property; and with regard to political refugees, I inclose for your information and guidance a copy of a letter from Mr. Addington to Captain W. A. B. Hamilton, respecting the reception of political refugees on board British ships of war, which I received from the Secretary of the Admiralty on the 14th instant.

"You will cause officers and men to be cautioned

carefully to avoid taking part in any political discussions or disturbances.

"Given on board the *Marlborough*, at Malta, the 18th May, 1860.

"*To* G. RODNEY MUNDY, ESQ., C.B.,
Rear-Admiral."

"*Foreign Office, 4th August*, 1849.

"Sir,—I have laid before Viscount Palmerston your letter of the 30th July last, requesting, by direction of the Lords Commissioners of the Admiralty, his Lordship's opinion on a question which has recently occurred in Naples, as to the extent to which British ships of war in a foreign port are entitled to receive on board and shelter the subjects of a Foreign Government, who may be apprehensive of being persecuted if they remain on shore.

"Viscount Palmerston directs me to request that you will acquaint the Board of Admiralty that his Lordship is of opinion that it would not be right to receive and harbour on board a British ship of war any person flying from justice on a criminal charge or who was escaping from the sentence of a Court of Law. But a British ship of war has always and everywhere been considered as a safe place of refuge for persons of whatever country or party who have sought shelter under the British flag from persecution on account of their political conduct or opinions, and this protection has been equally afforded whether the refugee was escaping from the arbitrary acts of a monarchical government, or from the lawless violence of a revolutionary committee.

"There seems to be nothing in the present state of affairs at Naples, or in Sicily, which ought to make a British ship of war stationed in a Neapolitan or in a Sicilian port an exception to the general rule, and therefore, although the commander of such ship of war should not seek out or invite political refugees, yet he ought not to turn away nor give up any who may reach his ship and ask admittance on board. Such officer must, of course, take care that such refugees should not carry on from on board his ship any political correspondence with their partizans on shore, and he ought to avail himself of the earliest opportunity to send them to some place of safety elsewhere.

"Viscount Palmerston sees no reason, however, why the fact of a British officer having exercised this act of usual hospitality should entitle the Government of the country to order him out of the port, if the interests of Her Majesty's service should require that he should remain there.

"I am, &c.,

"H. W. ADDINGTON.

"*To the Secretary of the Admiralty.*"

It is remarkable that a public document of eleven

years' standing, written with reference to the discontent and disturbances in the Kingdom of the Two Sicilies at that date, should again be called forth as a guide for naval officers in the present difficulties.

May 19.—At sunset I passed within a few miles of the town of Marsala, when Captain Ingram, of Her Majesty's steam vessel *Argus*, at anchor in the roads, made known to me by signal that Garibaldi, on the 15th instant, had defeated the Royal troops at Calatafimi, and was marching towards the capital.

May 20.—During the morning watch, in the midst of storms of wind and rain, and with the atmosphere so overcast that glimpses of the land could only be obtained at intervals as the sea broke on the rocky coast, I steamed into the bay of Palermo, and soon after daylight brought the *Hannibal* to an anchor, within a few cables' length of the pier, to the eastward of the citadel.

I found here the *Amphion*, 36, Captain Cockran; the *Intrepid* gunboat, Commander Marryat; the French paddle steam frigate *Vauban*, Captain Lefevre, and two small Sardinian steamers of war. In the forenoon Mr. Goodwin, Her Majesty's Consul, came on board, and expressed himself in terms of high satisfaction at my opportune arrival.

He had received, only a few hours previously, an official communication from General Salzano, in command of the Neapolitan garrison, which, after alluding to the deplorable aspect of affairs in the Island, contained the following decisive paragraph:—"I judge it necessary to inform you, that if an insurrection takes place in this city the royal troops will have recourse to all those painful extremities which war imposes in order to repress it, and I should neither know, nor should I be able to be responsible for, the consequences that might happen to foreigners who may remain in this city."

A document of this gravity, couched in language not over-courteous, and which, when made known to the foreign community, would be certain to create an alarm, required immediate response. I, therefore, informed Her Majesty's Consul that I should transmit to him, in writing, my opinion that the British merchants and residents should at once seek an asylum on board the ships of war in the bay, and that I should forthwith express my surprise and regret to the Viceroy, General Lanza, at the terms of a public circular which seemed to imply an inability or a disinclination to control the action of the troops.

I also requested Mr. Goodwin to inform the Consul and all other subjects of the United States of America who might be desirous of availing themselves of the protection of Her Majesty's ships under my orders, that I should have much pleasure in receiving them on board, if such should be their desire.

The city is now declared in a state of siege, is deserted by the upper classes, all business at an end, and the shops entirely closed. Of the movements of Garibaldi nothing certain is known. He is reported to be in the mountains with his volunteers and armed peasantry, called *squadre*, but what their numbers are, and what his plans, no one as yet seemed to know.

May 21.—At 8 A.M. I fired a royal salute, hoisting the Neapolitan flag at the main, which was immediately returned by the guns of the citadel.

At 11, I landed in full uniform with my staff, and proceeded to the palace to pay an official visit to His Excellency General Lanza, the Royal Commissioner Extraordinary and *Alter Ego* of His Majesty the King of the Two Sicilies. The streets of the city, as I drove slowly through them, seated in an open barouche, presented an extraordinary appearance. It was as if passing through a city of the dead, or one decimated by the plague. Containing two hundred thousand persons, not an inhabitant was to be seen, nor was there a vehicle abroad, save that which I occupied. Troops were everywhere posted, and the only sound which I heard was the tramp of the soldiery, who, either on patrol, or on guard, or on bivouac in the squares, held possession of the avenues leading to the forts and the military stations. In outward look these men had a martial bearing, and the equipment of the artillery was remarkable for efficiency.

At the principal gateway of the palace I was

received by a guard of honour, and on the staircase by an aide-de-camp, who accompanied me to the reception room. I was met at the entrance door by the Royal Commissioner, and by him introduced to the chief director of the police, Signor Manascalco, and to the chief of the staff, Colonel Polizzi.

General Lanza is a man of a benevolent disposition, and his manners replete with dignity and courtesy; but approaching fourscore years of age, with the infirmity of deafness, and weakness in the limbs, he was not a proper substitute for Prince Castelcicala, whom, only five days ago, he had superseded and replaced.

Having expressed to him the satisfaction which I had felt at saluting the Royal standard, and the hope that paying my respects to the *Alter Ego* of His Majesty so immediately on arrival would be agreeable to His Excellency, I entered at once on a subject of a more practical kind. I acquainted him without reserve that I had no mission from the English Government, but, as the officer second in command of the Mediterranean fleet, had been ordered to the Bay of Palermo by the naval Commander-in-Chief to afford protection in case of need to British residents and merchants, and that I hoped I might rely on the co-operation of the Royal authorities in any measure I might adopt for the security of the vast property which my countrymen held in the city. I did not think it advisable at this first visit of ceremony to proffer a remark on General Salzano's uncourteous notification, conceiving that a written despatch on so irritating a subject would be preferable to the risk of personal discussion.

General Lanza, in his reply, was equally careful not to make allusion to political matters. The name of the great adventurer who was known to be in possession of the whole country round was not even mentioned, nor any comment hinted at the deplorable condition of the city.

To the famous police chieftain, Manascalco, whose deeds of oppression and cruelty had long made him the terror of every inhabitant of the Island, I did not address a word; but, during the whole interview, he stood by the Governor's chair, anxiously listening to the turn of the conversation, and certainly could have learnt nothing calculated to make him regret the advent of the British Admiral.

At the foot of the staircase I found one of the Vice-regal carriages ready to re-convey me to the Marina, and my own hired vehicle sent back to its owner.

On my return to the ship I addressed the following letter to the Royal Commissioner:—

"*Hannibal*, at Palermo, 21 May, 1860.

"SIR,

"I take the earliest opportunity of conveying to your Excellency my regret that Marshal Salzano, in a letter addressed yesterday to Her Britannic Majesty's Consul, should have expressed himself as unable to afford any protection to British persons and property in the event of there being an insurrection in the city of Palermo.

"I have therefore thought it necessary to recommend all British subjects to seek an asylum on board Her Majesty's ships at anchor in the port.

"It being currently reported that in the event of such insurrection a bombardment of the city by the forts and Neapolitan ships of war is in contemplation, I have earnestly to desire that should such be determined upon, you will be pleased to give me ample notice, in order that if possible the property of British subjects may be saved from destruction.

"I trust, however, that a measure so extreme and deplorable as the bombardment of an open town may not be resorted to.

"I have, &c., &c.

"*To His Excellency* GENERAL LANZA,
"*Royal Commissioner Extraordinary.*"

I also issued the following general memorandum to the captains and officers under my orders :—

"It being desirable that Her Majesty's ships stationed at the various ports in Sicily for the protection of British subjects and property should maintain a strict neutrality with regard to the insurrection against the Neapolitan Government, it is my direction that the captains and officers commanding Her Majesty's ships and vessels under my orders, cause their respective officers and men to be cautioned to avoid taking part in any political discussions or disturbances, which would frustrate the object of their presence and compromise the British Government.

"Officers who may land are to appear in their proper uniforms, and are to return to their ships by sunset."

The reports which I received from the interior relative to the state and condition of the insurgents being very contradictory, I sent the *Intrepid* at daylight this morning to the town of Sicciara, which is situated twenty miles to the westward of Palermo, giving Commander Marryat instructions to ascertain from competent authority what were the positions held by Garibaldi and the calculated number of his armed adherents.

In the evening an Austrian squadron, consisting of the *Schwartzenburg*, 60; *Dandolo*, 21; and *Santa Lucia*, 6, under the command of Commodore Baron Von Wullersdorff, anchored in the bay, half a mile to seaward of the British ships.

May 22.—Strong north-east winds and rain. The *Intrepid* returned early, and brought me reliable intelligence of the movements of Garibaldi and his armed bands up to yesterday morning, when he was only eleven miles distant from Palermo, with a mixed force of volunteers and *squadre*, amounting to five or six thousand men.

I also received interesting documents, giving me, with some detail, a succinct account of the proceedings of the self-constituted Dictator, from the hour of his arrival at Marsala to his passage through Partenico on the 20th. This history will be given at length, as the source from which it has been obtained enables me to pronounce it as worthy of credence in all its essentials.

Garibaldi landed at Marsala on the 11th instant, with nearly eleven hundred men, four hundred of whom were professional gentlemen, either engineers, law or medical students. They came in the Sardinian merchant steamers *Piedmont* and *Lombardo*. The former succeeded in reaching the Mole, the latter was stranded: both, however, managed to get every one safely on shore. As the last company was put on *terra firma*, a Neapolitan frigate and two steamers of war opened fire upon the party, and one volunteer was wounded. The only other damage effected by this cannonade was the destruction of two casks of wine by a round shot, which entered the storehouse of Mr. Wodehouse.

Early on the 12th, the volunteers marched out of Marsala, with Garibaldi at their head. Before leaving, he sent a message to Commander Ingram, of the *Argus*, through Mr. Cossins, Acting Vice-Consul, requesting him to take care of the sailors belonging to the Sardinian steamers, who, under great alarm, had sought refuge in the wine establishment of one of the principal English merchants. This request was, very properly, not attended to by Commander Ingram. The men were Italians; their lives were not in danger; and it was most important, at a moment of lawless invasion, to abstain from an interference certain of misconstruction.

Passing through Salemi, the invading forces met the advanced division of the army of the King of the Two Sicilies, under General Laudi, within a few miles of the town of Calatafimi. Though strongly posted on high ground, they were immediately attacked by the intrepid chieftain; and an eye-witness of the engagement gave the following history to Commanders Ingram and Marryat:—

"On the 15th inst. the Neapolitans, about four thousand strong, under General Laudi, held a strong position on a mountain, having the town of Calatafimi in their rear.

"Garibaldi's force consisted of the men who landed from the steamers, six hundred who had joined him from Castel Vitrano, seven hundred from Mount Trapani, under Coppola, and three hundred who went with him from Marsala. Other small bands of armed peasants joined him from every village, swelling this mixed host to six or seven thousand men. Garibaldi advanced from the town of Salemi, and disposed of his men in the following order:—The

Piedmontese were placed on the right flank of the enemy, with orders on no account to return their fire; Coppola, with his force, on the left flank, and the remainder in front.

"The Neapolitans began their attack on the Piedmontese, who fell in large numbers, as if killed, though, in reality, steadily advancing on their bellies up the side of the hill. When close enough, they sprang to their feet, delivered one volley, and charged home with the bayonet. Those on the other side, under Coppola, had also gained the summit, and the united efforts of the two parties drove the Neapolitans pell-mell down the hill, in which descent they lost a great many men. They, however, took up another position; but were driven from this also, with the loss of one gun. At one time they reversed their muskets, putting the muzzles into the ground, and demanded quarter; but their general succeeded in shaming them out of it. The conflict ended by the Royal troops seeking shelter in Calatafimi and the insurgents sleeping on the ground last occupied by their enemy.

"On the following day the Neapolitans fell back on Alcamo, and Garibaldi passed through Calatafimi in chase.

"From Alcamo the retreat was continued to Partenico, and here the excesses of the Royal troops are spoken of as horrible. Forty houses were burnt down, and women and children murdered, without other motive than revenge and robbery. It was said that the soldiers carried small bottles filled with combustible matter, which they ignited and threw into the houses *en passant*. They, however, paid dearly for these atrocities, as the inhabitants, finding nothing would stop them, aroused themselves, and, making a sudden attack, killed thirty soldiers, and took several prisoners.

"The remainder of General Laudi's division, in a state of complete demoralization, and with the loss of waggons and baggage, entered Monreale, a small town a few miles from Palermo, on the 18th, on which day Garibaldi took possession of Alcamo, amidst the enthusiastic rejoicings of the people. Here he formed a Government, as at Salemi, in the name of Victor Emanuel, King of Italy.

"The principal persons who had already joined Garibaldi were La Masa, one of the first leaders of the Revolution in 1848, Carini, Callona, Orsini, a Colonel of Artillery, who deserted from the Neapolitans many years since, and Coppola."

During the afternoon I received a communication from three young ladies of the Sicilian aristocracy, whose husbands were confined in the citadel on charge of high treason, requesting me to intercede with General Lanza for the preservation of their lives. These noble ladies, the Princess Pignatelli, the Princess Niscemi, and Baroness Riso, of course assured me that their affectionate husbands were themselves the victims of a conspiracy, and innocent as lambs. They, moreover, begged me to grant them an interview, in order that they might explain in detail the injustice of their imprisonment, firmly persuaded that a word from the British Admiral would bring about their release. Believing that no good could arise from a personal interview, I declined the proposed visit, but let the petitioners know that I should speak to the Royal Commissioner in their husbands' behalf when he came on board.

Later in the day I landed in the city, and, proceeding to the Consulate, met a body of the principal merchants, who at my request had assembled there. I explained to them my views of the present aspect of affairs, and of the measures which I had taken for the protection of themselves and their property, and concluded by a recommendation that they should repair on board the ships of war, with their families, as soon as possible. Mr. Ingham, the oldest English resident, now in his eighty-second year, married to a Sicilian duchess, and in possession of immense wealth in the Island, was the only opponent of this measure. He felt convinced the Royal troops would be able to maintain order, and he should therefore refuse to leave his mansion and seek safety by flight.

On my return to the ship I found the following despatch from the Royal Commissioner in answer to my letter of the previous day :—

"Palermo, 22nd May, 1860.

"EXCELLENCY,

"The communication made by Marshal Salzano to the British Consul does not imply that no protection will be afforded to British subjects. On the contrary, I may assure your Excellency that orders have been given to guarantee as much as possible the dwellings and property of all strangers, should it fatally happen that an insurrectionary movement would oblige the garrison to make use of means which war dictates for repressing it.

"I am far from thinking to put the town to the horrors of a bombardment, and the sentiments of humanity which animate the Government of the King my Lord make me shrink from such an expedient. But your Excellency will comprehend that, if the army, while engaged in repelling the foreign invasion assisted by the rebels, should be attacked by the insurgents of the town from behind, I could not wait an instant to react with the artillery for saving the army I have the honour to command.

"The warning given by Marshal Salzano is in the usages of civilized nations, and the British subjects may avail themselves of it to secure their property.

"I hope that such extremity will not happen, but it is for the population to be wise, if they will not expose themselves to the horrors of civil war.

(Signed) "FERDINAND LANZA."

The *Iroquois*, American steam corvette, arrived in the evening, when Captain Palmer, in command, immediately visited me and expressed his thanks for the protection I had offered to his countrymen.

Five Neapolitan vessels of war also came to an anchor off the citadel.

CHAPTER IX.

1860.

Palermo.—Restoration of Arms to British Subjects.—General Lanza's Proposal of Intervention.—Garibaldi's Approach.—Celebration of Her Majesty's Birthday.—Endeavours to Prevent a Bombardment.

May 23.—It having been reported to me by Mr. Goodwin that General Letizia, who is employed on special service by the Neapolitan Government, had compelled all British subjects residing at Marsala and Trapani to surrender their arms to the local authorities, I made application to General Lanza for their early restitution. This demand was acquiesced in without hesitation, and at eleven this forenoon I despatched the *Intrepid* to Trapani, in the fortress of which town the arms had been deposited, giving Captain Marryat instructions to receive them from the Commandant and deliver them to their owners.

At noon the Royal Commissioner Extraordinary, accompanied by Colonel Polizzi, came on board in full uniform to return my visit. He was evidently in great tribulation, opening a discussion immediately on the present deplorable condition of his country, he being himself a Sicilian by birth. He informed me that nothing but a prompt intervention by myself in person between the contending parties could restore order, and he entreated me to accept the office of mediator. He acquainted me that General Garibaldi was at Parco, five miles from the city, that the armed peasants occupied the heights around, and that by my interposition an armistice might be arranged. I stated in reply that my instructions did not admit of interference; that my mission was to give protection to British residents and their families, many of which had sought refuge in the *Hannibal* and *Amphion*, when they learnt by Marshal Salzano's circular that they would not be safe if they remained in the city. I further observed that if affairs were really so desperate he would do well to make the truth known to his Government, and that in the event of my receiving instructions from Mr. Elliot, Her Majesty's Minister Plenipotentiary at Naples, I should be happy to lend my co-operation in such manner as might be desirable.

I next adverted to the case of the nobles imprisoned as conspirators. His Excellency at once offered to set them at liberty if I would guarantee their good conduct. This was of course inadmissible—for who should rightly interpret the meaning of such a phrase? —but in the most courteous manner he promised me that their lives should be spared, which joyful intelligence Mr. Goodwin undertook to convey to their wives. General Lanza subsequently took Mr. Goodwin aside, and stated that he saw no means of extrication from present difficulties other than a mediation, to be undertaken instantly by me in person, and entreated him as an old friend to support his application. The first step would be an armistice, and the next would be an endeavour to come to a conclusion satisfactory to both parties, and conservative of military honour. The Royal Commissioner also spoke of the desirability of proclaiming the Constitution of 1812. This decisive measure, he thought, might pacify the people.

It appeared that a complete change had come over the opinions of His Excellency during the last forty-eight hours; but that he should for a moment have imagined I could have power to act as he suggested, furnished ample proof of his unfitness for his post at such a crisis. A handful of adventurers were at the gates of the capital, and a well-appointed army of 25,000 men was ready to attack them. One vigorous effort of the rulers of this host would have sufficed; but, instead of action and reliance on their own resources, I was to be the pivot on which hung all their hopes of extrication from a dilemma occasioned by their own supineness.

After a visit of two hours General Lanza left the ship, under a salute of nineteen guns; and on his departure I received visits from the Austrian Commodore and the captains of the foreign ships of war, all of whom were anxious for information as to the progress of the insurrection. Though I discovered amongst them a divergence of opinion on many points of political interest, I found all were agreed that the officers of their respective ships should not have permission to go on shore, either in the city or in the country, and they appeared astonished when I apprized them that unless under the gravest circumstances I never interfered with the liberty of the officers. On the contrary, under proper regulations, I considered their moving about advantageous to public order, showing as it did a perfect confidence in the friendly disposition of both parties towards British naval officers, who, in the uniform of their rank, landed for the sake of exercise and amusement, and without a wish to intermeddle with the affairs of the Islanders.

During the evening the heights to the eastward of the city were covered with armed peasantry, carrying tricoloured banners at the heads of their companies, and at dusk fires were lighted at the different camps. It was reported that Garibaldi had slept last night at the house of the Eletto or Alderman of Parco, and had left early this morning for Bagaria or Misilmeri, villages about nine and ten miles to the eastward of Palermo. From Misilmeri there is a carriage-road to Palermo, and also a footpath behind the mountains to Mezzagno or Belmonte, whence another track leads through a gorge to the plain west of Maria di Jésu, and by this bye-path it is probable the great chiefs of the *squadre*, La Masa and Fuxa, will form a junction with the forces of the Sardinian Dictator. An attack from that quarter is talked of as fixed for to-morrow; and Count Tasca, who possesses a lofty mansion outside Porta Termini, has offered a ticket of admission for any officer I might select, in order that he might have an opportunity of watching and reporting proceedings. This kind proposition I begged leave to decline.

May 24.—At 8 in the morning the squadron dressed with flags, in honour of Her Majesty's birthday, the *Hannibal* hoisting the royal standard at the main; the Austrian, French, American, Sardinian, and Neapolitan ships of war, fifteen in number, following our example.

At noon a royal salute was fired by the ships of the combined squadrons, the report of which must have astonished the combatants, who at this time were engaged in skirmishes on the distant ranges of the mountains. Eight thousand of the Royal troops had marched out from Monreale yesterday, and taken the road towards the defile of Piano de Greci, in which direction the Piedmontese had been seen; and as their numbers were small, it was hoped they might be destroyed before they had joined the main body of the peasantry in revolt.

I had received intelligence in the morning through the French Consul, that eight Neapolitan steamers were preparing to throw shells into the city; and in the course of the day the alarm became so general that the British merchants requested me to make another appeal to the Royal Commissioner to dissuade him from such an aggression. I acquainted them in reply, that I should continue to do everything in my power to obtain that protection for their property which they were entitled to expect, and that they might reasonably hope the joint efforts of the foreign Consuls and myself would have a favourable effect.

At 7, I received on board the *Hannibal* at a full-dress dinner, in honour of the fête-day of the Queen, the captains of the ships under my orders, and the commodore and captains of the foreign ships of war, including Commodore Wullërsdorf, of the Austrian frigate *Schwarztenburg;* Captain Barry, of the Austrian steamer *Dandolo;* Captain Lefevre, of the French frigate *Vauban;* Captain Boyer, of the French steamer *Mouette;* Captain Palmer, of the American corvette *Iroquois;* Captain Flores, of the Neapolitan corvette *Ercole;* and Captain the Marquis d'Asti, of the Sardinian steamer *Governolo.*

The only toast proposed was the health of our gracious Sovereign, which was responded to by all my guests with a hearty good-will; and after "God Save the Queen" had been twice played by our excellent band, the master of which was a Neapolitan, the reserve hitherto reigning seemed to be sudddenly overcome, and the conversation became general. As the officer in command of the naval forces of His Sicilian Majesty was present, it was necessary to be guarded in speaking of the present condition of affairs in the city, and as much as possible to avoid allusion to passing events in the Island. Fortunately, due circumspection was observed, and nothing untoward occurred; indeed, as the party was kept up beyond the usual seafaring hours, and much hilarity and convivial feeling prevailed, the meeting may be pronounced in every way a success. I certainly remarked that the Marquis d'Asti, who represented the navy of King Victor Emanuel, and Captain Flores, who commanded the squadron of Francis II., did not exchange civilities during the evening, but probably, the ill-concealed desire of the Sardinian Government for the success of the rebels may have been the cause of this coolness.

May 25.—I addressed the following letter this morning to General Lanza, purporting to take it with me to the Palace, but only to deliver it into the hands of His Excellency in the event of my being unable to obtain satisfactory assurance of his intention of not ordering an indiscriminate bombardment. I must, however, mention that I should not have felt myself justified in making this strong remonstrance on the question of the extent of right which the governing Power might possess, in order to extinguish armed insurrection, had not the Royal Commissioner himself, when on board the *Hannibal*, entreated my interference, and shown an evident desire to consider me both as a friend and counsellor. He forced me, as it were, into the position of an adviser and a protester, and it remained for me to decide on my own responsibility how far interference might be carried in the cause of humanity and civilization:—

Hannibal, at Palermo, 25th May, 1860.

"SIR,

"After the conversation which I held with your Excellency on the subject of your letter of the 22nd instant, I observed with extreme anxiety several Neapolitan vessels of war take up a position with their broadsides swung towards the principal buildings along the Marina, bringing their guns to bear on points where they could only be used for the destruction of the city itself, without having the effect of quelling an insurrection of the inhabitants.

"I am still willing to believe that this change in the position of the Royal squadron is only intended as a demonstration, but as the panic is now universal, I feel it my duty again to repeat my earnest entreaties that your Excellency will not have recourse to an expedient so opposed to the system of modern warfare amongst civilized nations, and one which could in no way accomplish the result you are so desirous to attain.

"I have, &c.,

(Signed) "G. RODNEY MUNDY.

"*His Excellency*

"*The Royal Commissioner Extraordinary.*"

At noon I repaired to the Palace in company with the Consul, and found General Lanza, Colonel Polizzi, and Signor Maniscalco in the reception room. On this occasion I opened the conversation at once on the subject of the bombardment, explaining to His Excellency that as he had unreservedly spoken to me when on board the *Hannibal* of the alarming state of the situation, and had requested my mediation, I had now ventured to pay him a second visit, hoping to receive a distinct avowal of his intentions in the event of an insurrection of the inhabitants, and of the measures he proposed to adopt for the security of the vast foreign property distributed about the city.

The reply of General Lanza was frank and decisive. He told me he had well weighed every possible contingency; that he considered the notice of Marshal Salzano as quite in accordance with the custom of civilized nations in similiar conjunctions, and served to remove all responsibility from the hands of the Royal Government. He entertained a firm hope that Palermo would not become the scene of a sanguinary civil struggle, and all his endeavours were directed to remove from its walls the calamities of war. He should oppose the foreign invasion outside the city ; in fact, he had yesterday dislodged the band of Garibaldi from their strong position at El Parco, seven miles from Palermo, and had pursued them to the summit of the mountains of Piano dei Greci. If, however, in spite of his endeavours, the rebels should make the city rise, the fire of the artillery by sea and by land would concur with the troops in the repression of revolt. In this sad eventuality he would not order fire to be opened until two hours after the commencement of hostilities, in order to give time to the Consuls, to foreigners, and all peaceful persons to repair to a place of safety.

When General Lanza had finished his address I rose to depart, thanking him for his candid statement, but, at the same time, remarking that there was a vast difference between the indiscriminate destruction of the edifices of a great city, and the use of artillery against a people in revolt. He then informed me that two Piedmontese prisoners had been brought to the guardhouse in the morning, who, though dressed as private soldiers, were evidently gentlemen. I asked him to spare their lives, which he said he would do.

During this interview Signor Maniscalco and

Colonel Polizzi entered into the discussion, with a view of justifying the resolutions which had been so clearly expounded by the Royal Commissioner. Unfortunately, in the heat of the argument the former asked Mr. Goodwin if he did not think a population deserved to be annihilated, should they rise up in insurrection against the constituted authorities.

To this unexpected and ill-timed demand Her Majesty's Consul indignantly replied that he could not have supposed such a question would have been put to him ; but that as Signor Maniscalco had chosen to do so, he had no hesitation in saying that when a people were tyrannized over they had an inherent right to take up arms, and to fight against their oppressors. This manly reply seemed to astonish the questor, and drew forth a remark from General Lanza that he did not imagine the English Admiral would endorse the Consular opinion. I declined entering on the subject, but reminded the Royal Commissioner that the indiscretion of the director of police had elicited the retort of Her Majesty's Consul.

On leaving the Palace I placed my official protest against the intended bombardment in the hands of His Excellency, and returning immediately to the ship informed the British residents by letter of the result of an interview which strengthened my former impression that no effective protection would be granted by the Royal authorities, either to persons or property, and that every one should at once seek an asylum in the ships of war in the Bay.

Colonel Ebor, a Hungarian gentleman, arrived yesterday, and hopes to obtain a command under Garibaldi.

CHAPTER X.

1860.

Palermo.—Excursion in the Neighbourhood.—Narrow Escape.—Misilmeri.—Impending Attack on the City.—Insurrection.—Bombardment.—Entry of Garibaldi.—Mr. Goodwin's Courage.—Refugees on Board.—Bombardment resumed.

May 26.—The Royal Commissioner having informed me that the rebels were driven into the mountains, and that all the low country was occupied by the Royal troops, I landed in the afternoon, to take a drive in an open carriage with Mr. Goodwin.

We proceeded through the line of sentries to the eastward, and visited the Capuchin Convent and the picturesque village of La Grazia. A small offering to the friars for the benefit of the poor was thankfully received, these holy and very dirty-looking men complaining bitterly of the prevailing distress. They seemed most discontented with their position, and, for reasons imperfectly shown, did not hesitate to proclaim themselves as favourable to the Revolution. But what advantages a fraternity of lazy drones expected to obtain from a reformation in the Government appears altogether inexplicable.

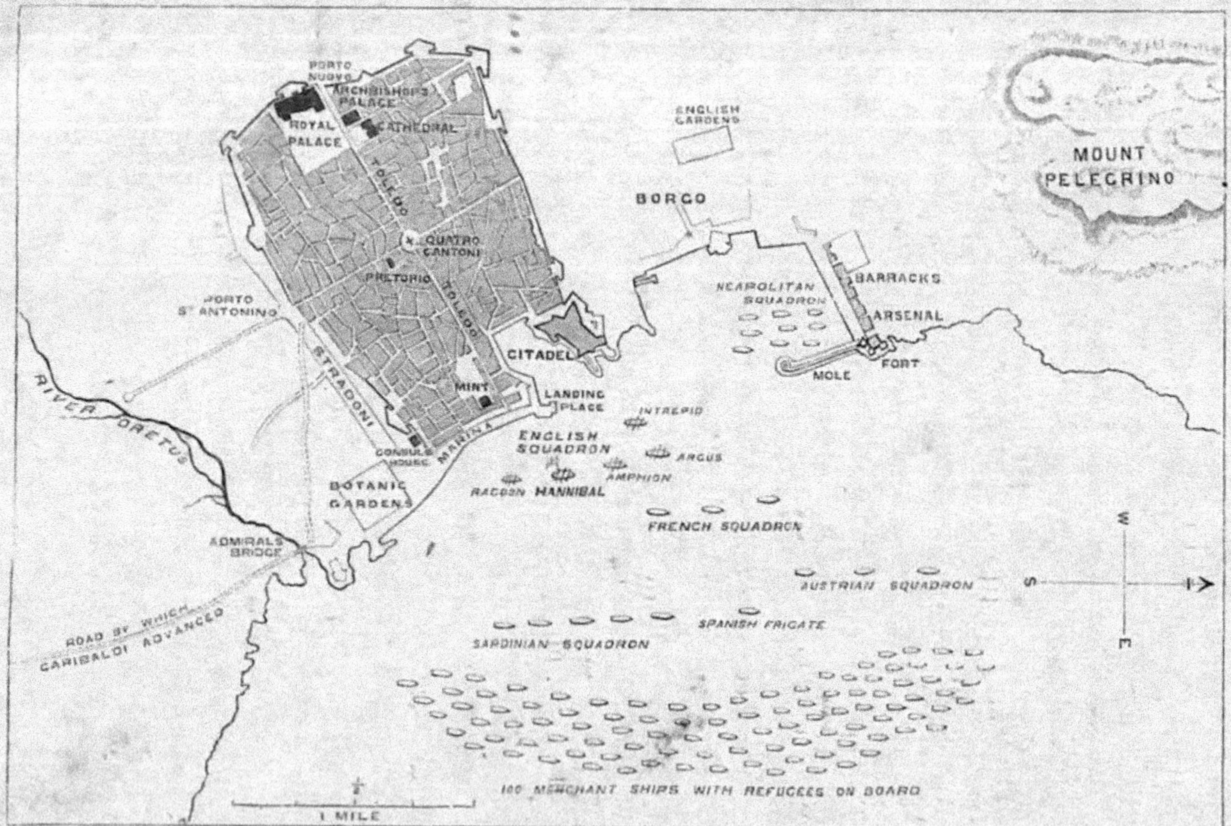

PLAN OF PALERMO AT THE TIME OF THE BOMBARDMENT.

As we entered La Grazia, through a narrow lane, hedged in on either side by high mud walls, our carriage was stopped by three suspicious-looking men, who presented their muskets at our breasts and demanded to know who we were.

"The English Admiral and the English Consul," was the immediate reply of Mr. Goodwin, in Italian, to the ruffians; who, apparently satisfied with the information, withdrew their weapons from the body of our vehicle, and exclaiming the two words, "*Bene: avanti!*" disappeared amongst some prickly-pear bushes. We afterwards learnt these heroes were the advanced sentinels of what they called the liberating army; and, though we were only a few miles from the city walls, it was clear from this incident that armed insurgents were in ambush between the divisions of the Royal forces.

On the outskirts of the city I gained admission into a mansion once occupied by the Moorish governors of Sicily, from the lofty turrets of which I witnessed the burning of several of the country palaces of the nobility who were supposed by the soldiery to be hostile to the Royal cause. In whichever direction I looked over this vast and richly-cultivated plain, the smoke of ruins and devastation presented itself to my view, whilst the constant report of musketry and the distant sound of cannon showed that armed men were in collision on the slopes of the hills.

As I drove down to the Mole on my return to the ship, I passed a number of men handcuffed, under escort of a body of police. These unfortunate people had committed no crime, but they had allowed a harmless curiosity to get the better of their discretion. They had spent the Saturday afternoon, which was the holiday of the workmen, on board the English ships of war, and on re-landing were surrounded by the myrmidons of Maniscalco, and thoroughly searched, under the suspicion that they had been supplied with arms and ammunition. Nothing was found on their persons beyond a little hard biscuit and tobacco, yet they were cruelly manacled and committed to prison. Verily, acts such as these, in violation of the first principles of justice, and tending to exasperate a class of the community which it should have been the effort of the ruling powers to conciliate, are beyond comprehension.

I was sitting, at a late hour of the evening, in my cabin, when a note was brought to me from an English gentleman, who, fearless of consequences, remained at his house in the city. The contents of the note were as follow:—

"DEAR SIR,

"I hear that a rising will take place at two o'clock to-morrow morning, at which hour or soon after, Garibaldi will be near Porta Sant' Antonino, through which you went out this afternoon, prepared to force his way into the city with the bayonet. Prince Lampedusa will let an officer go up to the tower at the end of the Palace to get a view of the combatants."

If information so concise and positive as this could be forwarded to me, it was reasonable to suppose it would be communicated through some reliable channel to the Royal authorities, and that necessary precautions would be taken to reinforce the quarter intended to be attacked.

I had previously received from Lieutenant Wilmot an account of an excursion he had made early in the afternoon, with Lieutenant Cooper, and Mr. Morgan, paymaster, as far as the village of Misilmeri, where, to their surprise, they heard the great national Chief had arrived from Parco, only a few hours before, and was then at dinner in a neighbouring vineyard. The General, on hearing that three English naval officers were driving through the village, sent one of his attendants with a message requesting them to visit his head-quarters. They accepted the invitation, and the following is the account which was given to me of the interview :—

Garibaldi was standing in the middle of a large enclosure, amidst a group of fifteen or twenty followers, who were clothed in grey trousers and red flannel shirts, the Chief being himself in a similar costume. His principal companions at the moment were his eldest son Menotti, a stout and tall youth of nineteen, with his arm in a sling from a recent severe wound; Colonel Carini, a Sicilian; Colonels Turr, Talecki, and Tukuri, Hungarians; and the priest Panteleo, who, cross in hand, had fought bravely at Calatafimi. The soldiers around were mere boys, of fifteen to eighteen years of age, who seemed to look with delight at the English uniforms.

Garibaldi, having invited the officers to be seated, and to partake of some strawberries fresh from the bed, alluded to the beautiful effect produced by the royal salutes from all the ships of war in honour of Her Majesty's birthday two days ago, and which he had witnessed from the heights of the Piano dei Greci. He spoke of his affection and respect for the English people as a nation, and of his hope that before long he should make the acquaintance of the English Admiral. He then moved to his tent, which was composed of a worn-out old blanket, supported on pikes, before which a child, under the name of a sentry, was pacing to keep off the crowd.

La Masa, the chief of the *squadre* of the Miselmeri district, was also on the mountain with three or four thousand men, armed with old flint muskets, spears, scythes, and rusty cutlasses. They were told off in companies, with innumerable tricoloured flags, green, white, and red, displayed around their camp, and were furnished with a host of musicians to incite them to martial deeds.

When the officers got into the vehicle to return to

Palermo, a friend of the driver endeavoured to mount up on the box, but this was prevented, conceiving that he might be a spy, who, under the protection of the British uniform, might desire to pass through the Royal outposts, and then return with intelligence for the insurgents.

This narration of my flag-lieutenant, coupled with the letter above-mentioned, showed a crisis to be at hand. Hitherto, trusting to the assurance of the Royal Commissioner that the country around was in possession of the King's forces, and that the officers might take their walks without fear of molestation, liberty till sunset had been duly given. The experience of this afternoon obliged me to curtail the indulgence, or reports would arise of encouragement given to rebels.

My last business of the day was to write the annexed memorandum :—

"*To the respective Captains and Officers commanding Her Majesty's ships at Palermo.*

"It having come to my knowledge that the armed bands under General Garibaldi have advanced to Misilmeri, a small town a few miles to the eastward of Palermo, and that several officers of Her Majesty's ships under my command, on returning from excursions into the country, had found themselves within the advanced posts of the above-mentioned forces; it is my positive direction that, until further orders, all officers, when on shore, keep within the limits of the sentinels of the Royal troops, and that the orders contained in my general memorandum of the 21st inst., relative to uniform, be strictly attended to.

(Signed). "G. RODNEY MUNDY,
Rear Admiral."

Whitsunday, May 27.—I was awoke at 4 o'clock this morning by continuous discharges of musketry, and on looking out of the port, observed a body of Neapolitan troops retreating at the double from the guardhouse at the eastern end of the Marina towards the gate of the citadel, the rearguard of which kept up an irregular fusillade at what must have been an imaginary enemy, for along the whole sweep of the broad roadway which skirted the sea, not an individual was in pursuit, nor was there a shot fired from any of the houses which commanded the position. These men had, however, scarcely passed the entrance of the main street of the Toledo, which abuts at right angles on the quay, when a party of the insurgents, with tricolour flags at their head, rushed in great numbers to the water's edge, and seeing the Royal troops in full retreat, advanced boldly towards the citadel, hoping to prevent their escape. The fire from the fortress then opened, which at once dispelled this illusion, and the rebels, falling back under shelter of the houses, commenced active work at the formation of barricades.

Shortly after six o'clock, the whole of the Neapolitan squadron opened an indiscriminate fire of shot and shell upon the town, which was very soon in flames in several places. The only reply given from the shore to this wanton act of revenge seemed to be an incessant peal from the bells of all the churches, which at the same moment were set ringing together, and was, probably, the preconcerted signal for a general rising of the inhabitants.

At eight o'clock, there seemed to be a lull, an intermission in the work of destruction, and by noon I received information that the whole of the city, with the exception of the Royal and Archiepiscopal Palaces, the Mint and the Citadel, were in the hands of the people, and that Garibaldi had established his head-quarters in a central position called the Piazza del Pretorio.

At the first report of musketry, I had sent the boats of the squadron on shore, to bring off any stray British subjects who might have still clung to their abodes under the hope of a pacific solution, and I gave directions that the aged Mr. Ingham, to whom I have already alluded as steadily refusing to avail himself of our protection, should be made acquainted with the fact of one of the cutters being specially told off to convey himself and family to the *Hannibal.* It was destined, however, that he should pay the penalty of his previous obstinacy. The mansion of the great merchant was at some distance from the beach, and before he could make his arrangements for reaching the ark of safety, the tide of battle had flowed onward to the outer walls of his domain. He was now compelled to remain within their circuit, and to trust to the good feelings of the combatants not to molest a British resident.

Her Majesty's Consul had informed me, on my first arrival in the station, that whether an insurrection of the inhabitants of Palermo took place or not, he had decided to continue at his post within the Consulate. He occupied the first floor of a large building, which otherwise contained a spacious courtyard and stabling. It was situated close to the broad roadway of the Marina, and was accessible through a back street running parallel to it, and extending to the landing-place abreast of the *Hannibal*. The English red ensign floated over the balcony, and it need hardly be said the area below was crowded by the women and children, who instinctively felt it to be a refuge for all who could shelter themselves beneath its folds.

A few hours after the attack by the Italian bands, this part of the city was completely in their power; and on my sending my flag-lieutenant to ascertain if Mr. Goodwin still persisted in his resolution of remaining on shore, he was allowed to pass the barricades by the Garibaldian officer in charge, and soon brought me word that the Consul would not move from his abode. He expressed himself as confident that neither party would act in any way injurious to a man who for forty years had dwelt amongst them, and who represented a nation whose good-will to all Italians, whether Northern, Southern, or Central, was well known and appreciated. I admired the pluck of Mr. Goodwin, and made no further effort to induce him to come afloat.

The English refugees on board the *Hannibal* amounted to thirty-nine persons, and fortunately for the ladies, the cabin belonging to Captain Farquhar, who had not yet joined the ship, was appropriated to their service ; temporary domiciles were also put up on the main deck, and one side of the gunroom was partitioned off as a nursery for the children, an arrangement, perhaps, not quite convenient to the mids and naval cadets. The officers of the wardroom, on their part, were equally considerate in the curtailment of their own comforts for the benefit of their homeless guests, and I believe every one was made as happy as limited accommodation would allow.

Captain Cochran, of the *Amphion*, gave up one-half of his cabin to the ladies of two of the principal firms of the city; and even the little *Intrepid* was not unmindful of the hospitality due on this trying occasion.

At three o'clock in the afternoon the general bombardment of the ill-fated city, by sea and land, recommenced. My own cabin, at the moment, was crowded with the wives and daughters of the merchants, who had hoped to spend the rest of the Sunday evening in quiet repose, instead of being spectators of one of the most awful scenes of destruction from civil discord that modern history has recorded. The citadel opened the cannonade by throwing shells in the direction of the Piazza del Pretorio, now known to be the head-quarters of the terrible Dictator; whilst solid shot of large calibre were launched at the churches and public and private buildings in the more immediate neighbourhood. The steamers of war, which, only a few years ago, had been built in England, and which were armed with 95 cwt. 68-pounders, next took up the fire, and were manœuvred under way with considerable skill. Captain Flores, of the *Ercole,* who had dined with me on the Queen's birthday, was above all others conspicuous in the ardour of his attack, as well as in the admirable manner in which he handled his vessel; but whether his crew would have been equally active in the face of opposition admits of reasonable doubt. Sweeping round within a few yards of the spanker boom of the *Hannibal,* he brought both broadsides alternately to bear on the Toledo, and raked with his heavy metal the whole of that magnificent street from the Marina to the Palace Square, to which it runs in a direct line of nearly a mile in length. So soon as the steamer drifted out of range, he turned again ahead at half a cable's distance from the shore, and thus kept repeating his circuit under the *Han-*

nibal's stern, and delivering his fire upon his countrymen, till darkness put a stop to the ruthless proceeding.

Again the loud ringing of the bells of the churches and convents gave evidence that the city still remained in the hands of the people, who were not to be turned from their enterprise by the havoc around.

Just before sunset the Royal troops, which, under command of Marshal Salzano, had marched upon Parco, were seen descending the hill from Monreale; but at its foot they were arrested by a body of the *squadre* who, having destroyed the main thoroughfare in connection with the Palace, now occupied the intervening space, and so prevented the junction of this division with the head-quarters of the Royal army. As darkness set in, the whole bay was illumined by the flames from the burning houses, and by the watch-fires of the peasantry, which were lighted on the slopes of the mountains. All night long, the conflagration continued, but by midnight the bells had ceased to toll, and at that hour, as if by mutual consent, hostilities were suspended.

CHAPTER XI

1860.

Palermo.—Escape of Political Prisoners.—Captain Cossovich.—My Intervention solicited. — Visit from Commanders of French and American Ships.—Lieut. Wilmot's Interview with Garibaldi.—Effects of the Bombardment on the City.

May 28.—As day broke, there was great commotion in the western suburbs of the city. The political prisoners who were in confinement in a large building in this quarter had effected their escape, and after a vigorous attack upon the troops, succeeded in capturing the outlying barracks and committing them to the flames, the soldiers retreating in much confusion to the fortified position on the Mole. Gunboats, in the meanwhile, swept close to the shore, and played upon the insurgents who ventured within their reach, whilst the mortars and heavy guns again re-opened upon the Pretorio.

I was watching the extraordinary scene with great interest from the stern gallery, when I observed an officer in full uniform leave the Neapolitan frigate *Parthenope* and pull towards the *Hannibal*. I had remarked that this vessel, during yesterday's bombardment, had abstained from indiscriminate fire upon the edifices of the city, and had directed her broadside against an encampment of the enemy which had been fixed at a short distance from the walls. I was much struck at the time with the manner in which the officer in command of this frigate had performed a most painful duty—so different to that exhibited by Captain Flores and his colleagues. When, therefore, Lieut. Wilmot entered my cabin and informed me that Captain Cossovich, in command of the *Parthenope*, was on board and earnestly requested that I would grant him an interview, I expressed my readiness to see him, and gave him a more cordial reception than I could have offered to Captain Flores. I asked him in French if he could speak English, to which he replied that he only knew his own language; but, hearing I understood Italian, he had dispensed with an interpreter, as the communication he had to make was most confidential and secret. I requested him to speak deliberately, and to make known his mission.

He first informed me that he had superseded Captain Flores and now commanded the naval force acting against the rebels; that all communication between the Royal head-quarters and the fleet was cut off by the insurgent population, and therefore messages could only be received through the medium of the semaphores on the turret of the Royal Palace and the citadel; that he had received a telegraphic cypher from General Lanza early in the morning, stating that an English merchant vessel had brought despatches from his Government, which he supposed might be in my possession, and if so, he should be obliged by my forwarding them to the Palace. Captain Cossovich then produced the telegram, which, when translated, ran as follows :—

"No. 1.

"*General Lanza to Captain Cossovich.*

"7 A.M., May 28.

"Ask the Admiral to have the courtesy to send the letters to me, as I have not the means of obtaining them; by which opportunity I would send two Generals to confer with the Admiral. Tell me quickly what he decides. If it be in the affirmative, I will discontinue to fire along the Toledo."

Now it certainly did not require much penetration to arrive at the conclusion that the request which was thus suddenly made to me by General Lanza through the naval officer in command was intended to ascertain how far the English Admiral would be ready to waive his declared neutrality, and act in a sense favourable to the Royal cause. The letters had been delivered by me to the nearest Neapolitan authorities on the previous evening, and I suspected the real object in view to have been the attainment of an opportunity for two superior military officers to survey the main defences erected by the inhabitants whilst screened by my protection, and so judge of the practicability of attacking them by the troops. The telegram also admitted of the supposition that I was in communication with the city, and had established an influence over the movements of the insurgents which would justify my interference in the manner proposed. Such an inference not being warranted by any previous action on my part, I felt the necessity of guarding against misconception by coming to a clear understanding with Captain Cossovich on the matter. I remarked to him that an application of this nature was tantamount to soliciting a mediation on my part, which I had expressly stated to His Excellency at two separate interviews I did not feel myself authorized to undertake. I added, however, that under the special circumstances of the case I was willing to receive the Generals, provided the firing upon the city by sea and land should immediately cease. I pointed out that the only construction I could put on the last paragraph was an intention on the part of General Lanza to discontinue the fire by the field-batteries in front of the Palace, in order that this particular line should be free for the passage of his Generals, but that I should be too glad to learn I was mistaken in this opinion.

Captain Cossovich, in reply, observed that he could not venture to give an interpretation of the meaning of the paragraph otherwise than as it applied to the main street called the Toledo ; but he was ready on his own responsibility to signalize to his squadron to cease firing on the town if there was a probability of the proposals leading to a satisfactory result, and he would furthermore invite the commandant of the citadel of Castellamare to do the same.

I then wrote the following response to the Royal Commissioner, which was immediately transmitted through the semaphore of the fortress to the look-out tower of the Palace :—

"No. 2.

"*Captain Cossovich to General Lanza.*

"Palermo Roads, May 28, 9 A.M.

"The English Admiral says he cannot send the letters, not being in communication with the city. As to the conference with the two Generals, he will receive them on board with pleasure."

Shortly before noon Captain Cossovich again came on board the *Hannibal*, and placed before me the following message :—

"No. 3.

"*General Lanza to Captain Cossovich.*

"Royal Palace, May 28, 10 A.M.

"Tell the Admiral that the Generals, in order to pass through the city and come on board, have need of the safeguard of the British flag."

This explicit declaration of the requirements of the Royal Commissioner at once cleared the ground from all ambiguity. My personal intervention was the great desideratum. The position of the Royal troops was evidently compromised, yet, probably, not sufficiently desperate to compel the General in command to the humiliation of treating directly with the rebels. Hence the endeavour to invest me with the character of mediator and adviser, whilst the existence of the insurgent forces was to be entirely ignored.

This was a position I could in no way accept. I therefore placed in the hands of the Marine Envoy the following reply, and informed him that in the space of two hours he should hear from me again :—

"No. 4.

"*Captain Cossovich to General Lanza.*

"Palermo Roads, May 28, 1860, Noon.

"The Admiral has said that he reserves his reply later."

I considered the announcement of a delay in my final decision would afford opportunity to the Neapolitan Commodore to submit to General Lanza details of our interview; and if the alarm at head-quarters was as intense as I imagined, more reasonable overtures would be made to insure my friendly co-operation. On my own behalf, I also required a short time for reflection, when a step in the wrong direction might have frustrated the one great object ever present to my mind, that of arresting the destruction of the capital without infringing the strict neutrality I had determined to observe.

At 1 P.M. I was surprised by a third visit from my naval friend; and on my remarking with good-humour that only half the period had elapsed which I had specified as necessary for the consideration of my reply, he apologised for the intrusion by reference to the terrible scenes which were passing around. The nervous anxiety he displayed whilst advocating the policy of the Royal Commissioner, and the earnest manner of his entreaty that an officer should be sent forthwith to the Palace to give escort to the Generals, told a tale of increasing difficulties which each hour was bringing about; but the exhibition of this emotion only furnished stronger evidence that unless General Garibaldi should give his consent, interference from a foreign quarter would be altogether out of the question.

Prefacing my answer with an expression of great disappointment that the bombardment should have continued after delivery of the message declaring my willingness to confer with the Generals, I proceeded to explain in detail the course I was ready to pursue. In the first place, as proof of my desire to meet the wishes of General Lanza, I proposed sending Lieutenant Wilmot on the dangerous errand of endeavouring to gain access to the head-quarters of Garibaldi, and if he succeeded in the attempt, he should make known to the General the proposals of the Royal Commissioner. Should the insurgent Chieftain agree to grant a free passage to the Royal officers through his lines to the beach, I would afford them the safeguard of the British flag from the Mole to the ship; but in this case I should expect a total cessation of hostilities during the remainder of the day.

I then reminded Captain Cossovich of the promise he had made of discontinuing the bombardment by sea, provided there existed a probability of a satisfactory result from our conference. I signified my opinion that as he had been commanded by the *Alter Ego* of his Sovereign to open fire upon the city when the troops had retired to the fort, he could not have done otherwise than obey his instructions; but that having once undertaken the mission on which he had lately been engaged, he became invested with the character of an envoy to a friendly Power, and in such capacity would be justified in acting independently without constant reference to the Palace authorities. I dwelt on the great responsibility I was myself willing to incur, by entering into official communication with an unrecognized individual, who, in command of a band of adventurers, had invaded the Island, and now, flushed with success, might scan my advances with no favourable eye. I summed up by a declaration that it would be trifling with the question before us to postpone its settlement any longer; and as the only solution possible was the one I had suggested, I strongly recommended his concurrence in its execution.

Captain Cossovich terminated the discussion by intimating considerable doubt as to his possessing the discretionary powers with which I had invested him, but as my suggestions were submitted in the form of an *ultimatum*, he would yield to my advice and acquiesce in their adoption. He would further give immediate orders for the cessation of hostilities by sea, and would proceed to the citadel and invite the Engineer officer in command to follow his example.

I then wrote and gave into his charge the following memorandum for General Lanza, which was forthwith transmitted by semaphore to the Palace, and within ten minutes after the departure of Captain Cossovich I had the satisfaction of seeing the signal flying from the masthead of the *Parthenope* to cease firing from all the ships; and as soon as they could be moved they took up other berths further out in the offing:—

No. 5.

"*Captain Cossovich to General Lanza.*

"Palermo Roads, May 28, 1860, 1.30 P.M.

"Admiral will ask General Garibaldi to give a safe escort to the Generals from the Palace to the Sanita, in order that they may go on board for a conference; but firing must be suspended."

Though I had secured the adhesion of the gallant captain to the wording of this note, I had misgivings as to the reception it would meet with from General Lanza, who, I felt persuaded, throughout the whole transaction had been acting under the guidance of the astute Director of Police, whose main object was to gain my support without recognition of his foe. This idea became more fixed as I observed the arms of the semaphore at work, yet no sign of any diminution of the fire from the fort; and shot and shell continued to fall in the direction of the Pretorio, to which spot I had already given orders to my flag-lieutenant to repair. His instructions were in writing as below:—

"*Hannibal*, Palermo Roads,
May 28, 1.30 P.M.

"You are to see General Garibaldi, and to inform him that General Lanza has desired the Captain of the Neapolitan frigate *Parthenope* by semaphore message, to ask me to grant him the protection of the British flag in order that two General officers may come on board the *Hannibal* to hold a conference; and that letters which had arrived by an English vessel from Messina might be sent to the Palace.

"I replied that I could not send the letters, not being in communication with the city, but that I should be happy to see the Generals. To this I received for answer that the Generals, in order to pass through the city, have need of the safeguard of the English flag.

"You are to ask General Garibaldi if he will allow them to pass through his lines for the purpose mentioned. If he agrees, I will have a boat at the Sanita to convey them to the ship. The Generals will of course have an escort back to the Palace, as I could not allow an English guard in the city.

"*To Lieutenant Wilmot.*"

In addition, Lieutenant Wilmot was verbally directed to inquire whether the English language was known to the Dictator, and if so, he was to read this document to him and request a categorical answer, but he was not to leave the paper in his hands. Should Garibaldi require it to be translated, and no one around his person was competent to do so, he was to seek for an interpreter at the Consular Office. Lieutenant Wilmot was also to make him distinctly understand that my communication emanated solely from an arrangement which had been entered into by the Neapolitan Commodore and myself, and might not be in exact conformity to the plans of the Royal Commissioner. Furthermore, should Garibaldi request, in the event of his acceding to the proposals offered, to be allowed to come on board the *Hannibal* himself, or to be represented by one of his officers, he was to be told that I would receive him, in the hope that, by a conference with the Neapolitan Generals, the horrors of the civil war might be mitigated and perhaps the terms of an armistice discussed.

At this stage of the proceedings I was honoured by a visit from the senior officers in command of the French and American ships of war. They were anxious I should join them in another protest to the Royal Commissioner against the continuance of the bombardment; but as I had already twice expostulated with His Excellency on the irregularity of his mode of warfare, I declined further interference as altogether useless. I informed them, before leaving, of the project now in contemplation of a conference on board the *Hannibal*, and invited them to be present if the scheme should be fulfilled.

About 3 P.M. Lieutenant Wilmot returned and gave me the following interesting account of his proceedings: —He was allowed to pass the first earthwork defence without question, the British uniform being recognized. At the second barricade in front of the Mint he was stopped by the officer in command, but when his mission was made known, he was conducted along the Toledo till he reached the Pretorio. Here he found Garibaldi, who, remembering to have seen him on the heights of Misilmeri, welcomed him to his bivouac.

The Dictator having stated that he was sufficiently acquainted with the English language to comprehend it when either read or spoken slowly, Lieutenant Wilmot read the paper to him, according to my directions. At the conclusion, Garibaldi remarked that he believed he understood every word of the document, but in order to impress it more strongly on his mind he should like to look it over carefully himself. This was done, and on returning the paper he said, "Tell the Admiral I am quite willing to allow the Generals to pass through the town, and I will give orders to my troops holding the defences opposite the Palace to cease firing immediately."

The following account of the damage done to the city, so far as was seen by Lieutenant Wilmot, from the Toledo, and in the streets leading to Mr. Ingham's house, to which I had desired him if possible to gain access, I give in his own words:—

"With much difficulty I found my way to Mr. Ingham's house, which is situated on the western outskirts of the town, near the English Gardens. The damage done throughout this district is very great, especially in the neighbourhood of Garibaldi's head-quarters; but, strangely enough, the vast Palace of the Pretorio, which he occupied, had not a single shell in it, although a church, convent, and other public buildings, which formed the other three sides of the square were riddled, the convent being in flames and completely in ruins. The shells were still falling, and several times I had to shelter myself in a doorway till they exploded. It was also very unpleasant crossing the Toledo and streets facing the Palace and Mint, as the troops were constantly firing down them with musketry and field-pieces. Close to Mr. Ingham's house there had evidently been a severe struggle. I saw several Royal artillery-men and horses dead, and still remaining where they had fallen

"The people seemed delighted to see a British officer in the streets, and crowded the balconies, clapping their hands as I passed. They were loud in their entreaties to know if the English Admiral was going to stop the bombardment.

"I was much surprised at the inefficiency of the barricades. Not one that I saw yesterday and the day before ought to have stopped any determined body of troops for a moment. In some places the pavement was not even torn up, but only furniture from the houses piled across the streets. In others, especially opposite the Royal Mint, omnibuses, carriages, and logs of wood, constituted the only defence. These did not form any protection from rifle bullets, and as the soldiers fired at random in hopes of hitting people passing, the passage to and fro was by no means agreeable.

"To-day a committee has been appointed to build the barricades, and great changes are in progress; many that were useless and ill-placed have been destroyed, and others constructed with paving-stones faced at the summit with sand-bags, and loop-holed for musketry. In the Toledo, particularly, they were quite strong enough to resist field-artillery."

At seven in the evening I received the following telegram, forwarded to me from the frigate *Parthenope*:—

No. 6.

"*General Lanza to Captain Cossovich.*

(Translation.) "The Royal Palace,
May 28, 1860, 6.30 P.M.

"Say to the English Admiral that I had telegraphed for the safeguard of the British flag. I am much obliged to him, but it is not necessary to speak to him any more."

This was conclusive. The arrangement which had been entered into between Captain Cossovich and myself had been disapproved of at head-quarters, and was not to be ratified. I could, moreover, conjecture from the not very courteous wording of the note, that the Neapolitan captain had been prohibited from again putting his foot on the deck of the *Hannibal*, or he would certainly have brought me the message in person, as he had done on three previous occasions. I felt this exceptional mode of operation was intended as a slight, and I regretted it much, as it appeared to exclude all hope of reconsideration.

Possibly the Royal Commissioner might now endeavour to effect his purpose by opening fresh negotiations with the Commodore in command of the Austrian squadron, or with the captains of the French and American ships of war; but in such a case would His Excellency obtain the acquiescence of the insurgent Chief in any measure he might propose? I thought not. It became at any rate necessary, in a spirit of fairness to both parties, that I should immediately acquaint Garibaldi with the failure of my project, or he would have continued under the impression that a conference would be held in the morning.

The flag-lieutenant was therefore again put in requisition, and despatched with all convenient speed to the great square of the Pretorio, with orders to make it known to the *de facto* ruler of the city, that my proposals to the Royal Commissioner had been peremptorily rejected, and that ulterior mediation on my part was entirely at an end. As darkness had set in, and the fire from Castellamare continued unabated, the performance of this duty entailed considerable danger. Yet it was promptly and satisfactorily executed.

The Dictator was found in the midst of his staff, inside the railings of the Quatro Fontani, and received the communication with perfect composure, simply remarking that he was grateful to the English Admiral for the exertions he had made in the cause of humanity, and that probably General Lanza, in a shorter period than he contemplated, would have reason to deplore his conduct in the matter.

At 10 at night, there was great movement in the Neapolitan squadron: the whole of the vessels which had shifted berth to the outer roads, after my negotiation with their Commodore, now hoisted signal lights, and steaming slowly in shore, took up positions as near to the Marina as the depth of water would allow, evidently in preparation to renew the work of destruction, if such should be the command of the Royal Commissioner, when daylight appeared.

I retired to rest little satisfied with the result of the day's exertion, but endeavoured to console myself with the reflection that my efforts had not been quite unavailing. The bombardment by sea had been arrested, and no small amount of human misery allayed.

CHAPTER XII.

1860.

Palermo.—Reinforcement of the Royal Troops.—Proposal for my acting as Mediator renewed.—The Bombardment resumed.—Narrow Escape of the British Consul.—Humiliating Position of the Royal Commissioner.—Preparations for the Conference.

May 29th.—Daylight showed us the Neapolitan fleet anchored in line of battle in close order before the city. Two large steamers were also seen approaching at full speed from the direction of Naples, the decks and paddleboxes of which were crowded with armed men. After communicating with the Neapolitan frigate, these vessels proceeded again to the northward, and remaining within signal distance continued cruizing about during the day. The troops on board were riflemen, part of the Bavarian Contingent, and were sent by the King as a reinforcement to the garrison.

In the course of the forenoon, a colonel of engineers, who stated himself to be in command of the citadel of Castellamare, presented himself on board the *Hannibal*, and asked if he might be permitted to have an interview with the Admiral. He was forthwith admitted, but before I invited him to enter on the subject of his mission, I begged him to inform me if he held command in the citadel yesterday, when I sent a message by Captain Cossovich to request him to cease firing whilst communications were going forward between General Lanza and myself. He replied in the affirmative, but set forth the impossibility of compliance with my wishes, as his orders were imperative to continue the bombardment, unless the answer which I should give was a full acquiescence in the proposals which had been made.

Having expressed my regret that he had not been able to assume the same independent attitude as that taken up by his naval colleague, I intimated my readiness to receive any statement he had to offer. He then produced a telegraphic message, addressed by the Royal Commissioner directly to me, which ran as follows:—

No. 7.

"*General Lanza to Rear-Admiral Mundy.*
(Translation.)

"Palermo, May 29th, 1860, 11 A.M.

"Referring to former correspondence, I send two Generals to confer with you. The fire will be suspended on both sides at noon."

I think any impartial person, on reading this telegram, would have arrived at the conclusion that not only were the necessary arrangements made for the passage of the Generals through the city to the Mole, but that if not already *en route*, they would certainly commence their journey at noon, when the fire on both sides by mutual agreement would be suspended. Yet nothing could be more erroneous than such a construction put upon the words; for on my expressing my satisfaction at the happy prospect before us of peace, and of my intention of immediately preparing the barge for the reception of my guests, I was met by the remark that I had not quite correctly interpreted the meaning of the note. The newly-appointed envoy then begged permission to explain more fully the nature of the instructions which had been transmitted to him by semaphore from the Palace. He affirmed, with due solemnity, that all the arrangements now proposed were still contingent on the supposition that I would afford the Neapolitan Generals the protection of the British flag from the head-quarters of the Royal army through the city to the ship, a safeguard which General Lanza felt assured would not be opposed by the leader of the rebel bands.

To say that I felt indignant at an explanation so illogical as that which was now offered, relative to the text of the telegram, would be far from giving expression to the sentiments I entertained; and I should certainly at once have broken off all further conference with the colonel, had I not perceived that since he had been on board the fire from the Castellamare had gradually slackened, and that the guns of the ships of war as yet remained silent. It was possible my words of quiet remonstrance, spoken yesterday, might have had effect on General Lanza, and that, whilst negotiations were in progress, he had ordered a reduction if not a cessation of the cannonade.

The interview was therefore prolonged until subject-matter of discussion was fairly exhausted. I then terminated the conversation by declaring it would be impossible for me to allow the British flag to be paraded through the streets of a city in open rebellion. It was unreasonable on the part of the Royal Commissioner to invite a second time my co-operation in a project so untenable, whereas, by agreeing to my amendment, every difficulty would be solved, and the conference on board the *Hannibal* immediately held.

The commandant of the citadel then took formal leave, carrying with him the following despatch for transmission by semaphore to the Palace :—

No. 8.

"*Rear-Admiral Mundy to General Lanza.*

(Translation.)

"*Hannibal*, at Palermo, May 29, 1860, Noon.

"Sir,—From your Excellency's last communication at 7 P.M. yesterday, in which you state it is not necessary to speak to me any more, I concluded the correspondence was finished. But as you again earnestly request my mediation, I consent to receive the two Generals on board, provided General Garibaldi allows them to pass through his lines. My boat will be at Porta Felice to receive them.

(Signed) "G. RODNEY MUNDY.

A firm determination to adhere to the plan I had originally formed would, I hoped, bring conviction to the mind of the Royal Commissioner. The arguments of the new envoy, who had been carefully selected from the most scientific of the military corps, had proved equally futile in changing my resolve as those of my naval friend who had been so summarily deposed; and, perhaps, the knowledge of this fact would eventually induce His Excellency to accede to my views.

The afternoon passed away, and the shades of evening were approaching, yet not a shot had been fired from the Neapolitan fleet.

To the good faith of Captain Cossovich the inhabitants owed this respite from destruction. Bound by his engagement made on board the *Hannibal*, an act of hostility yesterday would have been forfeiture of his word. To-day he was a free agent, with power to lay half the city in ashes, if such had been his will. He chose, however, to consider the re-opening of negotiations with me, though no longer employed himself, as warranty sufficient for extension of our contract, a decision in every way so honourable as to be worthy of record.

May 30.—The two steamers which had brought the Bavarian troops from Naples, and which had continued under way, with fires banked up, a few miles from the anchorage, moved in last night, and landed the greater part of their freight at the citadel, the remainder being carried on to the eastward, and put on shore near the village of Bagaria. The larger division sallied out from the citadel at a late hour, amidst great cheering and continued salvos of musketry, and, forcing their way through the western suburbs and the English Gardens, made the circuit of the city in rear of the Palace, and joined their companions shortly after daylight. The whole body, about seven hundred strong, were clad in light grey uniform, and admirably equipped. They were flanked by several squadrons of cavalry, which had also arrived during the night; and from the position taken up by this reinforcement within the walls of the Botanical Gardens, there seemed to be the intention of a desperate onslaught from that quarter.

The advance of this body of picked German troops, without hindrance from the armed peasants, who were supposed to be in possession of the whole country around, must have astonished the rebel populace, and filled them with dismay. The old scenes of Whit-Sunday morning were once more enacted. The bells from the towers of church and convent again tolled forth their solemn peals, calling every man to his post and every citizen to arms; to these the citadel instantly replied by thundering forth its cannonade, throwing shot and shell upon the Pretorio and the quarter held by the Piedmontese.

Meanwhile, the Neapolitan ships of war, by springing their broadsides to the shore, seemed to indicate an intention of discontinuing their late inaction, and of again taking part in the work of devastation. A glance at the upper deck of the steamers showed the seamen at their quarters, in readiness to open fire when the signal should be given, and which appeared only to be delayed by some of the vessels failing to warp into line. I still entertained a gleam of hope that these manœuvres of Captain Cossovich were in reality enjoined for the purpose of gaining time, or at any rate of postponing hostilities till all prospect of accommodation had entirely passed away.

Information had reached me during the morning watch, that the life of Her Majesty's Consul had yesterday been endangered by a 13-inch shell piercing the walls of his house, and subsequently exploding and destroying everything around.

I therefore despatched Lieutenant Wilmot to obtain particulars of this mischance, and to advise the worthy gentleman to seek an asylum on board the ship. It was immediately after the landing of my flag-lieutenant in execution of this service that the bombardment recommenced, and great was my anxiety for his safety, when I observed by the training of the guns from the Castellamare that the direction of the fire was in the line of the Consulate. I do not mean to assert that this change of the plan of attack was ordered for the purpose of annoyance to Mr. Goodwin; on the contrary, I believed it to have arisen with the view of forming a diversion in favour of the German legion, by throwing shells upon the buildings occupied by the insurgents in close vicinity to their encampment. If so, this might have been justified as a bold stroke of strategy, legitimately practised as a belligerent right; but then came the question, if war was to be renewed, why lead me to understand, that all arrangements were completed, and that yesterday at noon the Generals would come on board? These proceedings were a mystery I was unable to solve, and I ceased to puzzle my brain with further attempt to unravel them.

Shortly before ten, when to all appearance the struggle was assuming the proportion of a last desperate fight, and when it was reported a general assault would be made on the Palace, a cessation of hostilities from every quarter took place. Suddenly, and as if by magic, the din of battle was hushed, and over the late scenes of bloodshed a gloomy silence reigned.

This unexpected, simultaneous suspension—what

could it portend? Was it to be the harbinger of an era of peace, a signal for the staying of the slaughter of brethren, or only a lull to gather strength for more determined attack?

Half-an-hour passed away. It was eleven in the forenoon when Lieutenant Wilmot, entering my cabin, brought me intelligence direct from the field of the combatants. The Royal Commissioner had yielded to the advice I had given, but in a manner humiliating both to the Royal cause and to himself. Instead of a message, assenting to what I proposed, he indited a public despatch almost in the form of a suppliant, and forwarded it under flag of truce to the enemy's camp.

A suspension of the firing on both sides was the immediate result.

The original despatch was then forwarded for my perusal, with a message from Garibaldi that he had acceded to the petition, and would himself accompany the Neapolitan Generals on board the *Hannibal*, if I was still willing to receive him.

The following is a literal translation of the letter:—

"*General Lanza to His Excellency General Garibaldi.*

"Palermo, May 30, 1860.

"Since the English Admiral has let me know that he would receive with pleasure on board his vessel two of my Generals to open a conference with you, at which the Admiral would be mediator, provided you would grant them a passage through your lines, I therefore beg you to let me know if you will consent thereto, and if so (supposing hostilities to be suspended on both sides), I beg you to let me know the hour when the said conference shall begin. It would likewise be advantageous that you should give an escort to the above-mentioned Generals, from the Royal Palace to the Sanita, where they would embark to go on board.

"Waiting your reply,

(Signed) "FERDINAND LANZA."

What must have been the distress of the Royal army, before the *Alter Ego* of the Sovereign could have condescended to pen so humble a letter as this! The man who, up to the present hour, had been stigmatized by epithets degrading to human nature, and denounced in proclamations as a pirate, rebel, and filibuster, now elevated to the title and rank of His Excellency and of General! It was equivalent to the recognition of his character as an equal, and an acknowledgement of inability to subdue him by force.

My own feelings on the subject were those of infinite satisfaction. Strong in the knowledge that the presence and moral ascendancy of the British flag had arrested the conflagration, I held it as certain that, once let the representatives of each belligerent Power tread the deck of the *Hannibal*, hostilities would cease and Palermo be saved.

Arrangements were forthwith made for boats to be in readiness at the landing-place of Porta Felice, and intimation conveyed both to General Lanza and his great opponent that I should be happy to receive the negotiators at any hour after noon.

The captains in command of the French, American, and Sardinian squadrons were also made acquainted with the programme of the intended conference. These officers since my arrival on the station had been constant visitors on board the *Hannibal*, and had warmly seconded my endeavours, in conjunction with their respective Consuls, to deter the Royal Commissioner from an indiscriminate bombardment.

The Austrian Commodore, on the other hand, had studiously abstained from offering any opinion on existing complications, nor did he join in the protest submitted by other foreign nations in hope of saving the city from destruction. I wished much to have had the benefit of the presence of Baron Von Wullersdorff during the meeting of the Generals, but as he showed a disinclination to mix in any way in matters connected with the war, and had not been to my flagship since his first official visit, I did not venture to invite him to attend at the conference.

Lieutenant Wilmot had scarcely landed for the purpose of giving information relative to the hour fixed for the conference when, to my utter dismay, I heard a loud report of musketry in the direction of the Consular House, followed by continued discharges at intervals, as if from file and volley firing. This was succeeded by heavy guns from two of the men-of-war steamers at anchor off the Marina in face of the Botanical Gardens. It was past the hour of noon, at which time it had been distinctly made known, by messengers despatched to every barricade and to the posts occupied by the Royal forces, that all firing should cease.

It is impossible for me to describe the indignation which I felt at this recommencement of hostilities, when, with every due formality, a truce had been proclaimed. It seemed a contemptuous defiance of every understood law of honour, and a marked affront to the majesty of the British flag. At the moment of assurance of a great moral victory, obtained through the influence of that boundless confidence which each belligerent entertained for the nation I represented, a castastrophe had occurred which promised to throw all back into anarchy.

Great, then, was my relief at the sudden cessation of the cannonade, after ten minutes' duration. Could this breach of good faith have arisen from the wild passions of the undisciplined men over whom the Patriot Chief had no solid control, or was it a treacherous act on the part of the Royal troops? This question was solved on the return of Lieutenant

Wilmot, from whose journal of events I give the following extract:—

Lieutenant Wilmot's Statement.

"On my way up to General Garibaldi's head-quarters, by the same route I had taken on the preceding days, I found myself close in front of a body of Bavarian troops, who had suddenly advanced from the Botanical Gardens into the town, and were firing as they marched forward. Some of the *squadre* behind a barricade immediately returned the shots, and I was then between two fires. I at once took out my handkerchief, and, waving it, walked as quickly as possible up to the nearest officer of the foreign troops, telling him I was an English officer going to Garibaldi's head-quarters, and that it was distinctly understood all hostilities should cease at noon. I then took out my watch, and showed him it was already some minutes past that hour. He and his men were very much excited, and seemed determined to push on, and apparently intended to keep me with them.

"A Neapolitan colonel who had been sent from the Palace to Garibaldi, at this moment came up and told me the whole affair was entirely a mistake, and he then apparently gave orders for the Bavarians to halt, but to hold the position they had gained.

"Not many minutes subsequently, Garibaldi himself reached the spot, accompanied by thirty or forty of his Italian band. He was *furious,* and a very angry conversation took place between him and the Neapolitan colonel. Whilst this parley was going on, a shell fell close to us, thrown by a steamer which had been firing on the town in support of the Bavarians as they advanced.

"Both parties at length seemed pacified. We adjourned to the head-quarters in the Pretorio, and it was decided that the Generals should be at the landing-place at 2 P.M. As I passed over the same ground on my return to the ship, I found both townspeople and Bavarians busily engaged building barricades, so the latter evidently meant to hold the position they had so unfairly gained. Colonel Carini, whilst standing on the top of a barricade with a white flag in his hand, and restraining his own men from firing, was severely wounded in the arm. The flag must have been seen, and my firm belief is that the whole affair was planned to surprise and capture Garibaldi."

CHAPTER XIII.

1860.

Palermo.—Arrival of Generals Garibaldi, Letizia, and Chretien on Board.—Violent Conduct of General Letizia.—Articles of the Proposed Convention.—Armistice agreed to.

GENERAL GARIBALDI, and the Neapolitan Generals Letizia and Chretien, came on board the *Hannibal* at a quarter past two o'clock.

General Garibaldi was the first to step on the quarter-deck, the Royal officers having insisted on his taking the precedence. Whether this arrangement was an act of simple politeness on their part, or a premeditated scheme for ascertaining if he would be received with military honours, I do not pretend to say, but as they did not immediately follow him up the accommodation ladder, it struck me the delay was not entirely accidental.

Garibaldi appeared in the uniform of a Sardinian general officer, and was saluted by the guard of Marine Light Infantry according to his rank. The same honours were paid to the general officers of His Sicilian Majesty.

The French, American, and Sardinian captains accompanied them into my cabin, and I was on the point of addressing a few words to the assembled party in a friendly way, relative to the object of their visit, when General Letizia stepped forward, and, in a manner which I thought quite uncalled-for, interrupted me by an exclamation that he was not prepared to enter into communication with me, or to accept my mediation, in the presence of the captains of ships of war of other nations. He must therefore request that I would give directions for those officers to withdraw. He also desired to inform me, that although he had consented to meet General Garibaldi on board my flag-ship, he did not intend to recognize him in any official capacity or to confer with him personally on any subject whatever. All mediation must take place between the British Admiral, himself, and his colleague, and it would be for General Garibaldi to confirm or to disallow such terms as we might think proper to make. These were the instructions he had received from General Lanza, and from them he would not and could not depart.

The dictatorial tone in which these phrases were uttered, and the tenour of the language held, were certainly not the best calculated to smooth the difficulties which already beset the path of conciliation; but possibly the gallant General imagined that a bold initiative would disarm opposition and petrify the filibuster Chief.

A brief remark, in the form of a recommendation to look more calmly into the object of our meeting, and not to preclude all hope of accommodation by unreasonable proposals, was all I offered in reply.

I then turned to General Garibaldi and asked him if he felt the same objection to the presence of the captains in command of the squadrons of three friendly Powers as that which had been notified by the Neapolitan General. He answered that any arrangement I thought fit to make would be perfectly agreeable to him, and that he should be glad if they remained.

General Letizia now recapitulated in yet stronger terms the substance of his former observations, producing at the same time a copy of the letter from the Royal Commissioner to General Garibaldi, and endeavouring to show that the paragraph relating to the conference of which I was to be the mediator, clearly implied that the negotiations were to be undertaken between the English Admiral and the Neapolitan envoys, in which General Garibaldi had no right to take part. He again repeated his determination not to enter upon any subject whatever, unless the foreign captains left the cabin.

Captain Lefevre, of the French steam frigate *Vauban*, an officer evidently of keen sensibility, now came forward, and with great precision in his native tongue, expressed his astonishment at the conduct and language of General Letizia. He was seconded by

Captain Palmer, of the United States frigate *Iroquois*, whose indignation was equally great, but, who not being so thoroughly acquainted with the French or Italian language, was necessarily unable to give the same force to his expressions. The Marquis d'Asti, the Sardinian senior officer, remained silent, and the countenance of the Dictator betrayed no emotion at what was passing.

The altercation had now become so unseemly and noisy, that I deemed it absolutely necessary to stop further discussion by a decisive movement. I told General Letizia I was utterly unable to comprehend the meaning of the violent conduct he had exhibited, and I plainly intimated to him that, if he did not at once waive the objections he had offered, and consent to treat personally with General Garibaldi, and in the presence of the foreign captains, I should be obliged to re-land himself, his colleague, and General Garibaldi, and declare the negotiations to be at an end.

The captains, in the meanwhile, had walked out to the quarter-deck, in well-grounded displeasure at the proceedings they had witnessed, and they would, doubtless, have returned forthwith to their ships had I not requested them to wait till I received a reply to my demand.

General Letizia, perceiving I was in earnest in the matter, now gradually subsided into a calmer frame of mind, and eventually consented to the terms I had proposed.

As soon as the captains had returned to the cabin, I explained to the envoys that, as they were about to confer on the best means of restoring peace, it would be my duty to abstain from interference in their deliberations. I wished them thoroughly to understand that, from the moment they trod on the deck of the *Hannibal*, and so came under the protection of the British flag, they met together on terms of perfect equality; and in such capacity all discussion must henceforth be carried on. I added that I felt bound to make this opinion known to General Garibaldi, who might justly feel aggrieved at the attempt to ignore his character of negotiator, whereas he was entitled to the same courtesy and respect as that which was due to the high officers of the Royal army.

The three Generals then seated themselves before a small round table in the centre of the cabin, and the work of the afternoon began by General Letizia producing a paper on which six articles were written, the adoption of which he trusted would be agreed to by his opponent.

I was now in hopes that business would really begin. But, no: there was to be another passage of arms of minor import, and then a terrible explosion, with high dramatic effect. General Letizia, speaking abstractedly of himself, remarked to General Garibaldi that he was a very old officer, and had seen a great deal of active service; he had fought through many campaigns, had witnessed much bloodshed, and though with this experience he thought little of the present aspect of affairs in the city, he should be glad, for the sake of humanity, if a suspension of hostilities could be adjusted.

The Dictator, in a tone of ill-dissembled sarcasm, replied that he ventured to offer his congratulations to his brother General on his great good fortune. He could not himself pretend to equal experience in the art of war, though, perhaps, he knew something about it; he had, however, only acted once during his life with a regular army. Then, suddenly changing the subject, he requested that each article of the proposed convention might be read to him separately, when he would at once determine whether they were admissible or not. This was accordingly done, and the first, second, third, and fourth were agreed to without comment. They ran as follows:—

"1. That a suspension of arms should be concluded for the period about which the parties would agree.

"2. That during the suspension of arms, each party should keep his position.

"3. That the convoys of wounded from the Royal Palace, as well as the families of the *employés*, should be allowed to pass free through the town, in order to embark on board the Royal ships.

"4. That the Royal troops in the Palace, and the families of the refugees in the monasteries near, should be allowed to provide themselves with their daily provisions."

The delivery of the fifth article brought about the storm:—

"5. That the municipality should address a humble petition to His Majesty the King, laying before him the real wishes of the town, and that this petition should be submitted to His Majesty."

To this General Garibaldi, in a vehement and loud tone of voice, replied, "No!" Then, drawing himself up, he added, "The time for humble petitions, either to the King or to any other person, is past; besides, there is no longer any municipality. *La municipalité c'est moi!* I am the municipality! I refuse my assent. Pass on to the sixth and last proposition."

Astonishment and indignation were depicted on the countenance of General Letizia on hearing these words. Folding up the paper which lay spread before him on the table, he exclaimed, "Then, sir, unless this article is agreed to, all communication between us must cease."

Garibaldi, who, previous to the consideration of the fifth point, had maintained a phlegmatic demeanour, now burst forth in reply with language that showed he also had completely lost command of temper. He denounced in unmeasured terms the want of good faith, indeed, the infamy, of the Royal authorities, in allowing the foreign mercenaries, whilst a flag of truce was flying, to attack the Italian troops, who had orders to discontinue the fire. By this treacherous manœuvre they had severely wounded one of the bravest of his officers, the gallant Colonel Carini, and had acquired a position in advance which they still retained, in defiance of every principle of military honour. But perfidy, such as this, could not succeed; eventually it would recoil with terrific effect on the heads of the authors.

General Letizia retorted with equal warmth; then, turning to me, in the same dictatorial manner as on his first arrival, put a catalogue of questions in rapid succession. Was I not astonished at the answer which had just been given by the General? Had I not heard his master, the King, spoken of disrespectfully? Had I not accepted the office of mediator, and did I not think it incumbent on me to insist on the adoption of the article named? There could surely be nothing derogatory in the form of the petition which it was proposed should be humbly laid at the feet of His Majesty; he had trust in the justice of my sentiments, and now was the time to exercise my mediation.

When General Letizia had finished this harangue, which was in every respect as inconsequent in its conclusions as his original objections were untenable, I begged to remind him that it was quite a mistake to imagine that I was acting as mediator between the parties. It was true the Royal Commissioner had asserted in the despatch addressed to His Excellency General Garibaldi, that he considered me in that light, but my own official communications would admit of no such construction. The consent which I gave was, that the Generals might repair on board the *Hannibal*, provided arrangements could be made for their passage through the city, and there was no question of mediation in the proper acceptation of the term. In a spirit of strict neutrality, opportunity was offered to each contracting party to settle their differences; and if they neglected to profit by that opportunity, no blame could attach to any but themselves. I had once again to repeat that I should offer no opinion on any point in dispute, and if they found it impossible to arrive at an agreement there was no other alternative than to declare the meeting closed.

The Neapolitan envoy scarcely noticed this decision, but holding pertinaciously to his aggressive tactics, required to be informed, what could be the object of the presence of the foreign captains if they were not to give advice when a difficulty arose?

To this question so happily put, I replied by referring the interlocutor to the captains themselves, who would be able to explain that they were present at my invitation, to give a moral weight and friendly countenance to the conference.

Captain Lefevre, of the *Vauban*, who had been burning with indignation at this renewed exhibition of violent language, now relieved me from further debate, and by a masterly exposition demolished the fabric of objections which had been launched forth against the presence of himself and his brother officers.

Garibaldi, in the meanwhile, had risen from his seat, under the belief that the negotiations had been brought to a close. Such, however, did not appear by any means to have been the real intention of the Neapolitan General. Excusing himself on the plea of consulting his colleague, the two veteran diplomatists entered into a lengthened conversation, which ended by General Letizia announcing to his adversary that he would agree to the expunging of the fifth article from the convention, though by so material a concession he knew he should incur the displeasure of the Royal Commissioner.

The sixth and last article was then accepted without comment :—

"6. That the troops in the town should be allowed to receive their provisions from the Castello."

After a brief discussion, in order to carry into effect the articles of the convention, an armistice was agreed to until noon on the following day.

Before taking their departure, General Letizia and General Chretien asked me to give them a few minutes' private conversation. We retired into the stern gallery. All that I have already detailed having been publicly spoken, it has been freely related, but as what now passed was advisedly confidential, I will only say that I strongly recommended these ardent diplomatists to proceed at once to Naples, where they might fully explain the situation of affairs to the Sicilian Government, and that from the readiness shown by General Garibaldi to acquiesce in every proposal having for its object the stoppage of the effusion of blood, he would certainly agree to a prolongation of the armistice till they returned to Palermo.

I then requested General Letizia to express to the Royal Commissioner the mortification I had felt at the unaccountable conduct of the Bavarian Contingent of the Royal troops, in advancing upon the insurgents after a truce had been proclaimed. This breach of good-faith had compromised the British flag, and was an injustice to myself, after the great responsibility I had taken and the efforts I had made to meet the wishes of the King's Commissioner in support of constituted authority.

General Letizia did not attempt to justify the proceeding: it was entirely a mistake, attributable to a wrong transmission of orders, which he much regretted. Under the circumstances, I thought it expedient to accept the apology.

General Garibaldi did not ask to speak with me

privately, but whilst I was engaged with the Royal envoys he held an anxious discussion with the American and Sardinian captains. His manner throughout his visit, with the exception of excusable irritation on the subject of the flag of truce, was quiet and dignified. The demeanour of General Chretien, who seemed to stand in awe of his impetuous colleague, was courteous and conciliating, and he spoke from his heart when he thanked me for giving the opportunity of signing the armistice.

On re-landing at Porta Felice, the Neapolitan Generals invited their Piedmontese companion to accompany them in the Viceregal barouche to the nearest street leading to the Pretorio. This offer was accepted unhesitatingly, though not without misgivings on the part of the staff of the Dictator.

On arriving at the great square of the Quatro Cantoni, Garibaldi addressed the assembled multitude in the high-flown language of which he is so great a master, and which, though well adapted to the fervid imaginations of the Italian people, sounds bombastic and puerile in the ears of the more sedate Northman. His commands were to be up and stirring. To-morrow would be a day of life or death. The whole population must work during the night—he and his handful of soldiers must have rest. The barricades must be enlarged, multiplied and strengthened. The *squadre*, now designated the *Cacciatori del' Etna*, and every able-bodied man, must be armed and at his post in readiness to renew hostilities at the expiration of the armistice, and the first act must be to drive the foreign mercenaries from the advanced position they had treacherously gained under cover of a flag of truce.

At night the city was splendidly illuminated.

CHAPTER XIV.

1860.

Palermo.—Preparation for Renewal of Hostilities.—Extension of the Armistice.—Departure of General Letizia for Naples.—Visit to the City.—Frightful Results of the Bombardment.—Captain Vacca.—Murder of Police.—Interview between Generals Letizia and Garibaldi.—Battle at Catania.

May 31.—Since dawn of day the combatants on both sides had been active in the preparations for the renewal of hostilities. The barracks on the Fiera Vecchia, or Old Market Place, occupied by the 13th Regiment and Foreign Legion, which yesterday had treacherously gained this position, were now nearly enveloped in a network of barricades. The principal one, constructed of enormous stones and brick-work, had been erected at the junction of the Fiera with the Via Allora, a street opposite the house of the British Consul, which communicated with the Toledo and Senate House, the head-quarters of the insurrection. The new pavement of the main streets had also been removed, and the stones carried to the tops of the houses, which, with Orsini shells, were to be thrown down upon the Bavarians if they succeeded in forcing the first line of defences. The advanced position gained by these men within one hundred yards of the insurgents' pickets had now become one of imminent danger. They were closed in on three sides in a narrow street, and their lines of communication with the Palace entirely cut off.

During the night a Greek vessel had arrived, and powder had been supplied to the camp of the insurrectionists. It appeared that when the armistice was signed yesterday a very few cartridges remained for distribution. Garibaldi, who I mentioned as having been in earnest conversation with the Sardinian and American captains at the close of the conference, had confided to those officers the secret of his being entirely destitute of ammunition, and he entreated Captain the Marquis d'Asti and Captain Palmer to furnish him with a supply. I presume the Dictator imagined that the sympathy of these officers for the cause of the patriots might induce them to depart from the strict rule of duty. I have no reason to believe that they complied with his request; indeed, had they intended to do so, they would have thought it inexpedient to make me aware of the transaction, well knowing my sentiments on the subject of neutrality.

I now learnt from Lieutenant Wilmot that yesterday afternoon, when General Letizia and General Chretien had seated themselves in the boat to come on board the *Hannibal*, they were extremely astonished at observing General Garibaldi also step in and place himself by their side. They did not even know the self-created Dictator by sight, and had quite overlooked the small band of red shirts which had accompanied him as they drove down in state in the vice-regal barouche, with its blue and scarlet liveries and attendant outriders. A cynic might perhaps have discovered a spice of absurdity in the juxta-position of these antagonistic negotiators, and a feeling that he had been outwitted possibly shot across the mind of the chief Neapolitan envoy. He had thought, in conjunction with his colleague, to deal exclusively with me, and he found himself face to face with his redoubtable adversary. However, it was too late to remonstrate.

There is an old nautical saying, "Of sailing in the same boat," implying that the parties engaged must for the time being be reconciled to the position they occupy. In this instance the saying was literally, as well as morally, fulfilled. The parties were caged: orders were given to "out boat-hooks" and "shove off," and, though General Letizia was unable to disguise his dejection, the bitterness of spirit engendered by this incident did not explode till his arrival in my cabin, when, as already related, it found convulsive vent. I may also mention, that when Garibaldi and his son were standing at the landing-place, waiting the arrival of the Neapolitan Generals, several musket-shots were fired at him from the citadel, though the cutters were at the steps below him, with the English white ensign flying. As the distance across the inlet is not more than three hundred yards, any fair marksman with a rifle must have killed him on the spot. Garibaldi waved his handkerchief directly the shots were fired, and they were not repeated.

Before noon I received information that there was to be an extension of the armistice for three days, in order to allow time for General Letizia to proceed to, and return from, Naples. The state of affairs had compelled him to yield to the advice I had given, which, had he adopted forty-eight hours before, might have placed the Royal cause in a very different position. He was now a suppliant before the Dictator, who, standing on the vantage-ground gained by yesterday's proceedings, assumed the tone of the despotic ruler of the Provisional Government of Sicily.

In his walk to the head-quarters of this extraordinary man, Letizia had seen the mighty efforts made during the preceding night by the inhabitants; he had witnessed priests, women, and children working at the defences, and monks carrying the crucifix before them, everywhere exhorting the people to fight in the sacred cause of liberty.

Officers of the Royal troops had also begun to desert, though, to their credit be it said, few of the private soldiers followed their example. These men, so unfairly belied, had fought well, and had they been bravely led, very different might have been the result. For many days they had been short of provisions and water, the number of dead was great, and five hundred remained wounded in the Palace alone.

At dusk the city was again illuminated, and at midnight Letizia sailed for Naples.

June 1.—By the terms of the Convention signed yesterday by General Lanza and Signor Crispi, Secretary of State for the Provisional Government, the Finance or Royal Mint was delivered over to the insurgents. In its coffers were found one million two hundred thousand pounds sterling in cash, chiefly deposits. As the *squadre* at this date receiving pay numbered about twenty thousand men, this money allowed arrears to be settled, and an ample surplus for the purchase of arms and ammunition from Europe.

I sent Dr. Walker, M.D., first assistant-surgeon of the *Hannibal*, to visit Colonels Tuckory and Carini, who had been kindly received at the Tinacria Hotel by the landlord. The leg of the former had been badly amputated, and his life was in danger; the latter was doing well. Both were much gratified at seeing an English medical officer. About eight hundred wounded soldiers were carried off to the merchant shipping during the day.

June 2.—I landed this morning in plain clothes, with my flag-lieutenant as an escort, and visited all the principal parts of the city. When looked upon from the Bay the devastation could scarcely be perceived, the greater part of the missiles having been thrown over the buildings which face the Marina; but the interior of the beautiful metropolis of the Island presented a heart-rending spectacle. A whole district near the Royal Palace, about a thousand yards in length by a hundred yards in width, was a crushed mass of ruins, still smouldering in its ashes. Families had been burnt alive within the buildings, and the atrocities committed by some miscreants of the Royal troops in their retreat from the convents of the Benedictines and Annunziata were frightful. In the Toledo, and other streets adjoining, convents, churches, and palaces of the nobility had been demolished by the falling shells, eleven hundred of which were thrown from the citadel, and two hundred from the ships of war, before I arrested the fire. Solid shot, grape and cannister, in equal proportion, had also been launched in every direction to which the heavy guns could be trained, but their effect on the massive edifices was as nothing compared with the destructive power of the ten and thirteen-inch shells.

Mr. Herzell, the Swiss Consular Agent, gave me a written report of the sufferings of his own countrymen, he having personally visited the burning convents on the last day of the bombardment, and remained examining the devastation till finally driven from the scene of horrors, by the pestilential smell of the unburied corpses.

I was forcibly struck by the efficiency of the barricades, and by the determined attitude of the people. Carpenters, bricklayers, stonemasons, ironmongers, and artificers of every denomination, apparently under divisional leaders, were actively at work at the various depôts for preparing arms and materials for defence. Thousands of pikes, pitchforks, swords, and every imaginable rude weapon were placed out in the streets, ticketed and ready for issue, and boys and girls were assisting in carrying the lighter articles to and fro.

My flag-lieutenant seemed everywhere to be recognized; and as it was now generally known that the moral agency of the British flag had saved the city from further destruction, the gratitude and respect of the people were made unmistakeably manifest.

On my return to the ship, I received a visit from Captain Vacca, of the Neapolitan steam corvette, *Fiera Mosca*, who told me he was anxious to offer his respectful thanks for the prompt measures I had taken to prevent the continuance of the bombardment by the Neapolitan ships of war; these feelings, he added, were, with very few exceptions, universal throughout the squadron of the King of the Two Sicilies.

Late in the first watch, General Letizia returned from Naples, but the orders which he brought were kept a profound secret. On re-landing, he would have learnt that the hiding-place of a number of the sbirri, or police agents, had been discovered, and about thirty of them barbarously murdered in cold blood by the populace. All attempts to save the lives of these men were unsuccessful. The mob was implacable—many of them were stoned to death, and then torn to pieces. Against the Neapolitan soldiers, on the other hand, no feeling of resentment existed. The prisoners and the wounded were well treated.

June 3.—Letizia and Garibaldi had an interview early in the forenoon, and, as the re-conquest of Palermo by the Royal troops was hopeless, the armistice was indefinitely prolonged. The whole of the interior of the Island was now in revolt, and the garrisons of Girgenti and Caltanisetta had marched towards the fortresses on the eastern coast; yet up to this day the reinforcements received by the insurgents only amounted to one hundred men, landed at Marsala on the 31st of May, under command of Fardella, Marquis Torrearsa.

By the arrival of the *Caradoc*, Lieutenant Commander Buckle, in the afternoon, I received the following account of a severe conflict between the Royal troops and the insurgents at Catania, which ended in the retirement of the latter, after placing five hundred of the troops *hors de combat*.

At dawn, on the 31st of May, the city of Catania was attacked by bands of insurgents from the country, numbering about six hundred. The Royal forces, which were prepared for the attack, were concentrated in the Piano del Duomo, two thousand strong of all arms, with eight 12 pound field guns commanding the three principal streets to the north, east, and west, the Marina and its gate being commanded by the guns of the steam frigate *Guiscardo.*

As soon as the attack commenced on the part of the insurgents, the Royal troops commenced to sweep the streets with grape, case, shell, and round shot, and rifle bullets. The insurgents had also some artillery, which they applied with fearful effect upon the troops, keeping as much out of sight as possible, and gradually closing in from house to house, and by the bye-streets and lanes. The battle raged from daylight till noon, when the insurgents gradually retreated, after inflicting upon the Royal garrison a loss of two hundred killed and three hundred wounded.

Immediately after the insurgents left, the city was given over to the troops to pillage for thirty-six hours. Everything was taken from the houses of the four principal streets, centering on the Piano del Duomo, and the houses burnt. The insurgents, chiefly Catanese, behaved with great gallantry. They were composed of bands organized in the country, and concentrated at the village of Mascalucia. They were commanded by one Poletti, and by young men of the first families in Catania. Their object was to get possession of the city, or, at least, to inflict chastisement on the troops before the arrival of Marshal Alfon de Riviera, who, with his division of two thousand four hundred men, was known to be on his march from Caltinisetta, and who reached Catania the same night.

During this attack, foreign property and houses were respected by both belligerents. The only English subjects residents in Catania, at the time, were Mr. Jeans, the Vice-Consul, and Mr. Massey. The above account was furnished by the former to Lieutenant Buckle.

CHAPTER XV.

1860.

Palermo.—Evacuation of the City by the Royal Troops.—Return of Refugees to the Shore.—Excursion to the Camps.—Animating Scene in the Bay.—Narrow Escape of the Austrian Commodore.—Farewell Visit of General Lanza.—Celebration of Her Majesty's Accession.—Garibaldi's Visit to the Ships.

June 4.—I had, this morning, the satisfaction of receiving letters from the Honourable Henry Elliot, Her Majesty's Minister Plenipotentiary at Naples, and from the Commander-in-chief, Vice-Admiral Martin, fully approving the measures I had adopted for the purpose of arresting the destruction of Palermo. In the opinion of Mr. Elliot, I had acted right in refusing to mediate between Lanza and Garibaldi. He remarked that I had done all that was desirable in giving every possible facility for carrying on their conferences, for which they had much reason to be grateful to me; but that, as mediator, I should very soon have been accused of favouring one side or the other, and of not keeping to the strict neutrality I had hitherto succeeded in observing. The questions to be settled were simply of a military nature, for the principles at stake on the two sides rendered compromise impossible with regard to the political objects in view. I took note of these sensible observations, feeling they might be useful for my guidance as other difficulties arose.

By the same mail from Naples came also a copy of a circular which the Minister for Foreign Affairs had sent round to all the Foreign Missions, apologizing to the English Government for having previously affirmed that the English ships of war had interfered with the operations of the Neapolitan squadron during the landing of the expedition at Marsala.

June 5.—General Colonna, who commanded the garrison of the Royal Palace, had an interview with Garibaldi this morning, and an agreement was entered into between them, by which the Royal troops were to evacuate the Palace and all other places held by them within the city, except the fortress of Castellamare. They were to take up a new position on the Campo and arsenal near Mount Pellegrino, and to occupy the small fort of Castellacio on the Mole. It was also stipulated that the noblemen who had been so long confined in the citadel, and whose lives had been spared at the instigation of Mr. Goodwin and myself, should be released.

June 6.—General Letizia, who had made a second journey to Naples, returned to Palermo this morning, bringing with him full powers to treat with

General Garibaldi for the evacuation of the city by the Royal forces.

A convention was duly signed in the afternoon, the leading points of which declared that the Royal troops should be sent away from the city with their arms, baggage, and material, receiving all the honours of war, so soon as a sufficient number of transports could be procured. An exchange of prisoners was also to take place, and the citadel to be delivered up to the Dictator when the last detachment of the Royal army had left.

Colonel Orsini, with the artillery, consisting of six mountain field-pieces and a hundred men, arrived from Corleone, escorted by four thousand *squadre*. It was this small body of picked men that deceived Marshal Salzano, leading him on to the heights of Piano del Grece, whilst Garibaldi made the flank march to the left on Misilmeri.

In the afternoon the Sardinian screw frigates *Maria Adelaide*, 50, and *Carlo Alberto*, 50, anchored in the Bay, the former carrying the flag of Rear-Admiral Persano.

At 8 we had theatrical entertainments on board, performed by the ship's company, and dancing till midnight.

The bolder part of the refugees were now disposed to return to the shore, and this was the last evening of the general assembly. They had been sixteen days on board, and Commander Parkin deserved the greatest credit for the excellent arrangements he had made for their accommodation and comfort.

June 7.—During the forenoon, about fifteen thousand Neapolitan troops, infantry and cavalry, marched along the Marina, from the eastern suburbs of the city towards the Mole, to be in readiness for embarkation. It was one of the most humiliating spectacles that could have been witnessed, and I turned from it with disgust.

At the entrance of the Toledo, the son of Garibaldi, mounted on a black charger, with a dozen red-shirted youths near him, took up a position in front of the principal barricade. This advanced post was supposed to be the guard of the main defence of the city from the seaward, but doubtless the Dictator placed his firstborn in that marked locality, in order that the vanquished hosts of disciplined men might defile before him, and their degradation if possible be made more apparent. As soon as they reached the Mole the embarkation commenced, and by midnight four thousand were put on board the steamers, part of which took the direction of Messina, and the rest of Naples.

I landed in the afternoon, and visited old Mr. Ingham. I found him in good health, and was glad to hear that his house had been respected by both parties. The officer of the Royal troops had requested him to keep his windows closed, and not to let any one show himself; in that case he would answer that he would not be molested by his soldiers. There had been severe fighting in every direction around, but his mansion was uninjured.

I subsequently visited the military posts of the insurgents, and drove in an open carriage through the Campo, where twenty thousand Royal troops were in bivouac. I was everywhere received with marks of respect and by the military salute to which I was entitled by my uniform, showing that there existed no ill-feeling either to myself or to the English flag.

The commanding officers of the Austrian, French, American, Sardinian, and Spanish ships of war had not yet landed, and probably the confidence of which I gave proof, by trusting myself unhesitatingly amongst the armed legions of both parties in the midst of civil war, gratified their self-esteem. The officers and men of the Royal army were evidently equally glad as the leader and the insurgent people that hostilities had ceased. They knew to what quarter they were indebted for the benefit of the armistice, and to this feeling I attributed the deference that was paid to me.

Between two and three thousand men had been killed and wounded during the four days' struggle, and as many more were lying sick at the hospitals from exposure and want of nourishment. Pillage had been allowed where property was native, but houses and premises of foreigners were generally respected. One country house, belonging to Signor Fiamingo, who married an English woman, the sister of Frost, the Chartist leader, was threatened with sack and fire, and was saved by my sending an officer to give the lady protection as a British subject.

June 8.—The *Racoon*, Captain Chamberlain, arrived this morning to reinforce the squadron. Henceforth I discontinue my daily journal.

June 14.—During the past week, the Royal troops have been embarked with much regularity, and nine thousand only remain, for which transports have not yet arrived. The barricades in the city have been removed and confidence re-established. On all the public buildings, and on most of the private houses, printed papers are affixed, on which are written, "We want annexation to the Constitutional Kingdom under Victor Emanuel." Thus the annexionists have triumphed over the party desirous of a separate kingdom.

The English squadron on the coast of Sicily had been increased, and now consisted of the *Hannibal*, *Amphion*, *Racoon*, *Scylla*, *Argus*, *Intrepid*, and *Caradoc*; the Sardinian flotilla, under Rear-Admiral Persano, consisted of an equal number of vessels; and with the French squadron, under Rear-Admiral Jehenne, whose flag was flying in the screw ninety-gun ship *Donawerth*, and the Austrian, American, Spanish, and Neapolitan ships of war, and about a hundred merchantmen at anchor in the bay, presented an animating scene.

Admiral Persano paid me a visit yesterday, and informed me that he had seen the Dictator, who had expressed himself as most grateful for the courtesy I had shown him during the trying position in which he was placed at the conference on board the *Hannibal.*

I also received a visit from the Austrian Commodore, Baron Von Wullersdorf, who was extremely irate at the conduct of a Neapolitan picket stationed near the lighthouse. He was passing in his boat, with the Austrian flag hoisted at the stern, when a volley was fired at him, and subsequently single shots, as he pulled in haste out of range. Though the boat was missed, and he escaped from an ignominious death, the frigate *Swartzenburg*, bearing his broad pennant, was struck in the hull. Baron Von Wullersdorf declared to me that if they repeated the insult on his next boat excursion round the Bay, he should return the fire with a broadside from the guns of his ship. He had taken no part whatever in the conflict that had been raging, and he thought it most extraordinary that this animosity should have been displayed towards the Austrian flag.

I remarked to him that certainly the Neapolitans deserved a round shot or two from the frigate by way of a return compliment, but as the troops would now be leaving in a very few days, it was hardly worth while to go within range of their rifles again. With respect to their ill-will, I added, perhaps the reason he gave why he thought there should have been no animosity against the Austrian flag was the cause of their conduct. Austria was supposed to support and look favourably on the despotic form of Government, introduced by the late King of Naples and continued by his son, and when an Austrian squadron was at anchor in the Roads, and a dreadful civil war raging, the Neapolitans expected, if not assistance, at least advice or sympathy, neither of which had they received. He then observed that he had seen me frequently landing, both in the city and country, and seemed surprised that I should have ventured on so dangerous a step, and wished to know what kind of reception I had met with. I was glad of the opportunity of informing him that I had several times been on shore, and, after visiting most parts of the city, had driven for miles into the country round; and whether in the midst of royalists or rebels, patriots or priests, *squadre* or red-shirted Garibaldini, had always been received with respect and civility. I was proud to believe that the *prestige* and moral power of the British flag had exacted this willing homage from bodies of men who certainly had not been tutored by their Governments to look favourably on England.

June 18.—Last night General Medici, with a reinforcement of 2500 men for Garibaldi, reached Castellamare, a seaport town twenty miles west of Palermo.

The *Agamemnon*, 91, Captain Hope, arrived, bringing my flag-captain, Captain Farquhar. The Austrian squadron sailed for Naples.

June 19.—At 10 A.M. General Lanza came on board the *Hannibal*, attended by the whole of his personal staff, and was received with the honours due to his rank as Royal Commissioner Extraordinary and *Alter Ego* of the Sovereign. He was much affected at stepping on the quarter-deck, the remembrance of the horrors of the great civil struggle which had taken place since we had met three weeks before, doubtless passing through his mind. He was dressed in full uniform, and covered with decorations, and, with thorough gentlemanlike feeling, at once expressed his gratitude and thanks for the assistance I had afforded him in bringing about the armistice. "I have written officially to the King, my master, and have told him that you have done everything that could be done, to meet my wishes during the terrible crisis which has passed," were the words he used; "we have been unfortunate," he added, "but our military honour has been saved. I am grateful to you from my heart, and it is this sentiment alone which induces me at the moment of my departure to pay you a farewell visit."

The steam frigate which was to convey him to

Naples was lying-to, abeam of the ship, having the vice-regal standard flying at the main, and twenty-four other steam vessels were in the offing, each filled with troops, detachments of the great southern army, which had been so signally defeated by the Northern Italians. On General Lanza leaving the ship the white flag of the King of the Two Sicilies was hoisted for the last time in the waters of Sicily at the fore-top-gallant mast-head, and His Excellency saluted with nineteen guns.

By noon the whole flotilla was steaming towards Naples, at which hour the garrison of the citadel marched out with the honours of war, and the National Italian flag was displayed on the tower of the semaphore. Every part of the island, excepting the forts of Messina, Syracuse, and Melazzo, was now in the hands of the provisional Government. Augusta, Trapani, and Catania, had been evacuated.

At sunset the last steam transport sailed for Naples, and the insurrection was everywhere triumphant.

June 20.—At 8 A.M. dressed ship with flags in honour of the accession of Her Majesty to the throne, which ceremony was followed by the foreign squadrons at anchor in the bay, and at noon the whole of the ships fired a Royal salute. It so happened that Garibaldi had arranged to visit the flag-ships of the foreign Powers, without being aware of its being one of the days set apart for official celebration, both in and out of Her Majesty's dominions. The populace and peasantry within sight of this national demonstration and within hearing of the guns, believed the display to have been organized in honour of their victorious leader, and perhaps the Dictator himself, as he embarked in the barge of the *Maria Adelaide*, with the Sardinian standard at her prow, was not averse to the misconception which not unnaturally had gained the lower orders.

On board the flag-ship of Rear-Admiral Persano, Garibaldi was received with the same distinguished honours as I had paid on the previous day to the Royal Commissioner. He was considered by the Rear-Admiral as the *de facto* Viceroy and ruler of the Island, and as such had been welcomed and distinguished.

This salute of nineteen guns, if given without instruction from Turin, was indeed a bold measure, and could only be construed into a recognition of the dictatorship in the name of King Victor Emanuel.

From the *Maria Adelaide* Garibaldi came to the *Hannibal*. He was now dressed in his own costume, the red shirt, with the flowing coloured silk handkerchief loosely hanging down his back, grey trowsers, large curved sabre with steel scabbard, and the Tyrolese hat and black plumes. This dress was certainly more becoming to his figure than the closely-fitting coat and stiff collar of the Sardinian general officer. His narrow waist and broad hips allowing him to wear the lower garment without braces, gave an elasticity to his movements, and, doubtless, he felt more at home in his every-day apparel than when hampered with the accoutrements of pipe-clay and etiquette.

I went on to the quarter-deck to receive him, and the Guard of Royal Marine Light Infantry gave him military honours as on his previous visit, but I told him at once that I could not recognize his position as Dictator in the island, as had been done by Rear-Admiral Persano, nor could I salute him on leaving the ship as head of the Provisional Government of Palermo. He told me in reply that he neither wished nor did he expect me to receive him in an official capacity; the object of his visit was to thank me for arresting the bombardment, and for bringing about the armistice. For these acts of humanity he hoped I should allow him to consider me as his friend, and to express to me his lasting esteem and gratitude (*m'assurer de son estime la plus profonde, et de sa gratitude eternelle*). His love for England and the British people was unbounded, and their sympathy for the cause of Italian regeneration and for the oppressed in every land, had made the great English nation the admiration of the world.

I then mentioned that I had received instructions from Her Majesty's Government to use any influence I might possess with the belligerents to mitigate the horrors of war and to stay the effusion of blood, and I hoped that in the event of further hostilities in other parts of the Island, he would act in the same generous and humane manner as he had hitherto done.

He assured me of his desire to do so, but feared the approaching contest at Messina would be one of much obstinacy and bloodshed. He next alluded with great satisfaction to my having anchored the English squadron so close to the shore, he believed even with danger to the ships, in order that they might become a refuge to non-combatants flying from the destruction around. This magnanimous proceeding, he said, had been felt and acknowledged by all parties, and could never be forgotten.

I admitted the reasons he had assigned for the position taken up by the ships within the boundary line of the usual anchorage were perfectly correct, but reminded him that the circumstances were exceptional, and that when such was the case a bold attitude was desirable. I felt sure he would have noticed the proximity of the despatch vessel *Intrepid*, which, stationed at an easy stone's-throw from the Marina, could have been reached by any moderate swimmer in the space of a few minutes. I did not, however, tell him the whole truth, which was that I had placed this well-disciplined little craft, commanded by Captain Marryat, off the nearest rocks close to the Toledo, for the purpose of saving Garibaldi's own life should a stroke of adverse fortune compel him to look around for an ark of safety.

Garibaldi remained with me a quarter of an hour, and then proceeded to the *Donawerth*, bearing the flag of the French Rear-Admiral Jehenne, and then to the United States frigate *Iroquois*, Captain Palmer.

In the afternoon, Rear-Admiral Jehenne came on board the *Hannibal*, and expressed to me his surprise at the visit which the Dictator had made to him. It placed him, he said, in an untoward position, as he was obliged to tell his visitor that he could not recognize him even as a general officer, but only as a simple monsieur who had given him the unexpected honour of a call. My position, Rear-Admiral Jehenne admitted, was different, in consequence of the armistice having been signed in my flag-ship. He spoke sensibly relative to the imbecility manifested by the Royal authorities, from the time of the disembarkation of the Piedmontese at Marsala to the capture of the city by the insurgents, but he was not disposed to give up the Royal cause as irretrievably lost.

On the departure of the French Admiral, I landed and drove to the Palace Square, where a large number of the Italian forces was encamped, and on inquiry as to the cause of the assembly, I was told that the First Brigade of the Fifteenth Division of the National Army, three thousand strong, commanded by General Turr, was under review preparatory to setting out for Caltanisetta. After a halt of a few days in that city General Turr would proceed to

Catania, and organize the military establishments of the eastern departments of the Island.

These men looked remarkably well, and as they marched down the Toledo, received a complete ovation from the ladies, who, crowding the balconies, waved their handkerchiefs and threw down flowers on their path. Every house was decorated with the Italian banner and the white cross of Savoy, and the enthusiasm of the people was at its height. Colonel Peard, known as Garibaldi's Englishman, a fine, soldier-like-looking man, with the beard of a patriarch, was there; also Colonels Dunn and Windham, the former having been most active and successful in recruiting and organizing the Picciotti or Sicilian youths, both volunteer and conscript.

CHAPTER XVI.

1860.

Palermo.—Interview with Garibaldi.—Royalist Refugees on Board.—Proclamation of a Constitution.—Arrival of French Volunteers.—The Dictator and La Farina.—Unsatisfactory State of the Island.—Visit to Garibaldi.—His Farewell Letter.—My Answer.—Sail for Naples.

June 22.—In the forenoon I returned the visit of General Garibaldi, accompanied by Lieutenant Wilmot. I found him occupying a large suite of apartments at the end of a lofty terrace on the extreme left wing of the Royal Palace, commanding a magnificent view of the adjacent country, and of the expanse of water to the northward. He was truly glad to see me, and expressed himself as pleased with a visit which had been paid to him yesterday by the French Rear-Admiral. Of the French nation and people he spoke in kind terms, but he was unable to believe that their despotic ruler, the Emperor, had any true regard for Italy after despoiling her of the districts of Savoy and Nice. He was very sorry to say it, but he could never forgive the first minister of Sardinia, the

Count Cavour, for yielding his consent to this act of aggression.

I reminded him, in reply, that however galling it might be to know that these provinces had been ceded to France, on the plea of a necessity of a rectification of the frontier, it should not be forgotten that without the assistance which had been given by the armed legions of the Emperor Napoleon, Italy never could have conquered the position she now held. There were always two sides to a question, and it was only an act of justice to remember the benefits received as well as the injuries done. On this subject, however, I soon perceived that the Chief of the Provisional Government was self-willed and obdurate, and I hastened to change the subject to topics of a more general nature. I found I had to deal with an enthusiast, who, with the blandest manner in discussing ordinary matter, was apparently inaccessible to reason when the question of the regeneration of his country was to be taken into consideration.

June 30.—Several Royalist refugees of rank and station fled from the city this morning, and sought safety in the *Hannibal*. In the afternoon, I shipped four of them off in the *Intrepid* to Malta. They seemed equally apprehensive of the King's Government as of that of the revolution, and were unwilling to go to Naples. Amongst them were the Duke of Carcamo; late President of the Board of Health; Signor Nicastro, late President of the Supreme Court, and father-in-law of Maniscalco; Signor Napolitano, Councillor of State; Prince Manganelli, Prince Buonfortella, and Signor Marsala, the late criminal Attorney-General. The refusal of these gentlemen to trust themselves within the grasp of King Francis, whom they had endeavoured faithfully to serve, is inexplicable. Nothing but the firm conviction in their own minds of the unsoundness of the system they had upheld for years, and of their mistrust of their own companions still in power at Naples, could give me any clue to their conduct. As Roman Catholics and as absolutists, why ask English protection, when those of their own faith were on the spot to afford it? I was, however, glad to show that all who were in political distress might seek and be sure to find an asylum under the British flag. They had been arrested by Garibaldi for conspiring against the present order of things, and probably were allowed to escape.

I received despatches from Naples yesterday, giving me intelligence of His Majesty King Francis II. having granted a constitution to his Kingdom of the Two Sicilies, coupled with alliance with Sardinia, the adoption of the Italian colours, and a liberal amnesty. Mr. Elliot, in a letter, stated it to be his opinion that had this measure been effected six months ago, it would have saved the dynasty, which was now doubtful, as the people were incredulous of the reality of the concession and of the good faith of the Court. It was also uncertain if Sardinia would accept the alliance, the public feeling in Piedmont being strong against the Neapolitans.

At sunset General Medici, with a thousand men, marched out of Palermo, and took the sea-coast road towards Messina.

July 3.—Two seamen of the *Hannibal* were missing at yesterday's morning quarters, and, suspecting they had deserted to the patriot forces, I sent Lieutenant Wilmot to the Dictator, with a request that he would give orders for their apprehension, it such should prove to be the case. He complied immediately with my demand, and this afternoon they were brought on board by the Italian police, having been found in the mountains, endeavouring to gain the insurgent division which had marched on Caltanisetta. This promptitude of action on the part of Garibaldi was just what I expected from the character of the man.

July 6.—A French merchant steamer arrived yesterday from Genoa, with eight hundred volunteer soldiers, principally, Frenchmen. This reinforcement was greatly needed, as the state of affairs within the city had been for many days very unsettled. The Dictator had been compelled, by the clamours of a violent mob, to change his Ministers, and he was otherwise disappointed that scarcely a man of wealth or weight in the Island had joined his standard. The *squadre* were clamorous for pay, subscriptions had almost ceased, and funds were beginning to fail for the pressing exigencies of the State; but his greatest annoyance arose from the antagonism which existed between himself personally and the Government at Turin, on the subject of immediate annexation to the Kingdom of Sardinia. The Dictator was determined to rule absolute in the Island, until he could organize a sufficient military force to enable him to invade Southern Calabria; whilst Count Cavour, with equal pertinacity, had fully resolved to govern Sicily by his own agents, in the name of Victor Emanuel. For this purpose, he had sent over from Piedmont a tried friend and able administrator, the Signor La Farina, who, through the persuasive eloquence of Admiral Persano, was permitted by Garibaldi to assume the reins of government.

The Dictator, however, who possesses a deep astuteness of character, seemingly unrecognized either by his enemies or by his friends, never intended for a moment to relinquish the executive power. He allowed the installation in due form of the nominee of Count Cavour, but gave him unmistakeably to understand that he was to occupy himself solely with financial and commercial affairs: in short, he was to be the instrument by which money was to be procured for the prosecution of the war, and to assist in the pacification of the unmanageable populace.

La Farina, finding himself both in a false and in an undignified position, first remonstrated and then rebelled. A quarrel ensued, but the question was soon solved as to where real power was deposited, by an order from the Dictator to have the contumacious functionary arrested. He was seized by an armed force at the dead of night, and shipped off to the *Maria Adelaide*, the flag-ship of Admiral Persano, with a recommendation to quit the country with all convenient speed.

Thus ended the vexed dispute of immediate annexation. The Dictator had triumphed by an arbitrary act, but as he was resolute in his plan of carrying the war into the continental provinces of the kingdom, the violence of the proceeding might be excusable.

Garibaldi was also much chagrined at receipt of intelligence of the capture of the American clipper *Charles and Jane*, with nine hundred volunteers on board bound to Palermo. This vessel was taken off Cape Corse by the Neapolitan frigate *Fulminante*, and carried under the batteries of the fortress of Gaeta, when the passengers were made prisoners. The American Minister had made strong remonstrances on the subject, and hopes were entertained of their release. The clipper had been captured on the high seas, and doubts existed of the legality of the act.

The reports from the Vice-Consuls at this time relative to the state of the interior of the island were not satisfactory. The apathetic and volatile character of the Sicilians, joined to the total absence of sustained patriotic feeling on their part, frustrated all the efforts of the Dictator to gain able-bodied recruits by voluntary enlistment. His work was therefore one of increasing difficulty, and it was whispered abroad that he began to be doubtful of ultimate success.

On my return to the ship, after a long drive into the country with Mr. Goodwin, I had the satisfaction of receiving an official despatch from the Secretary of the Admiralty, forwarding to me the entire approval of Lord John Russell and Her Majesty's Government of the measures I had adopted to save Palermo from destruction, in which approval His Grace the Duke of Somerset and the Lords Commissioners of the Admiralty were pleased to concur. I also received instructions to proceed in my flag-ship to Naples, and on my arrival in the Bay I was to take under my command five sail of the line, a frigate and a gun-boat, which by their Lordships' directions Vice-Admiral Martin had despatched from Malta to reinforce my division.

As no further necessity existed for my presence in Sicily, I was glad to change the field of action to the waters of the capital.

July 7.—At 8 A.M. hoisted colours half-mast, and fired a gun alternately with the *Amphion* every half hour, in memory of Prince Jerome, deceased. All the foreign ships of war did the same and topped their lower and topsail yards.

At 11 I went to the Royal Palace, and paid a fare

well visit to the Dictator. I found him at breakfast, with several of his officers and staff around him. Amongst them General Cosenz just arrived from Genoa, whom he presented to me as one of the best officers of the Italian army, and a steadfast friend.

In appearance Garibaldi was much altered since I had seen him on board the *Hannibal*. He looked thin and careworn, and was evidently harassed in mind, and devoid of his usual composure. He told me he had received bad news from Turin. The Emperor Napoleon was decidedly hostile to Italian regeneration, and would never quit Rome unless the island of Sardinia was given up to him in compensation. This sacrifice Count Cavour was quite prepared to make, and a treaty was already in progress for the further humiliation of Italy, and for the aggrandisement of the French empire. He had received this information from competent authority, and should have it published forthwith in the free press of Sicily.

I expressed my unwillingness to discuss matters of this nature, but strongly recommended his abstaining from communicating intelligence to the public papers, which I felt convinced was untrue, but which, even if partially correct, had much better remain known only to himself. He finally agreed in my view of the matter, and renounced his intention of publication. I then cordially thanked him for the prompt and successful measures he had taken to arrest the deserters from the *Hannibal*, and for the protection he had granted to all British subjects in the city since his assumption of supreme power.

On my taking leave he again repeated his expressions of affection and admiration of the British nation and Government, and entreated me to believe that the generosity of my conduct towards himself individually could never be erased from his memory.

He should meet me again before very long at Naples, upon which city he should march as soon as Messina had fallen. I remarked to him, in reply to this unexpected announcement, that His Majesty King Francis II. had now entered his name upon the roll of constitutional monarchs, and was about to enter into an alliance with King Victor Emanuel.

Garibaldi gravely answered, "It is too late!" I then broke off the discussion and returned to the ship.

At 2 P.M. the *Hannibal* lifted her anchors, and steamed out of Palermo Roads.

Seven eventful weeks had passed since her arrival in the port. To me they had been days of great anxiety and of much responsibility, and I deemed myself fortunate in being able to record that I received the thanks of both belligerents for my endeavour to act impartially between them. With the Admirals, Commodores, and Captains in command of the squadrons of the various foreign nations with whom I had been associated, the best of good feeling at all times existed, and at frequent gatherings together at their table and at my own, though opinions greatly differed, cordiality was not disturbed.

The *Hannibal* had already gained some distance in the offing under easy steam, when a swift-pulling native boat shot up alongside, and brought me a despatch from the Palace. The letter was from the Dictator, written in Italian. I give the translation and copy of the original.

"*General Garibaldi to Admiral Mundy.*

"Palermo, July 7, 1860.

"ADMIRAL,

"You are leaving! . . . and in seeing you go far from us, a sentiment of deep gratitude penetrates the heart of every creature born in this land.

"You did not turn your terrible batteries against the servile bombarders of Palermo; you did not send your brave seamen, much as they might have desired it, to defend the city in peril; . . . your duty, as an officer, and the stern laws of policy, forbade it; . . . but, good and generous man, you did give us largely both of sympathy and esteem! . . .

"You anchored your ship close to the maritime threshold of the city, testifying your reprobation of the inhuman slaughter, and in readiness to receive on board those families which were driven to seek shelter from conflagration and destruction. . . .

"Thanks, Admiral! . . . thanks for your magnanimous conduct! Thanks in the name of Palermo, of Sicily—of entire Italy! . . .

"The departure of the *Hannibal* from the capital is felt as that of a friend truly dear. . . .

"May Providence ever protect that noble vessel, her valiant crew, and the esteemed and generous sailor who is her chief!

"With true regard,

"GIUSEPPE GARIBALDI."

Original.

"Palermo, 7 Luglio, 1860.

"AMMIRAGLIO,

"Voi partite! . . . e nel vedervi allontanare, un sentimento di mesta gratitudine penetra ogni creatura nata in questa terra.

"Voi non avete rivolti le terribile vostre batterie ai servili bombardatori di Palermo; voi non avete mandati i vostri valarosi marinari, benchè ne avessero molta voglia, alla difesa della citta pericolante! . . .

"Il vostro dovere di soldato, e le tristi leggi della politica ne lo vietarono . . . Ma voi—uomo buono e generoso, ci avete largheggiato di simpatia e d'affetto. . . .

"Avete serrato il vostro naviglio al limbo maritimo della citta dimostrando di riprovare la strage inumana,

. . . e pronto ad accogliere quelle famiglie che l'incendio e la distruzione potevano spingere verso di voi. . . .

"Grazia Ammiraglio! . . . Grazia del vostro magnanimo procedere! . . . Grazia in nome di Palermo, della Sicilia, dell' Italia intiera! . . .

"La partenza del *Annibale* da questa Capitale e sentito come quella d'un amico ben caro.

"Che la Providenza protega sempre il nobile legno, la cerra comitiva ed il venerando . . . generoso marino che la capitana!

"Con vero affetto,

"Vostro,

"G. GARIBALDI.

"*Al* AMMIRAGLIO MUNDY,
della Squadra Inglese, in Palermo."

The style of this letter may be that of rhapsody, but I thought the composition beautiful, and I felt the expressions to be sincere.

The armistice concluded on board the *Hannibal* had secured himself and the cause he represented from imminent peril, and he was not the man to disguise the debt of gratitude which he owed, although he knew the steps I had taken were at the express desire of the Royal authorities. The reply which I gave was, certainly, less poetical, though I hope not the less pertinent, nor opposed to any known law of the vexed question of neutrality.

"*Rear-Admiral Mundy to General Garibaldi.*

"H.M.S. *Hannibal*, Palermo,
"July 7, 1860.

"SIR,

"Your letter of this date reached me at the moment of my departure from Palermo. I thank you much for the sentiments expressed therein. I feel them to be sincere.

"It is true that I placed my ships near the marina of the city for the purpose of giving refuge to all who might flee from the terrors of the bombardment, and it is gratifying to know that I was enabled in some degree to mitigate the sufferings of the inhabitants.

"I shall always remember with satisfaction that my flag-ship became the neutral ground whereon was held the conference, the result of which stopped the further effusion of blood, and brought about that preliminary armistice, which ultimately led to the total cessation of hostilities.

"I thank you, sincerely, for your good wishes towards the *Hannibal*, towards her ship's company, and to myself.

(Signed) "G. RODNEY MUNDY."

At sunset, we lost sight of the high land around Palermo, and, taking a departure from the Islet of Ustica, steered a course direct for Naples.

CHAPTER XVII.

1860.

Naples.—The Prince of Syracuse.—Admiral de Tinan.—Overtures from Neapolitan Naval Officers.—Audience of the King.—Riot in the City.—Insult to the French Admiral and British Consul.—Prince Luigi and the British Sailors on Shore.—Captain Flores in a New Character.—The National Guard.

July 8.—At sunset, the *Hannibal* cast anchor in the Bay of Naples, within a few cables' length of the lofty arches of the Royal Palace, from the dark recesses of which, during the evening of the 21st of December, 1798, the ancestors of the present Royal Family escaped from the menaces of an infuriated populace, and, with the assistance of the boats of the English squadron, reached in safety the *Vanguard*, the flag-ship of Rear-Admiral Nelson.

At that period, the Bourbon dynasty, surrounded by internal enemies, betrayed by treacherous friends, and threatened by the invading armies of the French Republic, had only England to apply to for aid and protection. These were afforded with a lavish hand, were welcomed with a seeming gratitude in the hour of tribulation, only to be too surely forgotten in the day of prosperity.

Now, again, after the lapse of sixty-two years, the great grandson of Ferdinand IV., threatened also by an insurgent population, looked out from the same Palace windows, not on the fleet of one nation only to whom he might apply in the hour of need, but on the ships of the united maritime Powers of Europe and America, each of which was in readiness to grant all His Majesty might ask in the shape of refuge and protection to himself and the Royal Family.

No pressure from the restless ambition of a foreign nation now imperilled his throne. Firm in the sympathy and good wishes of the great military empires of France, Austria, and Russia, and of the semi-constitutional kingdoms of Spain and Prussia, His Majesty Francis II. might count with reason on a long and prosperous reign.

England, equally friendly, and whose predilection for monarchical authority gave earnest of her sincerity, had shown herself desirous, by many acts of generous counsel, to uphold the stability of this branch of the ancient House of Bourbon. She had honestly advocated the policy of non-intervention, which had been introduced by her powerful ally, the French Emperor; and acting up to the letter of this newly-created dogma, the King was left unfettered to appease the discontent of his people. If His Majesty possessed their affections and they were true to his house, the task of reconciliation would be easy. The invaders were a handful of undisciplined men, and were opposed by a powerful and well-organized host. The success of the Revolutionists against an army of a hundred and twenty thousand men was impossible, unless the whole population should rise and show themselves in their favour.

Moored in the Bay I found a French, Russian, Austrian, American, Spanish, Sardinian, and Neapolitan squadron; and from the Commodore in charge of the latter I borrowed the new constitutional flag, which, having hoisted at the main, I saluted with twenty-one guns, a compliment immediately returned by the battery on Castel Nuovo.

July 9.—In the forenoon I visited the French Vice-Admiral Barbier de Tinan, who had his flag in the *Bretagne*, 131. He saluted me on leaving his ship with thirteen guns, which was returned by the *Hannibal*. In the afternoon, I waited on Mr. Elliot, Her Majesty's Minister, and received an official visit from Mr. Bonham, Her Majesty's Consul.

Whilst at exercise aloft in the evening, shifting topsail yards, I observed a very portly gentleman, with a flowing red beard, in a very smart-looking boat, pulling round and round the ship, and at three different times he made an effort to mount the accommodation-ladder and gain the quarter-deck. The effort was each time unsuccessful. The topping up and unrigging the heavy spar directly over his head seemingly caused so much alarm that his courage failed, and a coil of rope from the top falling straight across the gangway, at last made him give up the attempt in despair. On inquiry, I ascertained that my intended visitor was His Royal Highness the Prince of Syracuse, uncle of the King.

July 10.—Vice-Admiral de Tinan came on board the *Hannibal*, and was saluted on leaving with fifteen guns, which was returned by the *Bretagne*. On my informing him that I had made application, through the Lord Chamberlain, for an audience, in order that I might pay my respects to the King, the Vice-Admiral told me he did not intend asking for an interview at the present moment. I also received visits of etiquette from the Russian Admiral, Nordman, from the Austrian Commodore, Baron Von Wullërsdorf, and the senior officers in command of the other foreign ships of war at anchor in the bay. The French Rear-Admiral Paris, with his flag in the *Algesiras*, 100, and two ships of the line, arrived as a reinforcement.

In the evening, the King and Queen pulled round the *Hannibal* in the Royal barge, passing close to the ship, and remained laying upon their oars, as if examining her with a critical eye. They seemed astonished at seeing so large a vessel at anchor so near to the shore. His Majesty looked downcast and sad, the Queen radiant in youth and beauty.

July 12.—I received overtures this morning from

fifteen Neapolitan naval officers employed in active service, who, having determined to resign their commissions, requested me to receive them for protection on board the *Hannibal*. They expressed extreme distrust of their King, and were apprehensive of being again called upon to fight against their Sicilian brothers. They stated that, by their *ordinanze*, or articles of war, they were entitled to send in their papers at any time when not before the enemy, and therefore the step contemplated could not be considered desertion. They only wished to seek the asylum of a British ship of war until opportunity occurred of leaving the country.

I acquainted them in reply, that I was astonished at their application, and that they would on no account be admitted on board any of the Queen's ships.

July 13.—At noon to-day, I proceeded to the Royal Palace with Her Majesty's Minister, and had an audience of King Francis II.

Captains Farquhar, Forbes, Chads, and Hope, Lieut. Wilmot, Mr. Shanks, secretary, and the commanders of the ships of the line also accompanied me. We were dressed in full uniform, and were ushered into the throne-room by the master of the ceremonies.

In a quarter of an hour the King entered, surrounded by his ministers. His Majesty was dressed in a close-fitting military coat, with a single large star, of great brilliancy, on his left breast. He seemed to be a well-knit, rather tall young man, with dark hair, very closely cut, and a bronze olive complexion. The expression of his countenance was that of distrust and despondency, and his manner extremely formal and ceremonious. He left the file of ministers, who were dazzling in a blaze of stars, crosses, and orders, marshalled in line at the door, and advanced by himself to our party, which had been formed in a semicircle in the centre of the vast apartment.

After presentation by Mr. Elliot, the King hastily remarked that he believed I had just arrived with the English fleet from the Island of Malta. Now, certainly, this observation was about the last I could have expected; as, considering the statement made to me by General Lanza, that he had written to His Majesty expressive of his thankfulness for my allowing the Royal Generals to hold conference on board the *Hannibal*, it was reasonable to suppose His Majesty would have remembered on what service I had been employed, and the part which I had acted in the late drama in Sicily. Indeed, Mr. Elliot had previously told me that, from the known gentlemanlike feeling of the King, he would certainly thank me himself for what I had done in favour of the Royal Commissioner.

I replied to His Majesty that I had not come from Malta but from Palermo, on which latter word I laid particular stress, where I had been stationed for many weeks.

The King, who stood with both hands deeply ensconced in the ample side-pockets of the pegtop trousers of the period, then asked several questions in rapid succession. Was the *Hannibal* considered a handsome ship? Had she any rifle guns on board? Had the French ships rifle cannon? How many ships of the line had England in the Mediterranean? Was the *Marlborough* as handsome a ship as the *Bretagne*? Were they both three-deckers? Were the English screw ships as good as the French screw ships?

Having given His Majesty to understand that there were no rifle guns in the English ships, but that there were a few in each French ship; that the English fleet mustered fifteen screw ships of the line and more than double that number of frigates and smaller classes of vessels, all propelled by steam, which was a force greater than had ever been previously sent into the Mediterranean during a time of peace; that the *Marlborough* and *Bretagne* were both three-deckers of equal beauty; and that the French screw ships were on a par with those of England; a dead silence ensued.

This was painful to every one. It had lasted certainly several minutes, when Mr. Elliot came to my relief by mentioning to the King that I was desirous of the honour of presenting the captains and officers of the squadron to His Majesty. This was accordingly done, and nothing could have been more courteous and even kind than the manner and address of His Majesty to each individual officer. He made minute inquiries into the state and condition of every ship, of the nature of their engines, their maximum speed, and apparently with the earnestness of a man really desiring instruction.

He subsequently entered more freely into conversation with me, and before giving the Royal bow which announced the conclusion of the audience, His Majesty was pleased to say that he had heard from General Lanza of the friendly disposition which I had evinced towards him during the calamities at Palermo, for which His Majesty begged to offer his thanks and gratitude.

It was satisfactory to me to receive this acknowledgement from the Royal lips, though it evidently cost His Majesty an effort to bring himself to make any allusion to the terrible proceedings in Sicily.

The King then took Her Majesty's Minister aside, and informed him that intelligence had been received in the morning of one of his steam-vessels of war, the *Veloce*, having been carried into Palermo, and treasonably delivered up by the captain to the rebel authorities. She afterwards put to sea again with a Sicilian crew, and captured two other small steam-packets in the vicinity of Messina, acts which His Majesty justly described as disgraceful to all concerned.

On descending the grand staircase we met the Russian Minister and suite, who with the Russian Admiral and officers of the squadron, were about to have an audience of His Majesty.

In the evening I gave liberty to five hundred seamen of the squadron for a run on shore for forty-eight hours. I had some misgivings as to the prudence of granting this indulgence, but the men had seen little of the shore for many months, and the change was desirable.

July 15.—In the afternoon, when I landed at the San Lucia steps, I observed an immense crowd gathered round my carriage, composed principally of lazároni and the lowest class of the population. On inquiry from a French officer who stood near, I ascertained that there had been a serious riot in the main streets of the city, that the troops had been called out to quell it, several arrests made, and that Admiral de Tinan, his captain, and staff had been grossly insulted by some of the *canaille*, who had shaken drawn swords in the Admiral's face as he passed in an open barouche at a foot's pace along the quay.

The British Consul, Mr. Bonham, whilst walking along the Largo Castello, had also been attacked by a band of these ruffians, had lost both hat and stick in the *mêlée*, and had eventually been obliged to seek safety in the main guard of the square.

As all now appeared quiet and the mob not disposed to molest me, I thought it advisable to take my drive. I visited the scene of the day's strife, found strong patrols at every point, and returned in a hopeful mood that my liberty-men were all right.

The *émeute* was supposed to have been planned in high places in a reactionary sense, the principal rioters being soldiers out of barracks for the day.

July 16.—Shortly before one o'clock this morning an aide-de-camp of Prince Luigi, Count d'Aguila, uncle of the King, came on board the *Hannibal*, and brought me a message from His Royal Highness requesting I would have the goodness to send on shore immediately for the English seamen on leave. The aide-de-camp stated they were in imminent danger from the anger of the populace, who had been outraged by the sailors spreading throughout the streets, crying out, "Long live Garibaldi!" Both the police and the Royal troops were acting energetically to save the lives of these misguided men, but no time must be lost, or it would be too late to extricate them from the just vengeance of a loyal people.

I had now been so long accustomed to the infatuated and senseless conduct of the governing powers of the Neapolitan House of Bourbon, in everything connected with their communications with me, that I had no place for astonishment at a proceeding so unusual, if not actually insulting. I felt perfectly convinced that there was gross exaggeration in the story thus detailed, but I considered it prudent to comply with the demand which had been made. Commander Parkin was therefore despatched, at dead of night, with an armed picket of Marines and a lieutenant from the other ships, to hunt up the unfortunate men who, as already named, were about five hundred in number, and up to this time had only completed half their leave of absence. They were found in their usual haunts, most of them housed and in bed, and, with the exception of a dozen stragglers, were brought to their respective ships in safety before morning's dawn. Not a man had been injured, or been even apprehensive of danger.

Being anxious to know the exact facts of the reported misunderstanding, which had led to the invasion of the city by the Marines of the squadron in the darkness of night, I sent Lieutenant Wilmot to Prince Luigi to intimate to His Royal Highness that if the hour of noon should be convenient, I would do myself the honour of paying my respects to him in person at that time. The Prince acquiesced, and I was admitted to an audience at his apartments in the Royal Palace at the hour I proposed.

His Royal Highness, who is noted for his extreme affability and open demeanour, came forward in a cheerful way, and shaking me warmly by the hand, as if delighted to welcome an old familiar friend, stated he knew I must be anxious for an explanation of his conduct last night.

I was in no way disposed to meet these advances

with the same spirit, feeling I had been treated in a cavalier manner neither dignified nor just.

His Royal Highness then said that in his capacity of Lord High Admiral and in chief command of the Royal Navy, it was his duty to act for the preservation of the public peace, whenever he might conceive it threatened by seamen either foreign or native. He had seen British sailors drunk; there had been disturbance near the Mole; and in his opinion it was desirable they should be immediately recalled to their ships. A full inquiry had been held this forenoon into all the circumstances of the case, and it now gave him great pleasure to be able to state that the evidence which had been taken completely exonerated the British seamen from blame. Some ill-disposed people had insisted on their joining in the cry of "Long live the King!" and they had resented this interference by shouting "Viva Garibaldi!"

I was of course obliged to accept this explanation, and immediately took my leave; but it did not require much sagacity on the part of His Royal Highness to discover that my displeasure was by no means removed.

Gentlemen of fifteen different nations honoured me with a visit on board the *Hannibal*, and left their names in my visiting-book. They were English, American, French, Austrian, Russian, Prussian, Spanish, Danish, Hanoverian, Swiss, Saxon, Belgian, Brazilian, Sardinian, and Neapolitan. I note this as a singular coincidence, in the same manner as I noted the visit of more than two hundred Ionian Greeks on the first day of this year. I think it a compliment to the nation I nautically represent.

July 17.—I paid Vice-Admiral de Tinan a visit this morning, and found him highly indignant with the Neapolitan Government for not keeping order in the streets of the capital. The threats which had been used whilst seated in his carriage, and the insults he had received, were a disgrace to the authorities.

It was now known that the riot was an outbreak of the soldiers of three regiments of the Guards, who, shouting "Long live King Francis the Second," rushed frantically through the Toledo, destroying everything that came in their way, and seriously wounding a large number of the people. This riot was supposed to have originated with General Nunziante and other reactionist field officers, and to have been looked upon favourably by the Princes of the Blood.

In the afternoon Captain Flores, my old acquaintance at Palermo, who had made himself notorious by his savage bombardment from the *Ercole*, came on board to ask my protection. He had abjured the naval service and taken up the cowl, but having been recognized by the mob, he was attacked upon the beach, when, leaping into a boat, he narrowly escaped with his life. He entreated me to give him shelter till an opportunity occurred of leaving the country. I complied with his request, and gave him over to the care of Captain Hope of the *Agamemnon*.

The Neapolitan naval officers, to whom I had refused admission in the squadron as refugees, sent in their resignations to-day.

The National Guard, nine thousand men, well dressed and equipped, made their first appearance to-day, and looked well. At night the city was illuminated in their honour.

CHAPTER XVIII.

1860.

Naples.—Battle of Melazzo.—Visit of the Lord High Admiral. —Admiral Persano.—Arrest of Prince Luigi.—Naples in a State of Siege.—Celebration of the Fête-Days of the Emperor Napoleon and the Emperor of Austria.—The French and English Squadrons.—The Marquis Villamarina.—Foreign Refugees on Board.—Landing of Garibaldi at Melito.—Visit of Alexandre Dumas.

July 24.—Intelligence arrived of the battle of Melazzo, named from a fortress built on a peninsula on the north coast of Sicily. It was fought on the 20th instant, between Colonel Bosco, in command of six thousand five hundred picked Neapolitan troops, principally riflemen, and Garibaldi, in command of four thousand four hundred Italians. Equal bravery was displayed on both sides, but victory remained with the insurgent forces.

Garibaldi fought hand to hand with a detachment of cavalry, and must have been killed but for the determined gallantry of his aides-de-camp, Missori and Stradella; who, with sabres and revolvers, brought the horsemen to the ground who had surrounded their leader.

The loss on both sides was enormous in proportion

to the numbers engaged. Eight hundred of the patriot forces lay killed or wounded on the ground; but the Neapolitans fighting on the defensive and under cover, suffered less severely. This victory decided the fate of Sicily. Messina alone now remained in the hands of the King.

July 30.—Prince Luigi, the Lord High Admiral, visited me on board the *Hannibal,* and a royal salute was fired on his leaving the ship.

His Royal Highness told me he had come on board to thank me for the undeviating kindness I had shown to the officers of the Neapolitan navy, both at Palermo and in this Bay, and especially for taking Captain Flores under my immediate protection; who was one of the best and most loyal officers in the service of the King. I fear His Royal Highness might with truth have added he was the only one really attached to the Bourbon dynasty. This unexpected visit of the Prince was evidently undertaken in order to remove from my mind the recollection of the unpleasant matter between us, relative to the expulsion of the seamen from the city on the night of the 16th ultimo.

August 3.—The screw steam frigate, *Maria-Adelaide,* with the flag of Rear-Admiral Persano, arrived and anchored in shore of the *Hannibal,* close off the steps of San Lucia. The Rear-Admiral came on board immediately to see me, and to inquire if I was satisfied with the position he had taken up.

I had, on two previous occasions, when he took up his moorings off Palermo, remarked that if he wished to show the Sardinian flag to advantage he should bring his ships as close into the land as the depth of water would allow; and I rather rashly added that at whatever port the *Hannibal* and her consorts might be found, it would not be an easy matter to pick up a berth between them and the shore. Bearing this little advice in mind, Admiral Persano had pushed his flag-ship boldly in near the rocks off Castel Ovo, and, rather proud of the achievement, paid me a good-humoured visit to receive my congratulations.

August 9.—Her Majesty's Minister paid me an official visit. His Excellency was received with yards manned, and was saluted with fifteen guns on leaving the ship.

August 14.—His Royal Highness Prince Luigi was arrested this morning, and ordered to leave the country. He had been conspiring for some weeks against the new order of things in the State, and was on the eve of an attempt to overthrow the Constitution by force, and to re-hoist the white flag, when the plot was discovered by means of the secret police. Five hundred revolvers, just imported, were found in his apartments; with which he intended to arm the most determined of his followers; and documents were brought to light exposing all details of the conspiracy. One paper, it was reported, gave the names of foreign officials who, as known enemies of despotic authority, were to be dealt with by stiletto, and prominent upon this list was the name of Mr. Elliot.

For my own part, I have no reason to regret that His Royal Highness is doomed to expatriation. My interview relative to the British seamen gave me no high opinion of his character.

In the evening the city of Naples was declared in a state of siege.

August 15.—All the ships of war dressed with flags at 8 A.M. and fired royal salutes at noon, in honour of the fête-day of the Emperor Napoleon. The French fleet on the station is composed of the following ships:—The *Bretagne*, 131, flag of the Commander-in-Chief, Vice-Admiral de Tinan; *Algesiras*, 100, flag of Rear-Admiral Paris; *Eylau*, 90; *Austerliz*, 90; *Impérial*, 90; *St. Louis*, 80; and corvettes *Prony* and *Mouette*; all in excellent order, well manned, and smart both in gunnery and exercise aloft.

The second division of the Mediterranean fleet under my command comprises, the *Hannibal*, 91; *Renown*, 91; *Agamemnon*, 91; *Cæsar*, 91; *London*, 91; and *Intrepid*, in the Neapolitan waters; the *Scylla*, *Amphion*, and *Argus* remaining on the coast of Sicily.

The Russian, Austrian, Prussian, Spanish, American, Brazilian, Sardinian, and Neapolitan ships of war and one Papal schooner, were also at anchor in various parts of the Bay, and gave animation to the scene.

I received an official visit from the Sardinian Minister, the Marquis Villamarina, and saluted him on leaving the ship with fifteen guns. He came on board with Admiral Persano, and stated the object of his visit to be to thank me for the many acts of consideration I had evinced towards his countrymen in the progress of the Great Revolution.

An attempt was made last night to cut out a screw Neapolitan ship of the line from under the fort at Castellamare by an Italian steam corvette. The attempt failed, but the Italian vessel escaped.

August 18.—This being the anniversary of the birth of the Emperor of Austria, the same ceremonies were carried out as on the 15th in honour of the Emperor Napoleon.

I waited on the French Admiral, and made arrangements with him for landing a combined English and French force to protect the Missions and Consulates in case of insurrection. De Tinan was prepared to put on shore a thousand *Marins fusiliers*, or seamen perfected in the rifle exercise at the port of L'Orient, and I should be ready with seven hundred Marines.

It was, however, my opinion, as well as my earnest hope, that General Viale, who commanded the Royal troops in Naples, would be able to maintain the authority of the Government, now the chief of the reaction had been arrested and banished. This General had behaved with much firmness during the military riot of the 15th of July, and His Majesty had personally addressed the troops at the barracks of Pizzo Falcone and Castello Nuovo, making them swear to be faithful to the new Constitution.

August 19.—I took the subjects of the Kings of Prussia, Denmark, Belgium, Hanover, Saxony, and of the Swiss Confederation, under my protection. The Consuls of these nations had made application to Her Majesty's Minister, who referred them to me, to act as I considered necessary. These gentlemen severally came on board the *Hannibal*, and received from me an assurance that all their compatriots, who considered themselves in danger, would find a welcome asylum in the vessels of the English squadron. I was certainly gratified at this proof of their confidence in my country. Of their own free-will they had made this selection, when the flags of other powerful nations were equally ready to grant their assistance.

August 21.—This morning we learnt by telegram that Garibaldi had effected a landing yesterday at Melito, on the extreme southern point of Calabria, with four thousand five hundred men. If the Royal troops are staunch, he must be annihilated in a week.

August 23.—Reggio was occupied by the Italian forces on the 21st.

August 24.—In the forenoon I received a telegram

from Sir James Hudson, Her Majesty's Minister at Turin, which informed me that an English steam-vessel, named the *Orwell*, had been forcibly taken possession of by armed Italians in the port of Genoa, who were supposed to be seamen engaged for the service of Garibaldi. The master was on shore at the time of the capture, and the steamer put to sea immediately.

I determined, without waiting for any details, to take steps for the immediate recapture of the vessel. I therefore directed Captain Forbes, of the *Renown*, to proceed to Messina, when, having acquainted Captain Lambert, of the *Scylla*, of this piratical act, he was to look in at the ports on the Peninsula where the ships of the Revolutionary party were known to be engaged in the transport of troops, and he was to capture and detain her till further orders.

Late at night Monsieur Alexandre Dumas, the French novelist, who had just arrived in a small yacht, came on board the *Hannibal*, and reported to me that he had received intimation that his vessel would not be allowed to remain in the harbour, as he was known to be favourable to the movements of Garibaldi. He therefore hoped I would allow him to anchor the *Emma* near my flag-ship, and that I would take her under my protection. I naturally expressed my surprise at this application, when there were two admirals of his own country and six sail of the line at their moorings in the Bay. The French

Admiral, I remarked, was the proper person to protect him.

To this he answered that he had already made a requisition to Monsieur de Tinan, and had been on board the *Bretagne*, where he was given to understand that he must not look for any countenance or guardianship from that quarter. I was unable to interpret satisfactorily the purport of this refusal, but the anomaly of interference on my part could not be removed by the information. I therefore politely declined the proffered honour of protector of the great writer, but recommended his communicating his distress to the Sardinian Rear-Admiral Persano, who, if unable to comply with his wishes, might enlighten him as to the course it would be advisable to pursue.

I received letters from Captain Lambert, of the *Scylla*, stationed at Palermo, complaining of the conduct of General Fergola, in command of the citadel, for allowing breaches of the convention entered into between him and General Medici. Fire had twice been opened by the garrison against the Sicilian outposts on the neutral ground of the Terra Nuova without any known cause, and several musket-shots had struck the corvette. As this vessel had been moved to her present anchorage on the invitation of the Commandant, and her position was without the line of fire of the two parties, the remonstrance made by Captain Lambert was in every way just.

CHAPTER XIX.

1860.

Naples.—Fête-Day of His Royal Highness the Prince Consort. — Magnificent Naval Spectacle. — Seizure of the *Orwell*. — Advance of Garibaldi. — The French Minister. — Signors Pilotti and Settembrini.

August 26.—The ships of war of eleven different nations, now at anchor in the Bay, dressed with flags and fired royal salutes in honour of the fête-day of His Royal Highness the Prince Consort. Probably this is the largest number of ships of war of different nations assembled together in the same port, either at this or any period of our naval history. As a grand nautical display of a pacific character, it may well be described as a magnificent sight, unequalled, probably, by anything of the kind which had yet been witnessed in Naples.

The naval representatives of the foreign Powers whom I had invited to take part in the celebration of the day, entered into the pageant with a feeling of hearty good-will, for it was the anniversary of the birth of a righteous Prince, honoured and esteemed throughout the world.

August 29.—Mr. Elliot received a second telegram

from Sir James Hudson, stating that the *Orwell* had put into the harbour on the Island of Monte Christo. I also received the sworn deposition of a seaman of that vessel, who had escaped at the moment of her capture, which proved the seizure to have been a violent outrage, if not a direct act of piracy. The seaman, named Richard Taylor, stated to Mr. Brown, Her Majesty's Consul at Genoa, that between seventy and eighty people, supposed to be persons going to join Garibaldi, were on board the *Orwell* as passengers; that they were apparently under the command of chiefs named Pilotti and Settembrini. "At ten o'clock at night, these Italians ordered the English engineers of the ship to move the engines ahead. This they refused to do, as the master was not on board. An hour was then given for the engineers to come to terms, Settembrini declaring that if at the end of that time the master did not come on board, and they still refused to work, he would find some one else to move the engines. The engineers remaining firm in their refusal, Settembrini called all his men aft to muster. They rushed along the deck, crying out—'Down with the engineers!' all of whom were overpowered. I then made my escape down the fish-tackle fall, and swam to an English vessel anchored near at hand. When on board, I saw the engineers and firemen, with irons on their hands, being put down below by force. In a few minutes from that time, the engines were moved ahead, and the vessel left the port."

Such was the substance of the declaration made by the only Englishman of the crew who had escaped at the time of capture. Details may be exaggerated, but the main features are, doubtless, correct; and if I succeed in recapturing the vessel, these Garibaldian marauders shall not go unpunished.

Garibaldi is now rapidly advancing through Calabria Citeriore upon Cosenza, the capital, with twenty thousand men, a large number of whom are Calabrese, under Stocco. The Royal troops either lay down their arms, or steadily retreat before them; yet the youthful King remains unmoved, and even is sanguine of final success.

At Salerno he determines to make a stand, according to reports rife in the city, and his faith in the loyalty of the divisions under Generals Ghio and Calendrelli remains unshaken, notwithstanding the defection of the thousands once equally trusted.

August 30.—Seven thousand troops left the city this morning, and marched on Salerno, leaving garrisons only in the forts of St. Elmo, Castel Nuovo, Castel Ovo, and del Carmine.

The National Guards, now augmented to twelve thousand men, took post at other points for the protection of the capital.

August 31.—In the evening I received, through Mr. Elliot, the following telegram from Sir James Hudson, relative to further doings of the *Orwell*:—

"Passengers of *Orwell* plundered Monte Christo, and then steamed south, presumed for Naples."

I thought it improbable that this vessel would venture into this neighbourhood, but had great hopes the *Renown* would fall in with her on the coast. In this I was disappointed. The line-of-battle ship returned in the afternoon, after a week's cruise, without any tidings of the vessel. It was, at any rate, satisfactory to know that I had taken prompt measures for her capture. Orders had been despatched to all the vessels on the coast of Sicily, with a concise description of the craft, and I wrote confidently to Mr. Elliot that she could not eventually escape.

In the meanwhile I sent the *Intrepid* to watch the channel between Ischia and Ponza.

September 1.—By the *Cressy*, Captain the Hon. Charles Elliot, which arrived this morning, I heard that the *Orwell* had been taken possession of by the *Scylla* on her arrival at Messina on the 29th ultimo. Captain Lambert stated that she was under the charge of Settembrini, Pilotti, her captain, having landed at Leghorn; that she had eighty-five passengers on board, comprising English, French, Americans, Swedes, Germans, and Italians, who had entered the service of Garibaldi as seamen. The depositions of the chief engineer and the mate had been taken by the Consul, and proved, in substance, the correctness of the statement which had been made by the seaman who had escaped in the port of Genoa. The chief engineer having refused to turn the engines ahead whilst the master was on shore, his life was threatened, and he gave up charge. Captain Pilotti then put his own engineers to work, and, refusing the petition of the mate and ship's company to be landed, steamed out to sea. They had all been well treated since.

Captain Lambert was of opinion that there had been collusion between Captain Pilotti and the agent and master of the *Orwell*, as an agreement had been seen by which five thousand pounds were to be paid under certain contingencies. Under these circumstances Captain Lambert would keep possession of the vessel and her passengers until he received further instructions from me.

September 2.—I went over this forenoon in the French steamer *Mouette*, with Admiral de Tinan, to pass the day with Monsieur and Madame Brenier, the French Minister and his wife, at their villa at Castellamare. We met Mr. and Mrs. Elliot, and a large party of French officers there, and had an agreeable *réunion*. Driving and riding in the beautiful chestnut woods which overshadow the town occupied the hours till sunset, when dinner was prepared, and it was not until midnight that I rejoined the *Hannibal*.

September 3.—I was taking my usual exercise in the stern-walk this forenoon, when I observed a small, rakish-looking steamer, with the English ensign flying, bring up at the anchorage between the

Sardinian squadron and the Mole. Taking up my telescope, I plainly discerned the word "*Orwell*" painted on the paddle-box, although it had been partially scraped off, and other figures written over. She had been discovered at the same moment by the signal-officer on the poop, who had orders to keep strict look-out on every vessel that arrived. Armed boats were sent immediately to take forcible possession, and the lieutenant in command had directions to secure the persons of Signors Pilotti and Settembrini, and send them prisoners to the ship. They were arrested accordingly, and brought on board in charge of a marine guard. The former protested loudly against this exercise of power as an arbitrary violation of his personal freedom, and maintained the vessel to be the property of the National Italian Government. He altogether forgot the fact of the pistol placed at the head of the chief engineer, Joseph Spiby, who, under the penalty of death, had been compelled to relinquish his charge, when the vessel was forcibly taken possession of at Genoa.

A despatch from Captain Lambert informed me that Signor Pilotti had arrived from Leghorn on the 1st instant, and having shown to him the contract for the sale of the vessel, and also a guarantee from the Commandant of Messina, on behalf of Garibaldi, that the money should be paid to the English owner, he had allowed Signor Pilotti again to take charge of the *Orwell*, on his giving his word of honour as a military officer that he would proceed at once to Naples and submit to my decision.

The article of the contract which affected the piratical part of the proceedings ran as follows :—

"It is provided and agreed that no forcible possession will be taken of the steamer, so as to deviate from her direct course to Messina, under the penalty of five thousand pounds sterling for the value of the said *Orwell*, besides becoming liable to other contingencies."

This was a very suspicious document, which justified Captain Lambert in his opinion of the probability of collusion, but it in no way detracted from the insult to the British flag, under which the vessel had cruized for six days in the character of a pirate. I therefore decided to send the vessels at once, with Pilotti, Settembrini, and the crew, in charge of Captain Mason, of the *Cæsar*, to Malta, where the whole circumstances of the complicated case might be brought under the tribunal of the Vice-Admiralty Court.

Before proceeding to the *Cæsar* these gentlemen requested an interview with me, but as I could perceive no possible advantage from a conference of this nature, I refused their petition. To a second entreaty, howev broughter, by Captain Farquhar, I yielded, and had subsequently cause to regret having done so.

Signor Pilotti, on being introduced into my cabin, expressed himself in a very off-hand manner as extremely astonished at the treatment he had received. He stated himself to be a gentleman by birth, an officer holding a commission, with the rank of captain, in the National Army under General Garibaldi, and to be the rightful owner of the *Orwell* by the terms of the bill of sale. He could, he said, easily have made his escape on his arrival at Messina, but, trusting to the honour of the British flag, and the high character of the Admiral, he had voluntarily placed himself and the *Orwell* in my power. He hoped, on reflection, I should order the release of Signor Settembrini and himself, and allow him to take his vessel and her passengers to join the national ships of war now on the coast.

Before replying to this charge I asked Signor Settembrini if he had any statement to make. He replied in the negative. I then told Signor Pilotti that I had wished to avoid the meeting between us, from the conviction that no good could arise from a personal controversy, but he chose to press the appeal, and I had yielded to his desire. The depositions on oath showed that an English vessel, with the English flag flying, was taken possession of by force, and the lives of the engineers threatened. It was for the committal of this outrage I had now made prisoners of himself and Signor Settembrini. I knew their family position, and I admitted that he had honourably kept his word in coming on to Naples, but the *Orwell* had already been re-captured by one of my cruizers, and could not have avoided a second detention wherever she might have gone. A sense of public duty compelled me to send the case before the judges of the civil tribunals at Malta.

The conduct of Signor Settembrini throughout the interview was that of a gentleman, who seemed to feel the humiliating position in which he was placed, whilst the bearing of his friend was scarcely becoming the character he assumed.

September 4.—The *Cæsar* sailed for Malta, with the *Orwell* in charge. Vice-Admiral Martin being at Beyroot, with the first division of the Fleet, I sent full particulars of this extraordinary case to Rear-Admiral Codrington, and closed my despatch with the following paragraph :—

" Having carefully perused the documents connected with the seizure and re-capture of the *Orwell* by the *Scylla*, after cruizing for a week off the coast of Italy, during which period she touched at and committed certain depredations on the island of Monte Christo, of which acts I had previously been informed by Her Majesty's Minister at Turin; and having also considered the report from Her Majesty's Consul at Genoa, which clearly indicates that the *Orwell* was forcibly taken to sea by Messrs. Pilotti and Settembrini, and the crew confined as prisoners, I have been unable to discover any justification of these piratical acts, although the document produced as an agreement, and the proof of complicity on the part of Mr. Sutton, the master, may be taken into consideration in extenuation of the crime."

CHAPTER XX.

1860.

Evacuation of Salerno.—Preparations for the King's Departure. —His Proclamation.—Flight of the King to Gaeta.—Deputation to Garibaldi.—Measures for the Protection of the British and French Legations.

September 5.—The *Intrepid* returned this evening from Salerno. Captain Marryat brought intelligence of the evacuation of that town by the Neapolitan troops.

Garibaldi was then at Eboli, twenty miles distant, with four thousand Northern Italians, and about fifteen thousand Calabrese and Sicilians.

It was now known in the city that the King was making preparations for his departure: alas! not to put himself at the head of his faithful soldiery, who had and would still have fought gallantly for his house and dynasty, but to secure the personal safety of himself and his brave young Queen within the walls of the impregnable fortress of Gaeta.

What an opportunity lost for the youngest sovereign in Europe to have made himself a name never to have been forgotten in history! The remembrance of the bravery shown by his troops at Melazzo should have made him feel they would not desert the Royal standard when properly led; and one act of daring resolution on his part might have checked the tide of invasion and gained him the approbation of the world. It was not the want of individual courage, but the absence of self-reliance, occasioned by priestly training, which led him to abandon his capital. Instead of action in the field, His Majesty had recourse to protest by the pen. He issued a farewell address, in language dignified and resigned, but it sounded the death-knell of his Royal House and of the cause of which he was the chief. I give the following translation of the document:—

"ROYAL PROCLAMATION.

"Among the duties prescribed to Kings, those of the days of misfortune are the grandest and the most solemn, and I intend to fulfil them with resignation, free from weakness, and with a serene and confident heart, as befits the descendant of so many monarchs.

"For such a purpose I once more address my voice to the people of this metropolis, from whom I am now to depart with bitter grief.

"An unjust war, carried on in contravention of the law of nations, has invaded my States, notwithstanding that I was at peace with all the European Powers.

"The changed order of Government, and my adhesion to the great principles of Italian Nationality, were not sufficient to ward off the war: and, moreover, the necessity of defending the integrity of the State entailed upon me the obligations of events which I have always deplored; therefore I solemnly protest against this indescribable hostility, concerning which the present and the future will pronounce their solemn verdict.

"As the descendant of a dynasty which has reigned over this Continent for one hundred and twenty-six years, after having preserved it from the horrors of a long vice-royalty, the affections of my heart are here.

"I am a Neapolitan, and could not, without bitter grief, address words of farewell to my most dearly beloved people, to my fellow-citizens.

"Whatever may be my destiny, be it prosperous or adverse, I shall always preserve for them a passionate and affectionate remembrance. I recommend to them concord, peace, and strict observance of their civic duties. Let not an excessive zeal for my dynasty be made a pretext for disturbance.

"Whether from the fortunes of the present war I return shortly amongst you, or whatever may be the time it please the justice of God to restore me to the throne of my ancestors,—a throne made all the more splendid by the free institutions with which I have irrevocably surrounded it—all that I pray from this time forth, is to behold again my people, united, strong, and happy.

"FRANCIS II."

September 6.—Shortly before 7 o'clock in the evening, the King and Queen, a few gentlemen of the Royal household, and the Ministers of Austria, Prussia, Spain, and Bavaria, embarked in the Spanish steamer of war *Colon*, and escorted by another Spanish vessel put to sea, and passing close to the *Hannibal*, proceeded on their course to Gaeta.

The King in his proclamation beseeches his loving people not to let excessive zeal for his dynasty be made a pretext for disturbance. They obeyed him only too well. He left the palace of his ancestors, and drove down to the Mole amidst a vast crowd of the inhabitants, but not a tear was shed, nor was a "God bless you!" even heard. It was the desolation of indifference. Indeed, a melancholy spectacle, which it grieved me to behold.

At the same hour in which His Majesty departed, a deputation from the municipality and National Guard of Naples left the city for Salerno, to invite General Garibaldi to the capital. A notification of this intention had been previously submitted by the first Minister, Liborio Romano, to the Dictator in the following terms:—

"Naples expects with anxiety the invincible

Dictator of the Two Sicilies, and confides to him her future destinies."

Comment on such fulsome language is unnecessary. The interpretation was easy. The Minister of the King was ready to become the Minister of the Revolution. How the invincible Dictator would act in the matter remained to be seen.

Late in the evening I was surprised at receiving a visit from Captain Villemaine, of the French ship of the line *St. Louis*, who brought me a verbal message from Admiral de Tinan, stating that, from information just received, he was under great apprehension there would be serious disturbances in the city in the course of the night, as, from the absence of the King and the disruption of the Ministry, there was in reality no effective government to control the population. It was therefore his intention to send on shore a body of his "marins fusiliers," for the protection of the Legation and Consulate, and would land them at the beach of the Chiaja, by the Villa Reale gardens, about one o'clock in the following morning, by which time the moon would be up, and facilitate the disembarkation. He hoped I should see the advisability of this measure, and give directions at the same time for a party of the Royal Marines to disembark and occupy the British public residencies with a similar object.

I requested Captain Villemaine to convey my thanks to Admiral de Tinan for the timely notice he had given me of the probability of disturbance, and to assure him of my acquiescence in the plan of landing a sufficient armed force from the French and English squadrons for the protection of the Legations and the subjects of our respective sovereigns in the event of danger being at hand. I should prepare three companies of the Marine Light Infantry for landing at the same hour as the French seamen; but in order to prevent the possibility of mistake as to the character of the disembarkation, I should immediately despatch my flag-captain to acquaint the Neapolitan General in command of the Piazza of the arrangement that had been made. He would then know that the armed men who were put on shore were friendly allies, ready to co-operate with his own troops if foreign property were attacked; whereas, without this intimation, with the bands of Garibaldi marching on the capital, our small force might be mistaken for an advanced division of the enemy.

Captain Villemaine did not seem quite satisfied with this announcement of making the Neapolitan General acquainted with our intended movement until further communication with his chief, and wished a short delay in the despatch of my envoy.

I thought it desirable, however, that no time should be lost. I felt sure Admiral de Tinan would hold the same opinion as myself that there would be danger of collision if we landed in force at dead of night without previous warning, and, as our joint object was identical, the sooner the mission of Captain Farquhar could be effected, the greater would be the chance of the maintenance of peace in the city.

Captain Farquhar, therefore, proceeded at once to the head-quarters of the Commandant, and having had the good fortune to find him at home, acquainted him with the apprehensions entertained by the French Admiral of a disturbance in the city, and that we were preparing to land a sufficient force for the protection of the Legation and Consulates. Captain Farquhar was furthermore directed to urge the Commandant on my behalf to use most stringent measures to keep the public peace, and so obviate the necessity of foreign interference.

The Neapolitan General received this communication in a friendly spirit. Captain Farquhar returned on board before midnight, by which hour the whole garrison of Naples was on the alert. The movement was plainly observable from the shipping by the numerous lights which were passing to and fro, by the tramp of armed men, and by the sound of the drum.

Neither "marine" or "marin fusilier" had occasion to leave his hammock during the night, and the dogma of non-intervention obtained another triumph.

CHAPTER XXI.

1860.

Naples.—Entry of Garibaldi.—His further Projects.—Great Rejoicings of the Populace—Interview with the Dictator.—Arrival of Piedmontese Reinforcements.—Garibaldi's Departure for Sicily.—Invasion of the Roman States by General Cialdini.—Saint Januarius.

September 7.—Garibaldi entered Naples at noon, having been joined by the King's Minister, Liborio Romano, at the station. He came by rail from Salerno, with General Cosenz and a dozen of his faithful followers, trusting himself implicitly to the care of the National Guards.

He took up his quarters at the Palace of the Foresteria, in the Great Square, and immediately addressed the people from the balcony, calling upon them to rally round the standard of Victor Emanuel, the model of all sovereigns, and the true Father of the Italians. He terminated his discourse with the ominous words that Italians were resolved henceforth to be masters in their own house, whether the powerful of the earth should wish it or not.

The Dictator subsequently gave audience to the

Sardinian Minister, the Marquis Villamarina, and to Admiral Persano. The Neapolitan fleet by decree was ordered to hoist the Sardinian flag, and to be placed under the command of the Sardinian Admiral; and General Cosenz was directed to form a Government.

In the evening Admiral Persano paid me a visit, and informed me that Garibaldi had written to him to say that, after a short rest at Naples, he intended to march onwards to Rome, and subsequently to Venetia; and that, when all Italy was restored to herself, he would transfer the united kingdom to the crown of Victor Emanuel.

The Rear-Admiral, adverting to the sense of gratitude which Garibaldi had told him he must ever feel towards me for the generous conduct I had evinced during the bombardment at Palermo, requested me to obtain a personal interview, and to use the influence I possessed in dissuading him from undertaking a contest which must eventually bring great misfortune upon Italy.

I replied that I had nothing to do with political matters, but that I was sure Her Majesty's Government would greatly disapprove any movement against the Austrian possessions; that if opportunity occurred, I would certainly give my own view of the subject to the Dictator; and that I should report the conversation immediately to Mr. Elliot.

September 8.—To-day the whole population of Naples was abroad from morning until night.

Garibaldi made the pilgrimage to the Piede del Grotto, and in the evening the city was illuminated.

I landed in plain clothes, and traversed the principal streets alone, in an open barouche. No words can express the frantic joy of the people, or the madness of the scene. Hundreds of the best-looking young women that could be mustered, many of them of respectable family, and others perhaps not the most discreet, were dressed in the costumes of ancient days, when excess of drapery was not required, and, formed in voluptuous tableaux and mounted on triumphal cars, were drawn in state along the great thoroughfares of the Toledo and Largo-Castello. Men, boys, and girls were also in requisition, in every imaginable garment, armed with swords, spears, and flambeaux; and following in their train were the very dregs of the population, denouncing with hideous yells the hated rule of the Bourbon, and forcing every one to join in the cry of "Evviva Garibaldi!"

The manner in which order was maintained amidst such a scene of wild fanaticism was indeed a miracle almost as great as the entry of the revolutionary chieftain into the city in which it occurred. Yet not a drunken person was to be seen, and on the word being passed amidst this impassioned throng that the Dictator was retiring to rest, the orgies were at once discontinued and quietude restored.

September 9.—Mr. Elliot received a telegram from Lord John Russell, desiring him to express to General

Garibaldi the hope that no attack would be made upon Venetia. As Mr. Elliot could not enter into direct official communication with the Dictator, it was arranged that a visit should be paid by me to the *de facto* ruler, and that when he returned my visit on board the *Hannibal,* Mr. Elliot would be there to meet him. I therefore called upon him in the forenoon, at the Palazzo d'Angri, where he now resided.

I found the General in occupation of a suite of apartments on the sixth story of the spacious building. He was engaged at the moment in conversation with Lord Llanover, Mr. Craven, and Mr. Wreeford the intelligent correspondent of the *Times,* and being much fatigued from incessant work was lying upon the bed in easy slippers, but otherwise habited in his usual uniform.

Lieutenant Wilmot having announced my being present in the ante-room, the Dictator remarked that it would not be becoming in him to receive the Admiral without his boots, so he commenced pulling them on, and had just succeeded in dragging the first over his foot when I entered the room. We were both much amused at this little disorder of dress, but immediately holding out his hand he said, "I am indeed glad to see you. I told you, Admiral, when we parted at Palermo that we should meet again at Naples."

There were no chairs in the room, so we sat down

upon the bed; and on my saying that I wished to speak to him privately, he requested Lord Llanover and his companions to leave us together. When alone I informed him that Her Majesty's Minister had a communication to make to him from Lord John Russell. On hearing this name, before I could finish the sentence, he exclaimed—"Mi Lord Russell, c'est un excellent homme, un veritable ami d'Italie."

I proceeded to say that if he would come on board the *Hannibal* to-morrow, Mr. Elliot would meet him in my cabin, and would then make known to him the message from Her Majesty's Government. Garibaldi, in his usual quick way, replied, "Certainly; anything you wish I am always ready to do. I will get a boat from Admiral Persano, and be on board the *Hannibal* at 11 o'clock, if that hour will suit. I shall be glad to make the acquaintance of Monsieur Elliot, who I believe is connected by marriage with Lord Russell."

I thought it strange that this circumstance, so entirely of a family nature, should have been known to the Dictator—and from whom could he have learnt it? Possibly it crossed his mind that, as the English Foreign Minister was believed by all Italians to be favourable to their regeneration, all public men who might be related to him would hold the same faith.

The city was again illuminated at night, and the

effect when viewed from the sea was extremely beautiful.

September 10.—General Garibaldi and Mr. Elliot met on board the *Hannibal* at 11 o'clock. The General was accompanied by Count Arrivabene, Colonel Bertani, Major Missori, Colonel Baggi, and another officer of his staff.

After I had made Her Majesty's Minister and the Dictator acquainted with each other, I requested the latter to desire his attendant staff to leave the cabin, as Mr. Elliot was desirous of a private conversation. Colonel Bertani, to my surprise, objected to the General being left alone with Mr. Elliot and myself, and lingered behind when the other officers had gone out to the quarter-deck. I then repeated my wish to the General, and, on a second invitation, Bertani joined his companions on the lower deck, where they had been taken by Captain Farquhar to watch the gunnery exercise.

Mr. Elliot having expressed to General Garibaldi the astonishment with which, in common with all the world, he had witnessed the marvellous results he had accomplished with such trifling means, informed him that, though he could have no official relations with him, he should remain at Naples until he received further instructions from Her Majesty's Government. This information appeared to give great satisfaction to the Dictator, who said he fully understood that official intercourse was not practicable.

Mr. Elliot then informed him that Lord John Russell had charged him to express the hope that no attack would be made upon Venetia, as, in his Lordship's opinion, it would be calculated to bring the greatest calamities upon Italy.

Garibaldi answered by saying that he would make no concealment of his plans, which were plain and straightforward. He intended to push on at once to Rome, and when that city should be in his hands, to offer the crown of an united Italy to King Victor Emanuel, upon whom would then devolve the task of the liberation of Venetia, and in which he would himself be but the lieutenant of His Majesty. If this liberation could be accomplished by purchase or by negotiation, so much the better. He added, he was sure that Lord John Russell, in counselling the abandonment of Venetia, did not fairly represent the generous feelings of the people of England towards the Italian nation, although he cheerfully recognized the obligations Italy was under to Her Majesty's Government for the sympathies they had exhibited.

Mr. Elliot, with great promptitude, then told the General not to deceive himself with regard to the feelings of the English nation; for that, although for the present undoubtedly almost to a man in favour of his efforts, that sentiment would quickly change if they saw him pushing matters so far as to be calculated to bring on a European war. Mr. Elliot next reverted to Rome, and pointed out in forcible language the danger which must accrue from probable collision with the French garrison, which would at once bring about the intervention of France in the affairs of Italy.

General Garibaldi replied with vehemence that *Rome was an Italian city*, and that neither the Emperor nor any one else had a right to keep him out of it.

The foregoing is an epitome of the main points which were discussed. The tone of the General throughout was that of an enthusiast, who had determined to risk all on the prosecution of his idea of Italian unity. He was evidently not to be swayed by any dictates of prudence.

In the afternoon Baron Brenier, the French Minister, paid me a friendly visit, and received from me an account of the circumstances which had led to the interview between his colleague and the Dictator. Furthermore, as there was nothing occult either in this or in any other transaction connected with the policy of England in the Italian question, he obtained a brief outline of the conversation which had taken place in the cabin of the *Hannibal*, so far as related to the friendly advice administered by Mr. Elliot, and to the earnest desire evinced by Lord John Russell to abstain from interference with the Roman States and Venetia. I remarked to Monsieur Brenier that the moral power of Great Britain was again exercised at this crisis, as it had been at Palermo, with the hope of staying further bloodshed and bringing about a reconciliation of parties.

September 11.—Six steamers, laden with red-shirted men, arrived for the new Government.

In the afternoon the Royal troops evacuated the forts, and the National militia took possession. The arsenal at the same time was occupied by two battalions of Piedmontese Bersaglieri.

At sunset the Royal troops marched out of the city towards Capua. I took up a position at the extremity of the Toledo to watch their exit. Every opportunity was given for desertion from their ranks to the army of the Revolution, but few availed themselves of it. There was a sullen determination and defiance in the look and bearing of the men, which gave no evidence of sympathy with the cause of the Dictator.

At midnight the Sardinian squadron, under Persano, sailed on a secret expedition.

September 14.—General Ebor's division arrived, and went on to Caserta.

September 16.—Late intelligence from Sicily having described the state of affairs in the island as bordering on anarchy, Garibaldi left early in the morning in the mail steam-boat *Ellettrico* for Palermo.

The majority of the islanders desired immediate annexation to Sardinia. The Prodictator de Pretis was favourable to their views, but the Mazzinian

Minister of the Interior, Crispi, was against them. Both were friends of Garibaldi, and both came to Naples to plead their respective suits.

Garibaldi, under the influence of Bertani and the extreme republican party, decided to support the opinion of Crispi, and for that purpose crossed the channel to quiet the population.

September 17.—Intelligence was received this morning that the Sardinian troops, under Cialdini, had crossed the frontier into the Roman States, with the intention of attacking the foreign mercenaries under the command of Lamoricière, and of delivering the inhabitants of Umbria and the Marches from the yoke which oppressed them.

This invasion is a very questionable proceeding, and only to be justified by the greatest emergency. King Victor Emanuel, for the safety of his dominions, may be compelled to move onward. On the one hand he is confronted with the increasing strength of the party of reaction, subsidized by the alms of the Ultramontanes of the Roman Catholic world; on the other by the masses of the Mazzinian and Republican factions. Of the danger of this position the King, Cavour, and the Government can alone be the judges. If the political situation appears desperate, the application of the remedy must be determined.

September 18.—Garibaldi returned from Palermo, having installed Signor Mordini, an Anti-Annexionist, as Prodictator.

September 19.—This is the day on which the miracle of the liquefaction of the blood of Saint Januarius is performed. It is the universal belief of the lower classes of the people that when the spirit of this holy man is satisfied with the administration of the government of the Neapolitan Kingdom, he makes it manifest to the faithful by the melting of the few drops of his precious blood which was collected at his martyrdom in the year 305, and has since been safely preserved in a small glass bottle. It may readily be imagined that during so long a period as fifteen hundred and fifty-five years this bottle or phial must have had many adventures and many narrow escapes from destruction. It was carried at various epochs to other cities in Italy, but in the year 1497 eventually found a resting place in the Duomo at Naples, where it has continued to remain in quiet repose, by the side of the head of the saint, which had been also miraculously preserved.

As the capture of Naples by an unrecognized adventurer was an event in every way likely to give displeasure to the saint, it had already been circulated by the chiefs of the Church that there was much probability of the non-fulfilment of the usual rite. Noon was the hour at which the process of change from congelation to liquefaction was generally completed. Great, then, was the astonishment of the pious inhabitants when, at 9 o'clock in the morning, salvos of artillery from the forts announced that the saint had approved the downfall of the Bourbon dynasty, by a three hours' advance in the time of the performance of the miracle.

Sceptics indulged in remarks on the extraordinary departure from traditional routine, and some even suggested that magic and witchcraft had been at work. Others boldly declared that orders had been sent from the Dictator which admitted of no other solution than that which had occurred.

September 21.—Baron Brenier, the French Minister, and his family left the Bay of Naples in the French ship of the line, *Algesiras*, and proceeded to Marseilles.

September 24.—Intelligence arrived of the defeat of Lamoricière and the Papal mercenaries by Cialdini at Castelfidardo, and of the approaching siege of Ancona.

Affairs at Naples meanwhile continue without amelioration. The siege of Capua makes no progress, and the division of Turr had been severely handled in a battle beneath its walls, though the undisciplined youths under his command fought with great gallantry.

September 27.—This being the Octave, or last day of the miracle of St. Januarius, I went to see its performance. I found not more than a hundred people, all of the lower class, and mostly old women, within the balustrade of the chancel, and the officiating priest busily engaged in carrying round the phial for the faithful to examine and to kiss. An acolythe accompanied him, with a lighted taper in his hand. This was held close behind the bottle, by which means the saintly blood was made transparent to the beholders. The bottle has a diameter of three or four inches, is circular in form, and quite flat at the sides, like a pocket scent-flask. As I stood outside the rails it was brought up for my examination, and as it was made to revolve in the priest's hands the liquefaction of the pitch-like substance it contained was made clear to the view. The priest wished me to kiss the bottle, which I politely declined.

With regard to this miracle I may mention that one large class of the community has derived much advantage from the late change of Government. The saint held theatres in abhorrence, and by order of the archbishop, during the time of the liquefaction of the blood, and for three days before and after its completion, these places of amusement were closed and the army of actors were without any employment. Twice in the course of each year this miracle is performed, occasioning a loss of thirty days' wages to all performers on the stage.

Garibaldi, by an official ordinance, worded so as not to be offensive to the prejudices of a priest-ridden people, declared that actors must, as other people, have opportunity of gaining their livelihood, and that henceforth theatres and all places of amusement would only be closed for one day during each octave of the miracle.

CHAPTER XXII.

1860.

Naples.—Address of the Dictator.—Great Battle on the Volturno.—Visit to Mr. Elliot at Castellamare.—Fall of Ancona.—Proclamation of King Victor Emanuel.—Arrival of English Volunteers.—Departure of Admiral de Tinan for Gaeta.—Decree on Annexation. — Meeting of Victor Emanuel and Garibaldi.—The *Orwell* again.—The *Sylphide*.—Father Gavazzi.

September 28.—The following address was issued this morning in the official gazette by the Dictator.

"*Caserta*, September 27.

"Our brethren of the Italian Army, commanded by the gallant General Cialdini, combat the enemies of Italy, and conquer.

"The army of Lamoricière has been defeated by these valiant men. All the provinces enslaved by the Pope are free. Ancona is ours.

"The valiant soldiers of the army of the north have passed the frontier, and are on Neapolitan soil. We shall soon have the good fortune to grasp their victorious hands.

"G. Garibaldi."

These words show no jealousy of the regular army. Indeed, Garibaldi must at last perceive that his undisciplined men, although brave in the field, are incompetent to lay siege to an impregnable fortress, and in his heart he must hail the advance of the Piedmontese divisions as a stroke of good fortune, which will enable him to extricate himself from increasing difficulties. Yet he continues to maintain the extreme faction of the Mazzinian party in power, against the wishes and advice of all moderate men.

October 2.—A great battle was fought yesterday on the Volturno. It continued during the whole day, and terminated in a decisive victory on the part of the army of the Revolution.

The Royal troops mustered thirty thousand effective men on the field, under the command of their best generals, and under the eye of the King and of Count Trani, his half-brother. Garibaldi had twenty-five thousand men, one-half of which were Calabrese recruits, the other half Northern Italians and Sicilians, with a few French and Hungarians.

Each party fought gallantly, the Royalists having for a prize the recapture and plunder of Naples, the Revolutionists the abstract idea of advancing the unity of Italy.

The Neapolitans lost between two and three thousand men in killed and wounded, and five hundred prisoners ; the Garibaldians about thirteen hundred killed and wounded, and more than half that number prisoners. Generals Cosenz, Medici, Bixio, Ebor, and Melvitz, commanded under Garibaldi, and had opportunities at various periods of the battle of greatly distinguishing themselves. Three Englishmen, Dunn, Wyndham, and Dowling, also made themselves a name by many acts of daring; and the former, in command of a Sicilian division, was seriously wounded.

October 6.—I went yesterday to Castellamare, and spent the day with Mr. and Mrs. Elliot, at their neat little villa near the town. The change from long confinement in a ship's cabin to the agreeable society of an English home was thoroughly appreciated, and I cannot say I was well pleased when the hour struck for my return to Naples.

October 8.—Large detachments of prisoners are brought by rail daily from the seat of war, and the last hope of King Francis seems rapidly passing away. Intelligence has been received of the fall of Ancona, and that Lamoricière and his mercenaries are prisoners of war.

During the siege of this fortress, Admiral Persano had greatly distinguished himself by a vigorous attack, with the small but well-disciplined naval force under his command, on the sea defences of the place, and its reduction in so short a space of time was mainly attributable to this flank movement of the ships of war and their effective cannonade.

Garibaldi, now entirely occupied by the operations before Capua, had appointed Signor Pallavicini Pro-dictator of Naples, in the room of Sertori, who had resigned the civil office in order to follow his Chief into the field. Bertani, having failed to give satisfaction to any party, had at last taken his leave, and had proceeded to Turin, where, as a member of the Legislature, he would have opportunity of detailing his grievances before Parliament.

Mazzini continued in the city, and although his influence over the Dictator was supposed to be increasing, he was equally out of favour with the Patriot generals, as had been the late Chief Secretary of the Government.

October 14.—The last week has been one of expectancy. All eyes are turned towards the north, and the hopes of the people are centered in Victor Emanuel. The King had taken command of the army at Ancona on the 9th, and had already crossed the frontier into the Neapolitan dominion. To the peoples of Southern Italy, His Majesty had issued a stirring address. It was a programme of intended action, not a vain protest. It was throwing down the glove both against the Reactionist and the Republican.

The following are the leading paragraphs of the bold proclamation:—

"I have proclaimed Italy for the Italians, and I will not permit Italy to become a focus for Cosmopolitan sects, who may meet there to contrive schemes of reaction or of universal demagogic intrigues.

"I have lavished the precious blood of my soldiers, not for myself, but for Italy.

"My troops advanced among you to maintain order. I come not to impose my will, but to make yours respected.

"You may freely manifest it. Providence, who protects the cause of the just, will suggest the vote which you should place in the urn.

"Whatever the gravity of events, I await calmly the judgment of civilized Europe, conscious of having fulfilled my duties as a king, and as an Italian.

"My policy will perhaps not be inefficacious in reconciling the progress of nations with the stability of monarchy.

"As for Italy, I know that there I bring to a close the era of revolutions.

"VICTOR EMANUEL.

"Ancona, October 9, 1860."

The Marquis Villamarina, and a deputation from the municipality of Naples, were at this date *en route* to meet the rising star of the new dynasty, and Garibaldi himself, mollified by the affectionate advice of the warrior king, though still defiant of the great Italian Minister Cavour, also put forth a proclamation to the Neapolitans, which recommending them to concord, terminated with the following patriotic words: "No more political colours, no more discords, no more parties. Italy one, as the people of this metropolis wisely determined it, the king galantuomo, are the eternal symbols of our regeneration, and of the grandeur and prosperity of the country."

In the afternoon two English steamers arrived, bringing the British Volunteer Legion, numbering about six hundred men. They were all dressed in scarlet uniform, and looked remarkably well. Unfortunately there is no longer probability of active work in the field for these hardy sons of Albion.

During the last fortnight numerous English tourists have arrived, and have had opportunities of visiting the prisons rendered famous or infamous by the atrocities committed therein, as portrayed by the pen of Mr. Gladstone during the reign of King Ferdinand.

I had the pleasure of receiving on board the *Hannibal*, Lord Llanover, Mr. Montagu Chambers, Q.C., the Honourable Evelyn Ashley, Mr. Russell, Mr. Saurin, Attaché of the Legation at Turin, Captain Keith Fraser, Colonel Baker, and Mr. Adam Smith, and was able to assure them that Garibaldi would welcome them to the front if curiosity should prompt them to visit Caserta and Mount St. Angelo.

October 16.—The *Bretagne*, 131, with the flag of Vice-Admiral de Tinan, and the *St. Louis*, 80, sailed to-day for Gaeta. I much regretted the departure of the Vice-Admiral, with whom, for a period of many months, I had maintained relations of friendly intercourse. Many and delicate had been the public questions which we had been called upon to discuss, as complications arose from the political chaos around, but in no instance had the difference of opinion which necessarily occurred disturbed the harmony of our private relations.

A decree has been issued by the Dictator, fixing the 21st instant as the day on which the votes upon the subject of annexation are to be polled throughout the kingdom of the Two Sicilies. They are to be given on the principle of universal suffrage, but under arrangements such as will exclude the possibility of the votes remaining secret.

It is believed that many persons, especially of the educated classes, would prefer that Naples should remain a separate kingdom, provided they were secure from the return of the Bourbon dynasty; but the terms of the Plebiscite declare that a simple declaration is to be made, "Yes," or "No," for the unity under King Victor Emanuel. Many, consequently, who are separatists at heart will give the affirmative vote.

The first Article of the decree affirms that—

"The people wish Italy united and indivisible, with Victor Emanuel Constitutional King, and his legitimate descendants. The vote to be expressed 'Yes,' or "No," by means of a printed ticket."

In the places destined for voting, three urns will be placed on a proper table. The middle one empty, and one on either side. In one of these tickets will be placed with the word "Yes," on them, and in the other those marked "No," in order that each voter may choose the one he wants and deposit it in the empty urn.

Yesterday, the Dictator issued the following notice, being the first official intimation of his intentions regarding the future government of the kingdom he had conquered:—

"The Two Sicilies, which owe their redemption to the blood of the Italians, and have elected me their Dictator, form an integral and indivisible part of Italy, with its Constitutional King, Victor Emanuel. I shall place in the hands of the King, on his arrival, the Dictatorship conferred on me by the nation.

"Sant' Angelo, October 15, 1860."

October 22.—Yesterday I visited a few of the polling-places in the city whilst the election was going forward. More than a hundred thousand people took advantage of the opportunity of recording their opinion, yet a stranger passing through the streets would have discovered no excitement, not even a crowd collected at any particular spot. Perfect order reigned everywhere; but I think, considering the general temper of the inhabitants, it would have required strong moral courage for anyone to publicly announce himself as an enemy to the sacred watchword of "Italia Una."

Every man privileged to the franchise had first to produce his paper from the mayor, showing that he was entitled to vote; he was then admitted through a file of the National Militia up a flight of steps to a platform on which the urns were fixed. The urns to the right and left of the central vase, and several feet distant from it, had the words "Si," and "No," painted on them respectively in a large type. Up to one of these the man had to walk beneath the gaze of a dozen scrutators, to thrust in his arm and draw out a card. It was, of course, open voting in the clearest sense of the word.

I remained an hour watching the progress of the election, and during that time I only saw three individuals who, after a few moments of apparent reflection, advanced slowly to the left and fished up a "No." I must, however, observe that no offensive remark was made either by the overseers or the bystanders at this open manifestation of preference for the Bourbon dynasty; but as voters had to deliver up their papers of identification, their names and calling were of course known. Under regulations such as these, I must chronicle my opinion that a plebiscite by universal suffrage cannot be received as a correct representation of the real feeling of a nation.

October 29.—We have intelligence this morning of the meeting of the King Victor Emanuel with General

Garibaldi on the 26th, in the district of Teano. They were both on horseback, attended by the officers of their personal staff.

Grave doubts had been circulated at Naples as to the reception which the Dictator would meet with at the hands of the King. They have been removed by the announcement of a sincere reconciliation. Unchangeable in his expressions of antipathy to the chief minister, Garibaldi's devotion to the monarch was incapable of change, yet there was a sadness in the whole interview. The devotion manifested by the Dictator was altogether personal in its character, and could in no way solve the increasing difficulties of their public relations.

The King represented a constitution which he had faithfully upheld, and he commanded a magnificent army of which he might well be proud. The Dictator represented a party strong in deeds of daring of unequalled audacity; but unsound at the core in its political structure. Amalgamation between elements so opposed was a simple impossibility, and the counsel given by Count Cavour that it should not be attempted at this time was worthy of the foresight of that eminent man.

After reviewing the divisions of General Bixio and Ebor, the King rejoined his army on march to the Garigliano, whilst the forces of the Dictator returned to Saint Angelo to resume the siege of Capua.

October 30.—Signor Pilotti has returned to

Naples, having been liberated at Malta by advice of the Crown Advocate.

The law in the case of this unusual seizure appears strange and unsatisfactory.

Rear-Admiral Codrington, holding the same view as myself of the magnitude of the crime of cruizing for a week under the British flag, in a vessel taken by force of arms from the British crew, and committing acts of robbery whilst sheltered by the flag, had officially requested that proceedings should be taken against the chief offenders, whom I had sent prisoners to Malta.

The Governor General, Sir Gaspard le Marchant, acting with his accustomed promptitude, laid the case before the Crown Advocate without a moment's delay; and the latter gave his opinion within the space of four days, which spoke well for the business-like habits of Doctor Dingli.

The prosecution could not be instituted, in the opinion of the Crown Advocate, for four substantial reasons:—

"1st. The master of the vessel was not present to prosecute, and there was reason to believe he connived at the seizure.

"2nd. The offenders were foreigners, and were arrested in a foreign port and brought prisoners to Malta.

"3rd. The master of the *Orwell* ought to have

appeared before the Consul at Genoa, and made his protest against the seizure.

"4th. Neither the mate, nor any other individual of the crew have shown any inclination to come forward with any action against Captain Pilotti, but declared themselves satisfied with their treatment since the capture."

No person had come forward either to claim the captured steamer, or to prosecute the men who had taken forcible possession at Genoa. The case, therefore, fell to the ground. The *Orwell*, however, was detained as property under care of the English Government till the rightful owner was found, and the vessel was lost as a ship of war for Garibaldi.

It is reported that Pilotti is now in prison in the city, by order of the Pro-dictator, for the irregularity of the act of seizure, so even the revolutionary flag would give no countenance to this outrageous proceeding.

Some days since I received a telegraphic message from the Lords Commissioners of the Admiralty directing me to place one of the vessels under my command at the disposal of the King of the Two Sicilies, in the event of His Majesty wishing to quit the fortress of Gaeta.

I sent the *Renown* the same morning to that place, giving Captain Forbes instructions to wait upon the Neapolitan Minister of Foreign Affairs, and to inform him of the communication which I had received from the British Government.

King Francis directed Signor Casella, in reply, to express to Captain Forbes, His Majesty's thanks to the British Government and to myself for the offer of a ship, but which under present circumstances he did not desire to avail himself of.

Whilst the *Renown* was in the Bay, in the execution of the mission above detailed, a small squadron of Sardinian ships of war appeared off the port, the commanding officer of which sent a boat with a flag of truce, first, to the flag-ship of Vice-Admiral de Tinan, and subsequently to the English vessel, in order to give notice that any French or English subjects at Gaeta should provide for their safety as an attack might shortly be made upon the place.

On receiving this intimation the French squadron immediately got up steam, and two line-of-battle ships placed themselves under weigh between the Sardinians and the shore. Admiral de Tinan then stated to the Sardinian officer that he should oppose with his force any attack upon the town. Upon the receipt of this answer the Sardinian squadron stood out to sea, and the French ships re-anchored in the Bay.

This is the first positive breach of the doctrine of non-intervention which has occurred during the progress of the Italian civil war, and is much to be regretted as an act of arbitrary power.

Admiral Persano sailed last night for the mouth of the Garigliano, having received orders to co-operate with the Sardinian army in its passage of that river to undertake the siege of Gaeta.

The *Sylphide* yacht, belonging to the Royal squadron, and the property of the Marquis of Downshire, arrived last week from Messina, having Lady Downshire, her daughter Lady Alice Hill, her two sons, and Major Earl on board. The size and beauty of this vessel, ship-rigged, gave her the appearance of a man-of-war, and great was the surprise of the officers of the health department when they learnt she was the private property of a private individual. The Marquis, who is an excellent seaman, soon discovered that the anchorage in the Bay of Naples at this season of the year is neither adapted to safety nor to comfort, and after riding out one gale of wind, during which the *Sylphide* rolled nearly gunnels under, his lordship wisely resolved to seek the shelter of the Mole.

October 31.—This morning, in the great square of the Palace, Garibaldi distributed new standards to the Hungarian legion, under Turr and Tekeli.

Subsequently, accompanied by the Pro-dictator and the Marquis Villa Marina, he addressed the assembled multitude from the balcony of the Forestieri, announcing the speedy arrival amongst them of the King of their choice, and he terminated his discourse by the following severe words against His Holiness, which, wonderful to relate, from so bigoted and superstitious a race, were received without a sign of disapproval.

"Personal ambition has blinded the Pope, and causes him to oppose the national movement—so great, so noble, so pure—and which stands alone in the history of the world.

"It is the Pope King who retards the complete liberation of Italy—he is the sole, the true obstacle to our unity.

"I am a Christian, and I speak to Christians, and I love and venerate the religion of Christ, because Christ came into the world to free mankind from the bondage for which God had not created him."

I had occasionally heard almost the same words from the ex-priest, Gavazzi, who, as an itinerant expounder either of Protestantism or of the reformed Catholicism of Father Passaglia, preached frequently in the open streets with the hope of getting converts, —but the good people of the city of Naples were certainly not as yet amenable to the persuasive eloquence of this bold innovator.

On one point of Church doctrine I must, however, do him the justice to say he invariably gained mute attention from the feminine portion of the community, and he handled the subject with a cautious knowledge of the dangerous ground on which he was treading.

The topic under discussion was the rite of auricular confession, and his desire was to set forth, without outraging religious prejudice, the frightful abuses which it involved.

In proportion as the excitable populace appeared to welcome or disapprove, he strengthened or softened down the language he used, and when the words "Bene," Bene" were shouted forth, he received them as tokens of assent on their part. He then ventured on denunciations on all wicked priests and their parasites, until the increasing violence of his epithets were drowned in murmurs of dissent. At one moment he would show that the Confessional was an institution well adapted to the early ages, when the perception of right and wrong was almost unknown; but repugnant to the present time, as destructive of family repose; and at another he would explain that it was the abuse, and not the use, of the rite, of which he complained. Above all, he exhorted the younger women, as they valued every moral quality and every chaste impulse of their nature, to open to God alone the secret thoughts of their hearts, and to avoid the inward contamination which auricular confession imposed.

Without assuming to be a judge on this delicate theological dogma, perhaps I may venture to say that I considered the advice sound and practical in its nature.

CHAPTER XXIII.

1860.

Naples.—Boat-Race.—Annexation to Sardinia.—Capitulation of Capua.—Distribution of Medals by Garibaldi.—Interference of the French Admiral at Gaeta.—Entry of Victor Emanuel into Naples. — His Devotions at the Shrine of St. Januarius. — Decorations of the City.—The King's Visit to the Theatre.—His Reception of Garibaldi.—Major Missori.—The Dictator's Farewell Address to his Army.

November 1.—Two events of importance came off in the course of the day.

In the forenoon the Piedmontese batteries, under the command of General Della Rocca, opened fire upon the fortress of Capua.

In the afternoon an interesting boat-race took place, between the thirty-foot cutters of the *Hannibal* and *Cressy*. The course was two miles in length. The race was run in seventeen minutes, and I regret having to record that the flag-ship's boat was not the victor. The *Cressy's* cutter won by eight strokes of the oar, or sixteen seconds of time.

November 3.—The forts and Sardinian ships of

war saluted, in honour of the annexation of the Kingdom of the Two Sicilies to Sardinia. The official accounts of the total number of votes given is not yet published, but the approximate result shows the following figures:—

	Naples.	*Sicily.*
Si.	1,303,064	432,054
No.	10,312	667

The Sardinian troops which landed in the Gulf of Manfredonia, under General Sonnaz, have passed Benevento, and are making a flank march to join the King on the banks of the Garigliano.

After a bombardment of forty-eight hours, Capua capitulated yesterday. The garrison, ten thousand men, were made prisoners of war, and were forthwith sent by sea to Genoa.

November 4.—This forenoon, in the square of San Francisco de Paolo, Garibaldi distributed medals to the survivors of "The Thousand who had landed at Marsala." The Dictator, surrounded by his staff, and supported by several ladies of the southern aristocracy, alluded in a speech of touching eloquence to the loss their ranks had sustained since they had disembarked on the shores of Sicily. The name of each man, or rather boy, of this heroic band was called over alphabetically, and the insignia was fastened to his breast by the hands of the Duchess of Verdura. One recipient was a child not thirteen years of age, yet he had come unscathed through the fights of Marsala, Calatifimi, Palermo, and Melazzo.

November 6.—Vice-Admiral Persano returned to-day from the waters of Gaeta. On the 2nd instant, with the squadron under his command, consisting of three screw frigates and five paddle-wheel steamers, he covered the passage of a division of the Sardinian army across the river Garigliano near its mouth; the main body, under the immediate orders of the King in person, effecting the passage higher up the stream.

When the French Admiral, who was at this time at anchor with five sail of the line, observed that Persano was manœuvring in line of battle for the purpose of taking up a position at the entrance of the river, he sent an officer on board the *Maria Adelaide*, to inform him that he could not be permitted to act on the offensive even in that quarter, though it was several miles distant from the fortress off which it had hitherto been supposed the Imperial squadron had been stationed, solely for the protection of the young King and the Royal family.

Admiral Persano, in reply to the astounding communication made to him by the French captain, stated that he had received instructions from the King to anchor off the Garigliano, and those instructions he should endeavour to carry into execution; if he was arrested by superior force, the responsibility must remain with the Admiral who gave authority for such an extraordinary proceeding.

Orders were then given for the *Maria Adelaide* to steam slowly ahead towards the point of land near the river's mouth; and as further opposition was not offered by the French squadron, it is reasonable to suppose the menace was in reality never intended to be enforced.

Two days subsequently the Sardinian squadron commenced an attack on the town of Gaeta, but in this instance Admiral de Tinan showed he was in earnest in intervention. Several shots were fired from the *Bretagne* across the bows of Persano's flag-ship, and the Sardinian Admiral was informed that he would not be allowed to approach within six thousand metres, or three and a half miles, of the French ships at anchor off the fortress.

Later in the day the Sardinian troops drove the advanced division of the Neapolitan army, ten thousand strong, from the town of Mola. These troops retreated *en masse* along the narrow isthmus which connects Mola with Gaeta, and must have been cut off by the Sardinian squadron, had not the latter been prevented by the French ships of the line from acting offensively against them.

The effect of this armed foreign intervention will be to protract for many weeks the civil war in the kingdom of Naples, and be an encouragement to Francis II. to defend himself to the last. His Majesty had the opportunity of safe retreat, and might probably have availed himself of it, had not false hopes been held up to view of assistance from without. Cooped up in a casemate, his resistance henceforth will be without dignity; whereas had he awaited his Royal rival, the great North Italian potentate, on the plains of Sessa, he might there on equal terms have fought the Sardinian army, and whether victorious or defeated, would have handed his name down to posterity with honourable fame.

November 7.—Shortly before ten o'clock in the forenoon, and half-an-hour earlier than notified by public decree, King Victor Emanuel made his triumphal entry into Naples. He came from the railway station in one of the Bourbon Royal carriages, and was accompanied by the Dictator, the Pro-dictator, and the Minister of State, Signor Farini.

The storm of wind, rain, thunder and lightning, which had swept with moderate force over sea and land from the middle of the previous night, burst forth with redoubled vigour at the moment of the entrance of the newly-elected Sovereign within the city walls; yet the masses of an excited populace manfully stood their ground, and welcomed the hero of San Martino with enthusiastic expressions of joy. Long and loud were the *vivas* for the Constitutional King, and for the people's idol Garibaldi; and these hurrahs became more vigorous when it was shouted abroad that His Majesty, as a fervent Catholic, intended to pay his devotions without delay at the shrine of Saint Januarius.

For this purpose, the Royal carriage turned into the great square of the Duomo, where the King and his companions alighted, and entering the sacred building, proceeded at once to the high altar, where mass was duly performed by the officiating priest. The King alone knelt down; Garibaldi, Pallavicini, and Farini standing apart, a few paces behind, and a little in advance of the multitude of the curious who had assembled to join in the thanksgiving for their country's regeneration. After a few minutes' contemplation of the relics and sacred phial, containing the blood of the Patron Saint, His Majesty returned to the cathedral square, re-entered the lumbering antique vehicle, and, driving through the Toledo in a continued storm of rain, gained the shelter of the Royal Palace shortly before noon.

The King, who was dressed in the uniform of a general officer, presented himself in the balcony, with Garibaldi by his side; and, as at this time the weather had in some degree cleared up, he was enabled to survey the elaborate works which, by order of the Municipality, had been erected to do him honour. The gigantic triumphal arches in face of the church of San Francisco di Paolo, and at the angle of the Café d'Europa, were structures of beauty and solidity; and the paintings with which they were adorned did credit to the Neapolitan artists. At the summit of one of these pyramids, as a compliment to the great nation, the moral influence of which had been so steadily exerted for the benefit of Italy, and against which not the shadow of suspicion existed of interested motives, two large silken flags, being the Union Jacks of Great Britain, were suspended on lofty staffs, and blowing out firmly in the breeze, were objects conspicuous to every quarter of the town.

The statues of the hundred principal cities of the kingdom, represented by female figures of colossal size, and fixed on pedestals, were also admirably executed, and, arranged at thirty yards apart throughout the whole length of the main street, gave a grand effect to the scene. They relieved the usual monotonous hangings of tapestry and banners, which invariably form the decorations of the streets of continental cities; but, unfortunately, several of these figures had only been partially completed, and the *coup d'œil* was thus destroyed.

The forts and ships of war had been garnished with flags since early dawn, and Royal salutes had been fired as the King entered the capital of his newly-acquired dominions.

Official notice had been addressed to me yesterday by Admiral Persano of the intention of His Majesty to make his public entrance into the city during the forenoon of to-day, and a programme had been supplied of the naval and military ceremonies which were to take place on the occasion. I considered it, however, my duty to inform the Sardinian flag-officer in command of the Italian squadron, that as King Victor Emanuel came to Naples by land, Her Majesty's ships under my orders could take no cognizance of his movements. Had His Majesty entered from the seaward, with the Royal standard of Sardinia flying at the mast-head of one of his ships, he would have received the royal salute which was due to a crowned head.

The senior officer left in charge of the French vessels of war, on the departure of Admiral de Tinan with the line-of-battle ships to Gaeta, had orders to follow my movements on the arrival of the King, and he seemed well pleased when he learned from me that neither salutes would be fired nor would a single flag be hoisted in honour of an event which was to change the face of Italy. The hostility of the officers of the French Marine to the progress of Italian unity seems nearly universal.

The American ship of war, *Iroquois*, in accordance with the usual custom of acknowledging every Government, followed the motions of the Sardinian squadrons, but the other foreign vessels of war in the roads took the inaction of the *Hannibal* for their guide. To me it certainly appeared self-evident that King Victor Emanuel, presenting himself on a sudden in the capital, and declaring himself King of Italy, could not be officially acknowledged by the naval force of any other nation, whilst King Francis, [illegible] head of his army, remained in any part of his dominions.

Yet many observers held an opinion that the squadron should not have continued at the anchorage unless prepared to take part in the programme of rejoicings.

Never was the working out of the principle of neutrality and non-intervention more open to criticism than during the phases it has presented since the first landing at Marsala, and right glad will all in authority be when the time shall arrive of a return to the normal state of international law.

King Victor Emanuel having announced his intention of visiting the theatre of San Carlos in state, I procured a box in the first tier at a fabulous price, and, accompanied by Lady Downshire and her daughter, Captain Farquhar, and Mr. Shanks, went early to witness what kind of reception would be given to His Majesty by the aristocracy and upper classes. The Opera House was magnificently decorated, brilliantly lighted with mingled gas and wax tapers, and every place, both in the boxes and pit, crowded with occupants, principally of the fair sex, all of whom, I need hardly say, were extremely well dressed, the toilets of the Neapolitan ladies being known throughout Europe as unexceptionable in taste as they are expensive in texture.

The King, attended by Fárini, General Della Rocca, Villa Marina, Persano, and his personal staff, entered the Royal box at nine o'clock, and was welcomed by a general waving of handkerchiefs on the part of the ladies, and by a continuous ring of *vivas* from the gentlemen of every class ; but there appeared to me to be want of concert in the demonstration, and an absence of that real enthusiasm which such an occasion should have inspired. In the first place, there was mismanagement at head-quarters. It had originally been arranged that Garibaldi should accompany the King, and a seat had been placed for the Dictator on the left of the Royal chair ; but, a few minutes before the arrival of His Majesty, and when excitement was at high pitch, a lackey entered the Royal box and carried off the Dictator's seat. It became immediately known throughout the house that Garibaldi would not be present, and low murmurs of disapprobation were distinctly audible amongst the throng.

It was at this inopportune moment that the doors of the Royal box were thrown open, and the elected King of the Italian people marched leisurely to the front. His Majesty was habited in military costume, and wore the star of the grand cross of the order of the Annunciata on the left breast of his coat ; no other decorations, if attached, being distinguishable.

His attitude and manner were essentially martial, the defiant expression of his countenance bearing testimony to the heroism of his nature. The boldness of his look, and I may add the severity of his aspect, did not quite comport with the part he was now called upon to act, but he was evidently agreeably surprised at the magnificent scene spread before him. He appeared to examine, with a scrutinizing eye, every person in every corner of the house, and to be struck with amazement at the vastness of the amphitheatre in which they were gathered.

At the conclusion of the opera the National Anthem was sung, when another outburst of popular applause greeted His Majesty's ear; and as the humour of the multitude seemed improved by the charm of music, the *vivas* were more hearty than those which had previously been heard.

The King, thoroughly fatigued by the incessant labours of the day, denied himself the pleasure of witnessing a new ballet which had been expressly composed for the edification of the Royal hero.

November 8.—At 11 o'clock this forenoon, the King, attended by his Minister of State and the superior officers of his staff, received the Dictator in the throne-room of the Royal Palace. Signor Conforti, the Minister of the Interior, under the Revolutionary Government, then made the following speech, which, as emanating from Garibaldi, may be considered the last public act of that self-sacrificing, but misguided man.

"SIRE,

"The Neapolitan people, in public meeting assembled, have proclaimed you their King by an immense majority.

"Nine millions of Italians are united to the other provinces ruled over by your Majesty with so much wisdom, and verify your solemn promise that Italy shall belong to the Italians only."

King Victor Emanuel made answer in his usual laconic style, and thus commenced the constitutional rule of Piedmont, and ended the dictatorial functions of Garibaldi in the Peninsula.

In the afternoon a second race came off between the cutters of the *Hannibal* and *Cressy*, each boat being manned by marines. It was neck-and-neck during the whole distance of one mile and a half, and was won by half a boat's length by the crew of the flag-ship.

In the evening I received a visit from the young Hungarian officer, Major Missori, who saved the life of his chief at the battle of Melazzo. He informed me that the Dictator had made his final arrangements for leaving Naples early to-morrow morning, and that he had desired him to go on board the *Hannibal*, to acquaint me that he hoped to pay me a farewell visit before he quitted the Bay. Major Missori spoke of his master in terms of great affection, and did not hesitate to say that he was dejected and low in spirits, from a belief that his followers would not be honourably treated by the Sardinian Government.

I at once negatived the idea of forming any judgment of the intentions of a Government which had not yet been installed twenty-four hours, and recommended the young Hungarian to look forward with hope, and not with despondency, on the future destiny of his late companions in arms, who, whatever might be the opinion of the justice of the war, had immortalized themselves in history by their self-denial and heroic bravery. I received at the same time a copy of Garibaldi's farewell address to his army, of which the following is an extract :—

"To my Companions in Arms :

"Arrived at the last stage but one of our regeneration, it is necessary for us to take into consideration the period which is about to finish, and prepare ourselves to terminate the stupendous conception of the elect of twenty generations, the execution of which has been designed by Providence to this fortunate generation.

"Yes, young men, Italy owes to you an enterprise which merits the applause of the world. You have conquered, and you will conquer, for you have now and for ever learnt those tactics which decide battles.

"To arms, all—all! and the oppressors, the all-powerful, shall be swept away like dust!

"And you, O women! put away from you all cowards: they will engender but cowards; and you, daughters of the land of beauty, have need of a brave and generous offspring!

"Providence has given Victor Emanuel to Italy. Every Italian should unite himself to him. All should gather close around him. By the side of the 'Re Galantuomo' every strife should disappear, every rancour be dissipated. Once again I repeat my cry to you. To arms, all—all! If the month of March, 1861, does not find a million of Italians under arms—oh, then! poor Liberty! Alas, for an Italian existence!

"Italians of Calatafimi, of Palermo, of the Volturno, of Ancona, of Castelfidardo, and of Isernia, and with us every man of the land who is neither servile nor a coward—all, one and all, gathered closely around the hero of Palestro, we will give the last shock, the last blow to the crumbling tyranny!

"Receive, young volunteers, honourable survivors of ten battles, one farewell word. It parts laden with affection from the depths of my soul. I leave you to-day, but for a short time only. The hour of combat will again see me among you, by the side of the soldiers of Italian liberty.

"We shall soon meet again, to march together towards the redemption of our brethren, still slaves of the stranger. We shall soon meet again, to march together to new victories.

"G. GARIBALDI."

CHAPTER XXIV.

1860.

Naples.—Farewell Interview with General Garibaldi.—Sketch of his Person and Character.—Visit from Admiral Persano.—Audience of King Victor Emanuel.

November 9.—At six in the morning, Lieutenant Wilmot informed me that General Garibaldi was in my cabin. I was in my cot at that hour, and hastily throwing on a few garments, came out from the sleeping apartment to see him. He was dressed in his usual costume, the red flannel shirt and grey trousers, but was without a sword. Looking out of the stern verandah windows, and pointing to an English merchant vessel blowing off her steam, at a cable's distance, he said, in a melancholy tone, "There is the ship which is to carry me to my island home; but, Admiral, I could not depart without paying you a farewell visit. It is the last which I make before leaving Naples. Your conduct to me since our first meeting at Palermo has been so kind, so generous, that it can never be erased from my memory. It is engraven there indelibly. It will last my life."

I assured him in reply, that every British naval officer who might have found himself in contact with the horrors of civil war, and had been invited to intervene, as had been my case during the bombardment of Palermo, must have acted in a manner similar to that which I had done. It was, in truth, the simple performance of a public duty, incumbent upon me from the position which I held. I added that I certainly had endeavoured to treat him with that courtesy and consideration which was amply his due, both from his own humane conduct, and from the acquiescence he had given to every proposal I had made for arresting the carnage around. Without his steadfast faith in the honour of the British flag, my action as a neutral power would have been inoperative for good, and the armistice which had brought about the cessation of hostilities might never have been arranged.

Garibaldi then invited me to pay him a visit at his cottage in Caprera, and spoke much of the beautiful harbour between the island and the main, where Nelson had once anchored for the protection of his fleet.

I told him eighteen months had yet to pass by before my time of service in the Mediterranean would expire, and I could hardly expect to find him at the same little spot at the end of that period. This remark appeared to strike a chord which threw the whole train of his reflections into a different channel.

From a tone of dejection and gloom he seemed suddenly to wake up to one of buoyancy and hope. He hastily exclaimed, "Before five months have passed I shall again be in the field! In March of next year we must have a million of men under arms, and the work of the regeneration of my country must be completed. I shall never rest satisfied till emancipation from foreign rule has been effected throughout the entirety of the Italian kingdom. Rome and Venice are not French and Austrian cities. They are Italian cities. They belong to Italy alone, and the powerful of the earth have no right to retain them."

This ebullition of sentiment led to the old point discussed between the Dictator and Mr. Elliot in the cabin of the *Hannibal*. The question was not one of right, but of prudence; and I ventured to assert decidedly that unless there was henceforth perfect accord between every section of the Liberal party, the real unity of Italy could never be established. I knew this would be the last time I should see the Dictator, and I determined at least to take advantage of the opportunity he voluntarily afforded me, of expressing firmly my opinion and, so far as etiquette would allow, my disapprobation of ulterior hostile measures in Italy, unless commanded by the King to undertake them in concert with the Parliament.

Two months' reflection, however, since the advice given to him by Lord John Russell, through Mr.

Elliot, had evidently made no change in his determination to agitate, even in arms if necessary, to force the foreign garrison from Rome. He stated again, as he had stated at Palermo, that the French Emperor was the prime enemy of Italy, and that the great Italian capital would never be delivered up unless the whole nation rose in arms, and compelled His Majesty to act justly. It was not the love of Italy, but the hope of enlargement of the Empire by the acquisition of Italian territory, that brought the French armies into Lombardy in the spring of last year; and, for his own part, he could never offer his hand to an Italian minister, however great he might be, who had acquiesced in the degradation of his country, by yielding to the will of the spoliator.

I found the attempt which I made on the present, as on two former occasions, to moderate the opinions of the Dictator on this question of State policy utterly useless. Rome, the Empress City of the world—Venice, the Queen of the Adriatic—to be in the hands of the alien! It was humiliation intolerable, and they must be rescued, at all risk.

With the insight I now possessed of the imaginative character of the man, I cannot say I was altogether astonished at the vehemence of his language on this particular head; but I was at a loss to understand the inveterate hatred he seemed to cherish for every act of the Chief Minister, and of his general distrust of everything Piedmontese.

The names of two persons only were ever mentioned by him to me. They were Count Cavour and General Cialdini. Of the former I have already written; of the latter, he spoke in the warmest terms of affection and respect.

During the whole of this interview the name of King Victor Emanuel was not once mentioned, in relation to His Majesty's entrance into the city, nor of the advance of the Sardinian army for the investment of Gaeta. It appeared to me the Dictator wished to avoid allusion to the subject, and it certainly was not for me to bring it into notice.

I next spoke to him of my astonishment at the conduct of Signors Pilotti and Settembrini, and of my recapture of the vessel which had been piratically seized for the naval service of the Revolution. Garibaldi expressed his entire disapproval of every part of that outrageous deed, and assured me that his agents had acted without any authority from him. He never could have contemplated or countenanced such a proceeding. I was satisfied with this statement, and abstained from further comment.

As he passed from the cabin to the quarter-deck, he observed my visiting-book lying on the table; on the same small table upon which, not six months before, the armistice had been signed, pregnant with such results. I asked him to be good enough to add his name to those of my former visitors. He sat down immediately, and wrote in French as follows:—

"G. Garibaldi

"Doit à l'Amiral Mundy par les preuves bien sincères et affectueuses d'amitié, dont il a été comblé dans toutes les circonstances, la reconnaissance la plus vive, et qui durera toute sa vie."

When Garibaldi rose to take leave, his previous animation had departed. He again became dejected, and his whole manner was that of a man who was suffering a poignant grief. I made no effort to elicit explanation of this change from his usual cheerfulness. It might have awakened another chord of melancholy reflection, and have brought about communications better left within his own breast.

After a visit of twenty minutes' duration, the ex-Dictator stepped into his little skiff, and, rowed by four boys, returned to the *Washington*. In a few hours the steamer rounded the Island of Ischia, and, turning her head to the northward, steered a direct course for Caprera.

I think I may be allowed, at this part of my journal, to introduce a slight sketch of the person and character of Garibaldi; and to that purpose I shall devote the following page.

GARIBALDI.

Garibaldi, when he came on board the *Hannibal,* was in his fifty-third year. He stands about five feet seven inches in height, and is well and strongly made. Broad shoulders, an expansive chest, a short and thick neck, and a small waist, with well-formed hands and feet, are the features in his person which are striking to the observer. The brow is lofty; the eyes are small and deeply set, and of a greyish tint; the hair, once a bright auburn, is now of a redder tint, and perfectly straight; the beard and moustache of the same colour, with streaks of grey.

The whole expression of his countenance is one of great benevolence and intelligence, without the least approach to fierceness; yet there is not wanting a look of profound astuteness, which would bespeak a more subtle temperament than that which he is generally believed to possess. There is at the same time a simplicity, and even a tenderness, in his manner and address which is most captivating; whilst his general bearing and attitude are marked with dignity and composure. No person of moderate observation could be engaged, even in a short conversation, with this remarkable man, without being struck with the clear, silvery tone of his voice, and with the originality of his style.

The delight with which he spoke of the certain

bright future of his beloved Italy, and of the overthrow of the blood-stained despotism under which she had suffered for so many centuries, would have appeared the mere ravings of the blinded enthusiast, had not the marvellous deeds he had performed given reality to the conception. He now became a voluntary exile from the land which he had conquered, and in his retirement he carried with him the personal respect and admiration even of those most opposed to his projects, and who were loudest in the denunciations of the lawlessness of his enterprise.

After several months of the exercise of absolute Dictatorship over Sicily and Naples, he is known to have been forced to borrow a few pounds to defray trifling debts; and, refusing all honours and emoluments from his Sovereign, has sought the repose of private life in the mountain wilds of his island home.

A general opinion prevails that he has not received at the hands of the King's ministers and advisers the consideration that his great services seemed to demand, and this has caused serious dissatisfaction among some classes of the population of Naples. King Victor Emanuel, however, in his individual character of a brother soldier and a friend, has expressed his sense of his services in the most handsome language, and would willingly have conferred upon him the highest honours in the gift of the Crown, had he not known that his powerful subject would have refused to accept them.

In the afternoon I received a visit from Persano, who had been promoted to the rank of Vice-Admiral for his brilliant services at Ancona. He informed me that he had received the King's commands to wait upon me officially, and to express on behalf of His Majesty his thanks for the consideration which I had at all times exhibited towards the Sardinian naval officers, and for the humane exertions I had used to arrest the civil war.

November 10.—I received this afternoon an official notification from the Lord Chamberlain of King Victor Emanuel in the following words:—

"The Lord Chamberlain in the service of His Majesty the King has the honour of announcing to Admiral Mundy that His Excellency and the Captain of the *Hannibal* will be received by His Majesty at an audience in the Royal Palace at 10 o'clock to-morrow morning."

This invitation or command took me rather by surprise, but I deemed it right at once to accept it, and sent an answer to that effect. Yesterday it was a leave-taking with the hero of the age; to-morrow it will be an introduction to the Sovereign of the people's choice.

November 11.—I landed at the San Lucia steps, and drove to the Royal Palace at the hour appointed, taking Captain Farquhar with me. As we mounted the grand staircase, and passed through the broad corridors to the ante-chamber, I observed that the hand both of the destroyer and the renovator had been actively at work since I had trod these marble halls only four months since to pay my respects to the last monarch of the Bourbon dynasty. Everywhere the lilies—emblems of ancient chivalry and despotic rule—had been carefully erased, and the white cross of Savoy—the symbol of modern civilization and progress—had been set up in their place. The paint, plaster, and mortar were not yet dry that had been employed in this transmography.

In the ante-chamber we found a large assemblage of gentlemen, habited in black evening dress and white neckcloths, many of whom held long rolls of paper and parchment in their hands. They were select deputations from the provincial cities, waiting an audience to do homage to their constitutional King, and one of these municipal bodies was already in the presence of His Majesty.

I was beginning to fear that I should have to exercise a vast amount of patience, and to resign myself to quiet meditation in the corner of the room until the rest of the functionaries had read their addresses, when a sleek-looking personage, evidently an upper retainer of the ancient *régime*, stole gently to the spot in which I was seated, and informed me that the King would receive me in the course of a few minutes. These minutes, however, rolled onwards, and more than half-an-hour had passed away when the same individual again entered the room, and in a loud voice proclaimed that His Majesty would receive the English Admiral.

When we were ushered into the presence-chamber, we found the King standing alone in the centre of the room. His Majesty was in full military costume, the front of his coat ornamented with the single brilliant star of the order of the Annunciata, as that of King Francis had been with the order of Saint Januarius.

Coming forward in the most friendly manner, the King shook us both warmly by the hand with the grasp of a giant, and welcomed us with a cordiality that disarmed all formality. Turning the conversation at once into a channel the most likely to be interesting to naval men, he spoke of a voyage he had lately made in the flag-ship of Admiral Persano in the Adriatic Gulf, when a violent gale of wind suddenly sprung up, and a day and a half were passed in a heavy sea on a lee shore. The vessel pitched and rolled with such violence that many of the oldest mariners were sea-sick, but he was delighted to find he suffered comparatively little himself. His Majesty confessed, however, to have been highly delighted when the sun re-appeared and the tempest abated.

The King next expatiated in glowing terms on the magnificent subject for a painter which the British squadron presented on the day of his arrival in the city. He had watched the ships riding heavily at their anchors for more than an hour in the evening, when at the height of the storm they appeared almost touching the rocks off the Mole, the waves dashing past their hulls with a power that seemed irresistible. His Majesty asked me if I considered them to have been in danger of shipwreck, and why they were collected in so close a space together.

I assured him that, for an open roadstead, the anchorage off the city of Naples was one of the best in the whole range of the Mediterranean; that the holding-ground was excellent, and that only when the breeze came strong from the southward could a swell be brought into the Bay.

It happened to blow a fierce sirocco on the morning of His Majesty's arrival. This was the worst point of the compass, as there was no break to the roll of the sea from the straits of Messina to the islands of Ischia and Capri.

After addressing a few kind words to Captain Farquhar, the King took me aside, and informed me that he had been desirous of seeing me at the Palace, in order that he might personally express to me those sentiments which he had commanded Admiral Persano to convey. He wished to thank me for the consideration I had so uniformly shown to the naval officers of his fleet, and to the Italians of every district during the progress of the civil war. My active exertions in the cause of humanity had been constantly brought to his notice, and my conduct in arresting the bombardment of Palermo, and in saving the lives of the people, had given him the greatest satisfaction.

His Majesty then spoke of the unvarying sympathy which had been evinced by the whole people of England, and by the Government of Her Majesty, for the welfare of the Italian nation. He mentioned Lord John Russell and Sir James Hudson by name as the truest friends that any country could possess. The earnest expression of the countenance of the King when he gave vent to these sentiments evidenced how deeply he felt the words which he had spoken. That severity of aspect and harsh look, half defiant, which I had so much remarked on his appearance at the Opera, had now entirely passed away, and was succeeded by a benignant smile agreeable to behold.

His Majesty seemed glad of the opportunity of announcing the force of his friendly sentiments, and of his high appreciation of the noble part England had taken.

With the exception of one American corvette, and one small French Aviso, the ships of war of every nation had either joined the fugitive monarch in the waters of Gaeta, or had sailed away for other destinations. The British squadron, undiminished in numbers, alone remained fixed at their moorings. For reasons which I considered imperative, it took no part in the present rejoicings, and certainly five sail of the line stationed close beneath the Palace windows, undecorated and silent amidst the roar of cannon around, might have been construed by the Neapolitan people as a sign of disapproval of the new order of things. But this misapprehension was unavoidable. I felt persuaded that Admiral Persano would have fully explained the grounds on which I demurred from joining in the ceremonials of the day; nor did I think it would be right to make any allusion to the subject unless some remark from the King should invite an explanation. The gracious reception I had met with showed the difficulties of my official position had been fully understood, and His Majesty must have known, through Admiral Persano, that Mr. Elliot had acquiesced in the course which had been pursued.

In speaking of the great pleasure it had afforded him at finding an English squadron in the Bay on his arrival, and of his hope that it would continue during the winter, he spoke also of the satisfaction it would have given him had he found the French fleet also at anchor in the roads instead of being at Gaeta.

He mentioned having received a letter from the Emperor, which had afforded him much gratification.

His Majesty subsequently gave a short description of the general features of the country through which he had passed on his route from Ancona. He made particular inquiries as to my opinion of the quality of the Neapolitan sailors, and was glad to learn that it was in many respects favourable. Of the Neapolitan soldiers His Majesty could not as yet speak in high terms.

In the field they had made no stand against the troops of Northern Italy, but this might have arisen from the difference in their *morale*, and their want of confidence in themselves and in their officers.

Finally, on my taking leave, he requested I would make known to Her Majesty's Government how deeply he appreciated their noble and magnanimous conduct, which had proved so advantageous to the interests of his country.

CHAPTER XXV.

1860.

Naples. — Sir William Codrington. — Decree respecting the Garibaldian Army.—Small-Pox.—Reported Participation of Seamen in the Revolution. — Attacked with Small-Pox.—Departure of the King for Palermo.—Excursion to Pompeii.—Dissolution of the English Legion.—Review of the National Guard. — Adventures of a British Seaman in the Royal Palace..

November 15.—Lieut.-General Sir William Codrington, the Governor and Commander-in-chief at Gibraltar, arrived in the Bay, and went on to Gaeta in the *Mohawk*, which I placed at his disposal. He was anxious to see the works of the Piedmontese in their advance to erect their breaching batteries, as well as the means of defence by the fortress. Signor Farini, who had shown great administrative talent during a nine months' rule in the Æmilian provinces, has been nominated Lieutenant-General in Southern Italy, and assumed the reins of government on the 12th.

The Italian Volunteers actually under arms are ordered to be paid a six months' indemnity before discharge, and those recommended for distinguished service in the field will otherwise be rewarded by the bestowal of medals.

A mixed commission is also to be appointed to examine into the title of every officer to the rank which he holds in the Garibaldian forces, and after the necessary eliminations are made, the remainder will form an integral part of the National Army. It is also expressly understood that the advantages and obligations, both of soldiers and officers, shall be equal with those of the regular military establishment. This decree of the King is eminently just, and no reasonable man forming a portion of the revolutionary bands could desire more; yet from the feeling of morbid discontent which exists in the republican ranks against everybody around the King, and against everything supposed to be Piedmontese, it will probably not give satisfaction.

November 20.—The small-pox, which suddenly broke out in my flag-ship, and in the *Renown*, ten days ago, is increasing in virulence. Ninety men have been struck down by the fearful malady, but only two have died.

On my application to Vice-Admiral Persano to allow me to land the invalids at the Lazarette, he informed me that he had forwarded my request to the proper department, and he had been desired to acquaint me that the large hospital buildings on the island of Nisida were entirely at my disposal. The men were immediately landed, and found ample space in the lofty wards of that establishment, furniture and other necessary comforts being supplied from the shore.

Lieutenant Pyne, of the *Renown*—a volunteer—took military charge of the island, with a detachment of marines under his orders. Dr. Walker, M.D., Senior Assistant of the *Hannibal*, became the resident medical man, and the Italian superintendent afforded every assistance. This act of real kindness on the part of the new Government was of the greatest benefit. The men must otherwise have been sent to Malta, whereas now, as cases occurred, they were transported to the shore, and the spread of the disease amongst the crew lessened.

I received intelligence this evening of the departure of the Queen mother, the princesses, and the younger princes from Gaeta. Counts Trani and Tapani still remained with King Francis in the fortress.

November 25.—I have received a despatch from the Commander-in-chief, calling upon me, by command of the Lords Commissioners of the Admiralty, to inform them if the report circulated in the newspapers, that seamen belonging to the *Renown* had taken part in the war now in progress in Italy were true. I was, moreover, reminded by their Lordships, that Her Majesty's Government had expressed its determination to show entire neutrality in the contest, and I was desired to afford a full report of all the circumstances of the case, if interference by anyone on board any of Her Majesty's ships, under my command, had taken place.

I have already stated in the early pages of this journal, that my principal object in giving publicity to matter originally written for private reference, was to rebut the accusations that were covertly made of my favouring the Revolution, and to show that in no instance had I swerved from a conscientious observance of the laws of neutrality.

The determination of Her Majesty's Government and of the Lords Commissioners of the Admiralty to enforce a rigorous obedience to the letter of their instructions is made evident, by official notice having been immediately taken of a mere newspaper report. Fortunately I was enabled, by written testimony, not only to prove the incorrectness of the charges brought forward against me, but to furnish additional proof of the complete neturality which had been observed. If, indeed, there had been any departure from the principle of non-intervention, it was not against the Royalists, but against the revolutionary party that I had acted.

I recaptured the vessel which had been purchased as a ship of war for Garibaldi, though at anchor in a harbour in the possession of one of his generals;

and I sent the two Garibaldian officers, the first and second in command, prisoners to Malta. That I took great responsibility on myself for so doing was clear from the Crown Advocate having declared his opinion that there was no case for criminal proceedings against them, and by their immediate release by orders of the Governor of the island. Had the vessel also been given up, I do not know how I could have met the action for damages of detention, which it was intended to have instituted against me.

The accusation of sending a body of armed men from the British fleet to fight against the troops of the King of Naples is one of so unusual a nature that I think it advisable to give at length the official explanation furnished to me by Captain Forbes, in command of the *Renown*, with an extract from the signal log of the *Hannibal*, showing the stringent measures adopted to prevent the crews of our ships interfering in the Revolution.

I subsequently received a copy of a despatch written by Count Ludolf, the Neapolitan minister in London, to Lord John Russell, in which His Excellency broadly charges me with sending seamen from the fleet to serve pieces of artillery against the troops of the King his august master. It was therefore doubly fortunate that I had already transmitted to England a full account of what had already occurred.

"*Captain Forbes to Rear-Admiral Mundy.*

"*Renown*, Naples, October 28, 1860.

"SIR,

"In accordance with your memorandum of the 25th instant, inclosing a copy of a letter from the Secretary of the Admiralty on the subject of some seamen of the *Renown* being said to have taken part in the war now in progress in Italy, I have to state as follows:—

"It appears that three seamen of this ship, being on leave, attracted by numbers of idlers from Naples doing the same thing, took a carriage, drove out to Caserta, and approached the environs of Capua when firing was taking place.

"A mounted officer, an Englishman, meeting these men, accosted them, saying that two field-pieces were lying dismounted in a field; that he had had his men (Garibaldians) out for a long time trying to mount them, but they had failed, and the officer asked the seamen if they could do so. They said they could, and being shown the guns they set to work; and being assisted by two Garibaldians, mounted the guns, then clapped on the drag-ropes, and assisted by two other Garibaldians, drew the guns within an adjoining field-work.

"Half-an-hour afterwards the seamen left the spot, and returned to Naples.

"These guns were not fired, nor were they intended

to be brought into action. They had, the men believe, belonged to the Royalists, and had been captured, or left in the field on a retreat. The object of the Garibaldians was to withdraw them within the work as a place of safety.

"Further than performing the act I have described, the men declare they took no part whatever in what was passing; they were not armed, and appear to have been attracted to the spot solely by curiosity.

"My information is necessarily derived from the men themselves, but I have examined them separately, and find no discrepancy whatever in their statements. The men are of good character, and I have every reason to believe that this is an exact account of what took place, and that they took no part whatever in the hostilities between the parties.

"I have, &c.

(Signed) "ARTHUR FORBES."

Extract from the Signal Log of Her Majesty's Ship "Hannibal."

July 16, 1860.—On account of state of city, no leave until further orders for the ships' companies.

July 26.—Leave for petty officers to-day.

July 29.—Ditto.

August 19.—Naples being declared in a state of siege, leave prohibited to the ships' companies until further orders.

August 19.—Limited number of privileged-leave men may go on shore.

August 26.—Leave as last Sunday.

September 9.*—No leave for ships' companies to-day.

September 16.—Leave for petty officers.

September 23.—Ditto.

September 30.—Ditto.

October 3.—Ditto.

October 7.—Leave for fifty privileged-leave men.

October 10.—Ditto.

October 14.—Leave for petty officers.

October 21.—On account of election no more leave for ships' companies to-day.

October 24.—Leave for petty officers.

October 28.—Ditto.

(Signed) EDWARD WILMOT,
Flag Lieutenant.

It will be seen by this copy from the signal log that the ships' companies had no leave on shore, from the date of their being brought on board in the dead of night at the demand of the Royal Conspirator, Prince Luigi, to the end of October, a period of three months and a half; and on the day of the battle of the Volturno, not even privileged-leave men had been allowed to land.

Privileged-leave men are a class of seamen placed

* General Garibaldi having entered Naples on the 7th.

on a separate liberty list, who, from their uniform steady behaviour and sober habits, may be trusted on shore upon occasions when it would not be advisable to give general leave.

I sought every opportunity of granting this indulgence to these men as a reward for their good conduct, and as an example to others, who, though well up to their duty on board, could not resist the temptation of the grog-shop when on land.

My own statement,* with the enclosures, were forwarded to the Commander-in-chief, Vice-Admiral Martin, an officer scrupulously exact in seeing that all orders are strictly carried out. I trust it may be considered satisfactory and conclusive.

November 26.—Mr. and Mrs. Elliott and family embarked on board the *Queen*, 91, Captain Hillyar, on the 21st, and proceeded to Marseilles. The Honourable Mr. Stuart and Mr. French accompanied them, Mr. Conyngham remaining at Naples in charge of the archives.

The departure of the Minister and family, with the secretary and *attaché* of the Legation, left me almost friendless in the great city, and was a real stroke of misfortune to the small communion of English society. The *Queen* sailed at 4 o'clock in the afternoon. I went on board shortly before the hour, to say adieu to my friends, and whilst standing on the poop in perfect health, suddenly felt giddy with a sensation of nausea, as if struck by a poisonous malaria shooting into the system. I returned forthwith to the *Hannibal*, and the small-pox declared itself in the course of the night.

I was engaged to dine with King Victor Emanuel on the following day. When His Majesty became acquainted with the serious nature of my illness he gave directions that a messenger should be sent daily to the ship to furnish him with a report of the state of my health.

November 30.—This forenoon the King embarked in the frigate *Maria Adelaide*, bound for Palermo, having the Royal standard of Sardinia flying at the main. His Majesty ordered Admiral Persano to steer between the *Hannibal* and the *Renown*, and to stop the engines when abreast of the former.

I was closely confined to my cabin, but I had given directions that the Captain and officers should be at their stations in full dress, and that the yards should be manned and a Royal salute fired as the Royal frigate passed. The King was in full military costume, and on the ship being stopped within a few yards of the stern of the *Hannibal*, "God save the Queen" was struck up by the band of the *Maria Adelaide*, during the performance of which His Majesty stood uncovered on the after part of the quarter-deck, and at its conclusion bowed graciously to Captain Farquhar and the officers, who now had assembled by order on the poop. As the frigate steamed slowly onward, the band of the English ships struck up the National March of Sardinia, and the ceremony terminated.

December 1.—The decorations throughout the city are now completed, and are most creditable to the taste and skill of the Neapolitan artists.

In remembrance of the services already rendered by France, and perhaps in tremulous fear of the future, a colossal bust of the Emperor has been erected in the Largo della Carita, on the pedestal of which is written the following magniloquent sentence :—

"I proclaim Italy free from the Alps to the Adriatic." But why this yet to be fulfilled declaration should have been promulgated in the Square of Charity has not been explained.

In token of gratitude to England, on the summit of the grand arch at the entrance of the Toledo, an elaborately-worked escutcheon, with the armorial bearings of Great Britain, was fixed between two English standards; and on a tablet underneath the following statement was written :—"Like generous France, the great country of Hampden and Stratford wishes, and will continue to wish, for a great, a free, a noble sister, and no longer a martyred Italy."

Here again it might be asked why a passing compliment could not be paid to England without bringing in another nation at the head of the sentence.

In the Palace square stood a huge transparent painting of King Victor Emanuel, having on either hand drawings allegorical of Rome and Venice. These were supported by gigantic statues in plaster, of Count Cavour and the Sardinian Generals, La Marmora, Cialdini, and Fanti.

The open space opposite the Jesuits' College was ornamented with a series of sketches in chalk and oil, commemorative of the exploits of Garibaldi and his followers. Statues and busts of Generals Cosenz, Medici, Bixio, Turr, Milvitz, Ebor, and the Englishman Dunn, were also conspicuous. In all the great thoroughfares of the city, flags, banners, and wreaths of evergreens were draped together in the windows and balconies, and across the streets at measured intervals massive paintings of the numerous victories of the revolutionary forces were suspended to captivate the imagination of the rising generation, and to give excitement to the lower classes.

For two nights the city was illuminated, and every part of this programme for a general rejoicing may be pronounced a perfect success.

December 14.—Little worthy of note has occurred during the past fortnight. I am recovering from the recent attack of small-pox, and have visited Pompeii. Thirty-eight years had gone by since my last visit to that interesting spot. I was then a midshipman of the *Euryalus*, commanded by Captain, now Admiral, Sir Augustus Clifford. All that I then so much admired, and which I now again inspect, is fresh in my recollection as if seen but yesterday.

On the 7th, the King returned from Palermo, and,

having the Royal standard flying at the main of the frigate, was received with the same ceremonies as when he sailed from Naples. His Majesty had cause to be well satisfied with the enthusiastic welcome given to him in Sicily, which far exceeded the demonstrations made on his entry to this city. The *Agamemnon*, Captain Hope, was stationed in the Bay, and joined in the festivities.

The English legion, which has been stationed during the last month at Salerno, has been dissolved, and the greater part have left for their own country. This fine body of men had made themselves very popular in that district, and a handsome address was forwarded to them on leaving the town by the Piedmontese regiment in garrison. The Hungarian force is now the only foreign contingent remaining intact in Italy.

We have had strong gales for forty-eight hours, the *Hannibal* and *Queen* rolling 18°. The *Renown* pitched heavily, and snapped in half her iron rudder yoke, and twisted the spill of the rudder-head in the wardroom as she dipped her stern into the trough of the sea. The *Cressy*, Captain Harvey, arrived to-day.

December 15.—I have made a minute inspection of the Lazarette at the Island of Nisida. The small-pox patients have been reduced from one hundred and twenty to seventy-three; six have died, and my valet, Harris, who had caught the disease from close attendance upon me, is now the only dangerous case. I found the building well adapted for an infirmary, from the extent and arrangement of the wards; but it had been much neglected by the late Government, and was out of repair.

December 16.—His Majesty reviewed the National Guard, under the command of the Marchese Tupputi. This body of men looked remarkably well. The uniform in good taste, and the arms excellent. They mustered fifteen thousand strong in the Square, and went through their evolutions creditably. The spectacle, as a whole, was brilliant.

December 20.—Admiral Persano has just given me a very amusing sketch of the humorous, but I must add highly inexcusable, proceedings of one of the crew of the *Hannibal,* who has lately been on liberty. This man, who did not belong to the class entitled to privileged leave, had partaken too freely of the vile spirituous compound of the country, and, being of a convivial and adventurous turn of mind when slightly effected by drink, he suddenly made known to his companions who were about to take seats in one of the "Mariners' houses of Call" that he had received an invitation to dine with the new King of Naples, and must therefore leave them for the present, and make his way to the Royal Palace.

An endeavour was naturally made by his friends to combat a resolution so evidently preposterous, but arguments were unavailing, and the man proceeded on his errand. As he approached the portico of the principal entrance of the Palace, he was confronted by two armed representatives of the National Militia, who, entertaining every sentiment of good-will towards English seamen as a body, yet considered it their duty to oppose the ingress of this individual within the enclosure of the Royal domain.

The seaman, finding the blockade of the gateway to be really effective, after giving vent to a few expressions not complimentary to the citizen soldiers, but which, being uttered in language only current on the lower deck, they fortunately did not understand, made good his retreat, and subsequently joined the throng of idlers which was collected in the Square.

It appears that from this position he continued to keep watch on the movements of the volunteer sentinels, who had so roughly accosted him, and so effectually prevented the success of his enterprize. He knew they were not military men, or, to use his own words when called upon for explanation, were not "real soldiers;" and he thought it just possible he might find them off their guard. In this expectation he was correct. At a moment when one of them had ensconced himself within his sentry-box to light a cigar, and the other was engaged in earnest conversation with a passing friend, he contrived to elude their vigilance, and thus effected an entrance unperceived to the interior courts of the building. Wandering onwards unmolested, he reached the foot of the grand staircase, where he met a portly menial, in full livery of the House of Savoy, who, with many gestures of indignation, and with uplifted staff of office, endeavoured to make the intruder comprehend that he was treading on forbidden ground, and must depart from the Royal precincts with all convenient speed.

Now the grand marble staircase of the Royal Palace of Naples, considered by competent judges one of the most splendid in Europe, from its works of modern sculpture and general design, possessed also another feature, which, though useful on state occasions, when the Sovereign received his subjects, proved, in the present instance, destructive to the peace of mind of its guardian. The width between the balustrades, as well as the space from step to step, were inordinately great, and therefore rendered defence difficult if an attempt should be made at escalade. Possibly had the original designer constructed this fair way of smaller dimensions, the issue of the dispute between the English tar and the Italian porter would have been different in result to that which I am about to relate.

The seaman, not having an inclination to yield the same submissive obedience to the verbal demand of the solitary warden as he had done to the cross bayonets of the citizen soldiers, but, on the contrary, evincing an intention of mounting to the next story, the liveried official thought it expedient to try the effect of a little force. Stretching out his baton of authority across the chest of the bold invader, he summoned him to stand back and desist from his rash attempt, or he would certainly pay the penalty of the madness of his conduct.

Jack seems, however, to have been constitutionally of a pacific disposition, or, at any rate, in an affair of this nature, to have resolved to avoid all symptoms of pugnacity. He made no overt resistance to this gentle act of hostility, which, in truth, he richly merited; but, stepping quickly aside from the grasp of his assailant, rushed across to the furthest balustrade, and with the agility of an active topman, reached the summit of the flight of steps before his bewildered opponent could recover from his surprise.

The adventurous nautical hero had now firmly planted his foot on the threshold of the grand corridor, and the magnificence of the scene which then presented itself to his view probably struck him with astonishment, and perhaps with some feeling of awe. He was observed to take off his hat with the respect due to the quarter-deck, to smooth down his hair, and then look around with amazement, and as if uncertain how to proceed. On recovering his composure, he made a movement in advance, and had traversed the tesselated pavement of the principal gallery, when his further progress was again arrested by two more of the Royal domestics.

An altercation now ensued between the parties

thus opposed, which soon became so vehement that it was heard by an officer of distinction who happened to be seated in one of the adjoining apartments. This was Vice-Admiral Persano, the Commander-in-chief of the Sardinian fleet. Speaking English with great fluency, he promptly demanded of the British seaman why he had ventured to introduce himself within the walls of the Royal Palace, and he as promptly received for answer that he had come, according to invitation, to dine with His Majesty King Victor Emanuel.

The Admiral, perceiving the man to be under the influence of free libation, made use of coaxing language to induce him to depart; but, finding this manœuvre unavailing, he whispered to one of the servants to descend to the guard-house, and to bring up a few soldiers.

Two stalwart privates of the Piedmontese Guard were in a few minutes upon the spot, and on the Admiral desiring them to convey the prisoner to the outskirts of the Palace, the seaman remonstrated against any exercise of force, and expressed his delight at joining company with such fine, noble-looking fellows. They were real soldiers, he said, and no mistake—very different from the feathered peacocks called the National Guard.

As he walked quietly away with his new friends, he made some passing remarks on the shabby treatment he had received at the hands of the King, with whom he still loudly maintained he had been invited to dine; but I believe he complimented the Sardinian Admiral on his knowledge of the English idiom, which, he contended, was the only language necessary for a gentleman to know.

Admiral Persano subsequently informed me that he had told the whole history to His Majesty, who was extremely amused, but seemed inclined to give him blame for not seeing the man well fed before he was ejected from the building.

British seamen of a certain stamp of mind, when under the influence of spirits, are amongst the most eccentric of human beings. I give the foregoing little sketch as a sample of their ingenuity, dogged obstinacy, and wit.

December 22.—I received a friendly note this morning from Vice-Admiral de Tinan from Gaeta. He told me the anchorage off the fortress was good, and that his squadron rode out the late gales easier than it would have done in the roads of Naples. He also informed me that King Francis, having fifteen thousand staunch troops, and a large supply of ammunition and provisions, intended to hold out till the last. This determination was in opposition to the advice given to His Majesty by the Emperor of the French, and the Ministers of the Foreign Powers who still remained with him. His noble young Queen continued in the fortress, and by her courageous addresses to the garrison, and her devotion to the sick and wounded, gained the admiration of every-one.

Yet this protracted resistance on the part of His Majesty is simply puerile. It is the exercise of the same blinded obstinacy which prevented his listening to the friendly counsels of England and France months ago, when a timely concession would have saved his throne and dynasty.

The Sardinian batteries are now rapidly getting into position, and the new guns invented by Cavalli will have an opportunity of trial.

CHAPTER XXVI.

1860-61.

Naples.—Dine with the King.—Sardinian and Danish Etiquette.—Grand Ball of the National Guard.—Departure of the King for Turin.—Reactionary Plots.—The Archbishop Sforza.—The Burgher Militia.—Prince Carignano.—Signor Nigra.—Armistice at Gaeta.—Departure of the French Fleet.—Dine with Prince Carignano.—Capitulation of Gaeta.

December 23.—I dined to-day with the King, accompanied by Captains Farquhar, Forbes, Harvey, and Hillyar. The entertainment was magnificent; covers laid for seventy people. Signor Farini was unwell, and did not attend; other civilians holding high office in the State, with General Della Rocca and the chief naval and military officers, both Sardianian and Neapolitan, were present; and about twenty ladies, two of whom were English.

According to the Royal Etiquette of the House of Savoy, His Majesty does not appear in the reception room. When dinner was announced, the guests were marshalled by the Lord in Waiting, and conducted into the saloon of *régalement,* where we found the King seated at the centre of the table alone, with the army of liveried menials standing around.

The Marchioness of Ely was placed on his right, a Neapolitan duchess on his left; the position awarded to me being that on the right hand of Lady Ely, with the Marchesa Casa Nova, an English young lady married to a Neapolitan nobleman of that name, on my right. The Marquis of Downshire and the captains of the ships of the line were shown to seats at other parts of the table, and selection made to give companions on either side, who, by their knowledge of the English language or by their amicable sentiments towards the foreigner, might in some degree relieve the formality of a Royal entertainment.

During the whole of the dinner, which occupied more than an hour, the King did not even remove the napkin from his plate. He neither tasted a morsel of food nor took a drop of water to drink, but sat like a statue of marble, with both hands resting on the hilt of his sword, patiently awaiting the termination of a ceremony which must under such rigorous discipline have been in no slight degree irksome.

I could not help contrasting this self-abnegation of the excellent viands which were presented for the choice of His Majesty to the royal customs which are in force in Denmark. When in command of the *Nile*, during the Russian war, I had the honour of dining with the Sovereign of Denmark, at Altona. The occasion was one of great state, and a hundred guests were assembled. His Majesty joined them in the ante-room, and after addressing a few words to each individual, led the way to the banquet hall. The King wore a full dress military uniform, with helmet and gauntlets. He dispensed with the latter on taking his seat, but the helmet and sword remained fixed to the Royal person. Upon the cloth immediately in front of His Majesty, two common quart bottles of wine were placed. Of these he partook generously, as a natural assistant to the excellent dinner which he made, and he conversed with great freedom with all around the board, within compass of his voice. The etiquette which surrounded King Victor Emanuel was evidently more severe than that of Frederic, King of Denmark.

At the conclusion of the dinner His Majesty retired alone to the drawing-room, and, some minutes afterwards, the ladies and the principal personages of rank of the party who had remained in the passing rooms were invited to enter. The King then came round and spoke for a short time with each of the ladies, and subsequently with each of the gentlemen. He had now put aside the formality of the dinner-table, and was extremely affable and full of animation. He gave a hearty welcome to the Captains and to myself; and when, in the course of conversation, I mentioned that I was daily expecting the arrival of the *Victor Emanuel* ship of the line, named after His Majesty, and commanded by Captain Clifford, he expressed a hope that she would arrive before he quitted Naples. He then spoke of the state of affairs at Gaeta, of the immense engineering works undertaken by General Cialdini in his approaches to the fortress, and of the probability of an effective fire being opened early in January. As on a previous occasion, His Majesty was reserved in speaking of the hostile part taken by the French squadron under Admiral de Tinan, but he seemed to be perfectly aware that the inability of acting by sea with the Italian fleet, could only delay, but not in any way prevent, the final capture of the place. The King retired to his private apartments at half-past eight, and the guests immediately left the Palace. It was understood that at ten he made his own dinner in the society of the staff-officers on duty.

December 25.—A fine Christmas day, with wind fresh from the south. I went round the lower deck at noon, and addressed a few words to the men before they sat down to dinner. The messes were neatly decorated, and the tables amply supplied with the best of everything from the shore. The crew were all well, and in high good-humour, for the scourge of small-pox had left, and the general health of the ship's company was now excellent. Liberty for a run on shore for forty-eight hours had been given, and the men had thoroughly enjoyed themselves, without meeting the same obstructions as had been offered during the reign of the Lord High-Admiral, Prince Luigi.

December 26.—The *James Watt*, 91, Captain Codd, arrived to-day, making up my squadron again to six sail of the line.

In the evening there was a grand ball given to His Majesty by the officers of the National Guard. I attended the festive scene, accompanied by the Captains of the squadron, Lieutenant Wilmot, Mr. Shanks, and a few of the officers from each ship. The crowd was enormous, and the rooms of the building in which the *fête* was held being small, dancing was almost impossible, and the crush greater than I remember to have seen in the most orthodox of London squeezes.

When the King arrived, and had mounted the hundred steps which led up to the third storey, on which lay the suite of apartments prepared for the evening's amusement, His Majesty found himself blockaded at the vestibule. At length, by the exercise of verbal persuasion, coupled with the use of a certain amount of gentle force on the part of the managers of the *fête*, a narrow lane was made, along which the monarch marched with giant strides, evidently much amused by the bustle which surrounded him. Arrived at the terminus of his promenade, a small circle was formed around him, and an attempt at a quadrille was immediately commenced.

I had already taken up my position in this quarter with Lady Downshire, Lady Alice Hill, and Mrs. Russell and her daughter, who were amongst the few

English ladies present, but the crush was so great that it became impossible to maintain our ground. I was swept fairly through the doorway by a current of crinolines flowing in that direction, and I had settled in my own mind to make an attempt at escape into the street, when I found Admiral Persano by my side, who told me the King would leave Naples at midnight for Turin by land, and wished to see me before he went. By a series of convulsive struggles, and to the destruction of epaulettes—but which ornaments I still hope will always be maintained in the full-dress uniform of an Admiral—I regained my lost position, and was welcomed by His Majesty with a hearty shake of the hand.

The King told me he should set out for Turin precisely at the hour of midnight, going by the high-road to Ancona, and, travelling night and day, hoped to accomplish the journey in about seventy hours. After making some happy allusions to the excessive heat of the rooms, and to the questionable pleasures of a crowded ball, he spoke again in kind terms of the satisfaction it gave him to observe the British fleet at anchor in the Bay; and as he inquired after the health of the crews, it gave me the opportunity of making known to His Majesty the great benefit we had received from the use of the Nisida Hospital.

He gave me a short account of the enthusiastic reception given to him at Palermo, and spoke of the presence of the *Agamemnon* at anchor in the Bay as adding m.... to the beauty of the naval part of the scene. He finally bade me farewell a little before midnight, and left the room, followed by the minister in attendance and his personal staff. His Majesty immediately got into his travelling carriage, and, escorted by a small body of lancers, set out for the frontier. The government of the Southern Provinces was left in the hands of Farini.

December 31.—Intelligence reached me of the arrival of the King at Turin on the evening of the 29th, having accomplished the journey without accident, in sixty-nine hours.

January 1, 1861.—The new year commences with reactionary plots in Naples and in the provinces. Four general officers are implicated, and have been arrested, and mobs of boys are running about, shouting, "Long live King Francis!" but the National Guard are at their post, and the attempt at disturbance has been suppressed by the firm attitude of this militia. The Cardinal Archbishop Sforza, who had refused to allow the midnight mass, according to annual custom on Christmas Eve, is known to be at work in opposition to the new Government; and his palace has twice been threatened with an attack from the populace. It is strange that this descendant of the renowned family of Sforza, once all powerful in Milan, should be so antagonistic to the national regeneration, when his connection, the Duke Sforza Cesarini, was the first of the Roman nobles who, at the risk of confiscation of his property, and of the loss of his titles, joined the movement of Emancipation twelve years ago, and, though a strict Roman Catholic, became an exile from his patrimony at the triumph of the reaction, rather than submit to the despotism of Papal rule. Probably his Grace, having in early life connected himself by marriage with a young and amiable English lady, imbibed, unconsciously, from her society, the ideas of patriotism and toleration.

The word patriotism reminds me of another English young lady, married to an Italian nobleman, whose acquaintance I had the pleasure to make. I was surprised one morning by a visit from the husband, who told me the Marchioness was on the eve of her confinement, and so great was her love for her native country that she could not be happy unless the child should first see the light of day under the shadow of the English flag; she therefore hoped I would lend her one of the British ensigns from the *Hannibal*, that it might be unfurled and hoisted in her chamber. The sight of this glorious banner she felt sure would give strength and courage in her hour of trial, and infuse into the new-born infant those heroic feelings she so much wished it to possess.

January 2.—To celebrate the new year, Miss Bonham, the sister of the Consul, gave a dance in the evening, which was well attended without being crowded. The rooms of the Consulate are spacious, and all the arrangements were excellent.

January 5.—Having received a telegraphic message, through Mr. Iggulden, from Mr. Elliot, in which he most kindly offered me the use of the fine suite of apartments in the Palazzo Nunziante which he occupied whilst accredited to the late King, I took possession of them to-day with the whole of my retinue.

January 9.—The interchange of the burgher militia is now in operation throughout the provinces, and with excellent effect. The people of a great country, numbering twenty-one millions of inhabitants, speaking the same language, though different in dialect, will now have the opportunity of becoming acquainted with each other, asperities will soften down, good fellowship be engendered, and a mutual confidence inspired. No race of men identical in tongue can be more opposite in moral perception and more antagonistic in feeling than are the Piedmontese and the Neapolitans of the present day; yet who would be bold enough to say that a few years of friendly intercourse may not mitigate this unnatural sentiment, and elevate them in the social scale? The middle and lower classes of the Piedmontese, reserved, manly, cold in temperament, first-rate soldiers, and proudly confident in themselves as citizens of a free and enlightened country, would impress some stamp of their national character on the vain, volatile, and light-hearted Neapolitan, who, degraded in mind by the bondage of the superstition in which he has been educated, could know little either of self-reliance or independence.

What could bespeak more the reproach of a city containing half a million of inhabitants, the great majority of which were known to hold in detestation the tyrannical Government under which they lived, than the fact of scarcely a man joining the liberating army after the Dictator entered the city? At the battle of the Volturno, the Inkerman of the Royal troops, not ten Neapolitan citizens were in the ranks of the patriot forces; whilst from the towns and the mountainous districts of the three Calabrias, fifteen thousand volunteers had marched to the field, determined to fight, through the length of the Peninsula, for the consolidation of the liberty they had at last obtained.

These reflections have been suggested by the arrival this morning of large detachments of the National Guards from Turin and Milan. As a body, they are not so tall as the Neapolitans, but they have a more soldier-like exterior, and marched proudly into the city amidst the cheers of the people.

The *Victor Emanuel*, 91, Captain Clifford, arrived to-day from Malta.

In the evening I attended a ball at the house of Madame Muricoffer, the wife of the Swiss Consul-General, and made the acquaintance of the Piedmontese General Sonnaz, who gave me an interesting description of his march from the Gulf of Manfredonia, through Benevento to the Garigliano.

January 11.—At noon His Royal Highness Prince Carignano arrived in the Sardinian frigate *Victor Emanuel*, escorted by the *Maria Adelaide*, bearing the flag of Vice-Admiral Persano. The squadron under my command, moored in order of sailing in two columns off the lighthouse, dressed with flags, manned yards, and fired a Royal salute. The Sardinian ships passed between the lines under easy speed. His Royal Highness and suite were in full uniform on deck, and whilst the National Sardinian March and Garibaldi's Hymn were played by the bands of the English ships, "God save the Queen" was given by the Italians. After crossing the bows of the English line-of-battle ship *Victor Emanuel*, the Sardinian frigate of the same name lay-to for some minutes, evidently with the intention of giving the Royal Viceroy an opportunity of examining the figure-head of the King, which was executed with much skill and was an admirable likeness.

After landing on the jetty of the arsenal, His Royal Highness proceeded direct to the Palace, and was exceedingly well received by the people. He was accompanied by Signor Nigra, as Minister Secretary of State, a young man of great promise, who had attracted the notice of Count Cavour at his first entrance into public life. His Royal Highness and the Minister appeared together on the balcony of the Palace, and as I was myself present beneath the windows, I can testify to the general remarks of the crowd being highly favourable to the Prince and to his companion. His Royal Highness stands six feet two, with a martial figure and handsome countenance, and is forty-seven years of age. The young Commendatore has scarcely numbered thirty years, is nearly equal in stature, and of comely exterior.

The Prince has been appointed to supersede Signor Farini, whose ill health and family afflictions have compelled him to resign the post of Lieutenant-General of the Southern Provinces.

January 13.—I met Commendatore Nigra at dinner at the house of Mr. Craven, who informed us that an armistice had been concluded at Gaeta until the 19th inst., at the expiration of which date the French fleet would return to Toulon, and further opposition to the blockade of the fortress by the Sardinian ships of war be removed.

January 17.—In the afternoon I had an audience of His Royal Highness Prince Carignano at the Palace. I was accompanied by Captains Farquhar, Clifford, Codd, and Harvey, and the officers of my staff.

His Royal Highness thanked me for the brilliant reception given to him on his arrival by the squadron under my orders, and subsequently gave me a short account of the proceedings of the Sardinian army before Gaeta. The works undertaken by the General of Engineers, Manabrea, seem to have been stupendous, and nearly two hundred guns were now in position. He did not think King Francis would hold out long after the departure of the French fleet, when a close blockade would be instituted, and the ships of war be able to attack from seaward.

I sent the *Mohawk*, Commander Howard, to Gaeta for intelligence.

January 19.—Admiral Persano sailed with the Sardinian squadron for Gaeta, and the French fleet left for Toulon. The Spanish ships of war also returned to Carthagena.

January 20.—I dined to-day with His Royal Highness Prince Carignano, accompanied by the captains of the squadron and my staff. The guests numbered fifty persons, including members of the new ministry, naval and military officers of rank and civilians of note; but neither at this dinner nor at the grand banquet given by the King did I observe a single dignitary of the Church. I was placed next to and on the right hand of the Prince; the Secretary of State, Signor Nigra, on his left. His Royal Highness was very cordial in manner, and spoke confidently of the speedy fall of Gaeta.

January 28.—A grand attack was made against the sea-faces of the fortress of Gaeta on the 22nd by the Sardinian squadron, and from trustworthy sources, I hear that the damage done was immaterial. The ships were manœuvred with skill, under a heavy fire from the batteries, and though they approached within eight hundred yards, the strength of the masonry and earthworks was proof against their heavy metal.

January 31.—Prince Carignano went by land to Mola, to watch the progress of the siege.

February 4.—I made the acquaintance of the Hungarian General, Klapka, to-day, who had arrived from the East. Both his appearance and manner are highly attractive. Admiral Sir Thomas and Lady Cochrane arrived from England in the afternoon.

February 9.—An armistice for forty-eight hours has been demanded by King Francis, and granted by Cialdini. Two explosions had taken place in the fortress, and four hundred soldiers buried beneath the ruins, and great damage done to the works. The accuracy of aim of the Piedmontese gunners, and the precision with which the shells were projected, appear to have destroyed the casemate of the magazines.

Whilst this havoc and destruction is going forward almost within sight of the Capital, the good people of Naples are quietly enjoying the Carnival; but I understand the revelry is tame in comparison with what was customary in other days.

February 13.—I went in the evening to the reception of the Duchess of St. Arpino, whose drawing-rooms are arranged in the best possible taste, and are thrown open every Tuesday to the Neapolitan world. Here the *élite* of the society, both foreign and native, may be met, and the rich toilettes of the aristocracy admired without a crush.

The custom of setting apart special evenings in each week by a few of the principal residents in the city, for a *réunion* of their friends, is a great resource to the casual visitor. I found it most agreeable to have the opportunity of making a few acquaintances, and so to while away a portion of the long evenings, and turn my thoughts occasionally from the professional routine of naval life. At the palaces of Lady Holland, Lady Strahan and Salza, the Countess Nocella, and in the picturesque villa of Miss McClean, I passed many agreeable hours.

Here I became acquainted with Count Poerio, whose health is broken down from the sufferings he underwent during his cruel imprisonment under King Ferdinand.

February 14.—Gaeta surrendered yesterday to Cialdini. The King and Queen of Naples embarked early in the forenoon in the French steamer of war *Mouette*, and proceeded to Terracina, from whence the fugitive monarch and his most gallant young Queen intended making the journey by land to Rome. The intelligence of this event was officially communicated to me by Signor Nigra, and I telegraphed the same immediately to the Admiralty.

When the capture of the fortress became generally known in Naples, the wild rejoicing of the inhabitants was manifested with the same extraordinary enthusiasm as was shown at the first entrance of Garibaldi. The news came late on the evening of

Ash Wednesday, one of the strictest of the fasts in the Roman Catholic Church; but vain were all attempts to arrest the delirium of the inhabitants. Every house was illuminated; and instead of a multitude of penitents, clothed in the garments of sackcloth, a real Carnival was kept, to the horror of the spiritual pastors of this excitable flock.

For some days past there has been a close search amongst the archives of the convents by the Government agents, but no important documents of a political nature have been discovered. The only manuscripts not touching on theological matter were fragments of light correspondence between the monks and the nuns. Many of these effusions were not devoid of poetic merit, but as they spoke of things of this world they were consigned to the flames.

CHAPTER XXVII.

1861.

Naples. — Suppression of Monasteries. — Farewell Dinner of Prince Carignano.—The English Protestant Church.—Refusal of the Grand Cordon of St. Maurice and St. Lazarus.—Departure from Naples.—Arrival at Malta.—Capitulation of Messina.—Termination of the Italian Civil War.—Departure for the Coast of Syria.

February 18.—A decree ordering the suppression of the monasteries was promulgated to-day. It is a lengthy document, but the main features will be seen from the following extract:—

"All monastic orders of both sexes in the Neapolitan Provinces, except such as are hereafter named, shall cease to be recognized, and the property of these corporations shall be administered by the Ecclesiastical Treasury of the State. Chapters of collegiate churches, unless with cure of souls, and simple benefices, chaplaincies, and abbacies, without cure of souls attached, will not be recognized by the law. Pensions will be granted to all of the present inmates, according to a fixed scale."

The number and quality of the monasteries which are to be retained in their present form is not stated in the decree, but it is known that all those establishments which grant instruction to youth, and minister to the wants of the aged and sick, and perform other functions compatible with the progress of the age will be allowed to remain intact.

It is the firm determination of the Constitutional Government that all mendicant friars, and the drones of every denomination, who fatten on the weakness and ignorance of their fellow-men, shall henceforth be totally suppressed; whilst those classes of the brotherhood which are moral and productive shall be proportionately increased. In the age in which we live, the great majority of these institutions are the depôts of sloth and superstition, and their *status* in society is corrupting and noxious. The proposed reforms, when carried out, must be greatly beneficial to the mass of the population; and, as the funds which will accrue to the State from the sale of the convent property, will principally be awarded to increase the stipends of the lower clergy, and to give pensions to dispossessed monks, the measure will probably not be opposed by the middle classes.

A decree has also been published, declaring to be terminated and void of effect the concordat concluded by the late Bourbon Government with the Papal See in February, 1818, together with all other conventions, anterior and posterior, between the expired Government of the Two Sicilies, and the Court of Rome.

February 20.—We had theatricals this evening on board the *Hannibal*, and a large party came from the shore to witness the acting of the seamen. The pieces were well chosen, and the entertainment went off well.

February 26.—Having received orders direct from the Admiralty to proceed with my division to Malta, leaving one ship of the line only at Naples. I waited yesterday on His Royal Highness the Prince of Carignano to take leave.

His Royal Highness expressed great regret at the approaching departure of the English squadron, and honoured me by a communication of his intention to pay me a visit on board the *Hannibal* before my departure.

February 27.—Prince Carignano gave a farewell dinner to the captains of the squadron and myself. In the course of the evening he informed me that the late reactionary movements in the provinces had been suppressed by the National Guards alone, and that in the Abruzzi General Sonnaz had defeated the brigands infesting that region, though they were constantly reinforced by the incursion of the Papal Zouaves, who were equal in acts of atrocity to Mussulman fanatics.

His Royal Highness spoke hopefully relative to affairs in the Roman States, and added that if the

Pope relinquished his temporal power, the King was ready to entertain any propositions having for their object the splendour and accommodation of His Holiness as head of the Roman Catholic Church.

February 28.—The piece of land given by Garibaldi to the English residents at Naples, as a site for the erection of a Protestant Church, and which the Sardinian Government had refused to confirm in consequence of some irregularity in the deed of gift, has at last been settled in a favourable manner. Signor Mancini, the Minister of the Interior, has declared that the English Protestant Church is an existing religious community, a "*culto esistente*," and as such entitled by the laws of Piedmont to recognition and protection. The ground will therefore be granted.

Surely, the English community in Naples owe much to Garibaldi for this spontaneous act of enlightened liberality, and to the Minister for his bold avowal of the right of religious association! Yet there are found men so wedded to the old system of bigoted misrule, that, although themselves members of the reformed faith, they will give no credit to the great Liberator for checking the abuses of superstition, and for laying the first stone of religious toleration in the Southern Peninsula.*

* The first stone of this church was laid, on the 14th of December, 1862, by the Duchess of St. Arpino, an English lady by birth, who, married to a Neapolitan nobleman of high lineage, has steadfastly adhered to the reformed faith.

The great principle is now established that Episcopalians and Protestants of every recognized denomination may hold property for religious purposes, instead, as heretofore, being obliged to perform their church service either at the Consulate or in a private house. One country alone remains in Europe where the demon of intolerance yet stalks triumphantly throughout the land. It is Spain. In that noble nation, the question of the right of private judgment has yet to be solved. No people can be great whilst it remains in abeyance.

March 1.—At eleven this forenoon, the Prince Carignano, accompanied by Signor Nigra, General Della Rocca, the Marquis Cortanza, chief aide-de-camp, Count Bardesono, and other officers of his staff, honoured me with an official visit on board the *Hannibal*. When the barge left the San Lucia steps the ships dressed with flags and the yards were manned; and on His Royal Highness reaching the quarter-deck, the Royal standard of Sardinia was hoisted at the main, and Royal salutes fired from each ship of the line.

The Prince, who is a Vice-Admiral, and has passed many years of his life afloat, went over every part of the vessel; and having signified a desire to see the crew at gun exercise, the drum beat to quarters, and from his position at the foot of the lower-deck ladder he witnessed the clearing for action and three rounds of quick firing with evident delight. The earnestness and rapidity of the work seemed greatly to impress General Della Rocca and his military companions, who more than once found it difficult to secure a safe berth against the rush of the men in shifting the train-tackles.

His Royal Highness returned to the shore at noon, under the same ceremonies as were given to him on his arrival on board.

Later in the afternoon the Marquis Cortanza returned on board, and informed me that he had been commanded by the Prince Carignano to deliver into my hands the first-class insignia or Grand Cordon of the Order of St. Maurice and St. Lazarus, which His Majesty had transmitted from Turin, with directions that it should be presented to me in the name of His Majesty as a token of the estimation in which he held the generous service I had rendered to Italy during the late Revolution.

The Marquis then produced the insignia from his pocket, and was about to place it on the table, when it became my duty to acquaint him that, deeply as I appreciated the high honour which King Victor Emanuel had done me in the bestowal of so magnificent a testimony of his favourable opinion, it was entirely out of my power to accept the decoration without having previously obtained the sanction of Her Most Gracious Majesty.

The Marquis, evidently surprised at the positive nature of my refusal, then pointed out the dilemma in which he would be placed by having to make known a determination so adverse to the expectations which His Majesty would have formed, and he begged me to reconsider the decision I had made. By way of enforcing his argument, he feelingly alluded to the many humane acts which he said I had carried into effect during the bombardment of Palermo, by which the lives of many of our fellow-creatures had been rescued from destruction, and which were hailed with equal thankfulness by the Italians of every party.

In reply I could only state, that although it was true that by stopping the bombardment and arresting the horrors enacted at Palermo I might be deemed to have rendered acceptable service to the people of Italy, yet even these exceptional circumstances would not justify my acceptance of the Order, in opposition to the stringent regulations of the Board of Admiralty. I added, that as the Marquis appeared to think I was taking too strict a view of the instructions which governed the acceptance of foreign Orders, I should be glad if he would ask the opinion of a naval officer of distinction, Admiral Sir Thomas Cochrane, who had lately arrived from England, and was now on board the ship. The Marquis Cortanza gladly availed himself of this proposition, and soon learnt from Sir Thomas Cochrane that my acceptance of the insignia without the Queen's permission was quite out of the question, a decision which was doubly fortified by the opinion of my friend Sir

Henry Martin, who also chanced to be in my cabin at the moment of the visit of the Prince's aide-de-camp.

The envoy next requested to know if the matter could be arranged by diplomatic application through the Italian to the English Goverment, and he was informed by the Admiral that whenever a foreign Sovereign intended to confer an Order upon a British subject, such intention may be notified to Her Majesty's principal Secretary of State for Foreign Affairs, either through the British Minister accredited at the court of such foreign Sovereign or through his Minister accredited at the court of Her Majesty.

This explanation of the state of the case appeared to give satisfaction to the Marquis, who took his leave, after expressing a hope that the intention of the King would now be made known to the English Government through the medium of the Minister at Turin.

At 5 P.M. the *Hannibal* got under weigh, and with the squadron in company, sailed with a light favourable wind for Malta. Excepting an occasional cruize to Castellamare, and to the offing between Ischia and Capri, for the benefit of exercise at sea, I had been nine months at anchor in the Bay, and I had witnessed the commencement and termination of one of the most astonishing revolutions of modern days. So far as depended on the declared will of the nation, the unity of the Peninsula had been accomplished, and the presence of foreign ships of war for the protection of their subjects became no longer necessary. Piedmont, a country small in itself, yet by the excellence of its institutions and the steady development of its internal resources, strong and respected abroad, had now fairly assumed the responsibilities of government. Let us hope it may continue to exercise both moderation and justice in the difficult task of reconciling provincial rivalries, and allaying the antagonism of hostile parties! A powerful Italian kingdom, containing twenty-two millions of inhabitants, may then be established and take its station in history amongst the great nations of Europe.

March 2.—Squadron under all sail, steering for the Straits of Messina. In the afternoon I spoke the *Exmouth*, 91, Captain Paynter, bound to Naples, who gave me a duplicate of a despatch from Vice-Admiral Martin, directing me to hold myself in readiness to proceed to Beyrout so soon as the *Hannibal* should have completed her necessary refit at Malta.

March 3.—The *Hannibal*, *Victor Emanuel*, *Cressy*, *James Watt*, and *Mohawk*, entered the Faro this afternoon, and stood off and on for two hours at the entrance of the port of Messina.

I communicated with Vice-Admiral Persano, and learnt from him that the fortress was closely besieged by sea and land, and would be summoned by Cialdini to surrender in a few days. Having ordered Captain Clifford, in the *Victor Emanuel*, to anchor off the town, I proceeded under sail with the rest of the ships, to the southward.

March 4.—This afternoon the squadron stood close in to Syracuse, and after procuring fresh provisions from the bumboats, bore up for Cape Passaro.

On entering the channel of Malta, we found a fresh gale blowing from the westward, and a considerable sea running. The sails were furled, steam got up, and before midnight, under full pressure, with fires under the four boilers, we were making seven knots on our course, and taking in the water fore and aft, in a manner picturesque but not agreeable. Sir Thomas and Lady Cochrane had given me the pleasure of their society during this short cruize; and I must do her ladyship the justice to say that she proved herself an admirable sailor.

March 5.—The *Hannibal* took in her moorings in the harbour of Valetta, and commenced refitting. I found here the Commander-in-chief, with his flag in the *Cæsar;* also the ships of the line *Algiers, Neptune,* and *Mars.*

March 9.—I paid a visit, with Sir Victor Houlton, the Colonial Secretary, to the oldest of the Italian patriots, Ruggiero Septimo, now in his eighty-fourth year. He had been invited by Cavour to take the post of Viceroy in Sicily, but wisely declined on account of his age.

In the afternoon I visited the different Government works now in progress, and also those which had been completed during the last year. I found a marked improvement in many parts of the city. The new market-place, the covered ways, the ornamental walks, the terrace and evergreens in front of St. John's Cathedral, and many handsome buildings erected at Floriana, were all real improvements, and were felt to be so by the Maltese, who owe much to the energy of their present governor, Sir Gaspard le Marchant.

March 13.—The citadel of Messina capitulated to-day to the Sardinian forces under Cialdini, after a few hours' bombardment. This terminates the Italian Civil War.

March 21.—Intelligence was received to-day that King Victor Emanuel had been proclaimed, by the Parliament assembled at Turin, King of Italy.

March 23.—The melancholy intelligence of the death of Her Royal Highness the Duchess of Kent reached Malta this forenoon. The Royal standard was immediately hoisted half-mast at the Palace, and the ensigns half-mast at the gaff-ends of the ships of war. This tribute of national grief will be continued for three days.

March 28.—The refit of the *Hannibal* was completed yesterday, and to-day I sailed for the coast of Syria, in company with the *James Watt*, Captain Codd.

The state of affairs in this quarter had become more and more complicated, owing to the impossibility of combining such measures for the pacification of the Lebanon as would be satisfactory to the rival factions of Druse, Maronite, and Mussulman, and prevent the renewal of the massacres of last year.

The Commissioners of the five Powers, England, France, Austria, Russia, and Prussia, had been indefatigable for many months in their efforts to solve the question as to what measures should be adopted to insure protection to the several denominations of Christians, after the departure of the French troops.

The 5th of June was the day fixed by convention for the complete evacuation of the country. Two months only remained, and as yet nothing had been settled. A prolongation of the foreign occupation was to be avoided, as trenching on the independence of the Porte; but, on the other hand, to leave the Christian communities to the mercy of the fanatical Druse and Mahomedan would be impossible. Under these difficulties it seems to have been decided that powerful squadrons of England, France, and Russia should be despatched forthwith to the coast of Syria, in order that they might be ready to act as a combined European force for the safety of their co-religionists when the French army quitted the country in accordance with the treaty. I was selected by the Lords Commissioners of the Admiralty to take a division of the Mediterranean fleet under my command for the execution of this service; and as the orders came by telegraphic message, it is probable the Government are anxious that the English flag shall appear in force in the extreme East with the least possible delay.

The crisis of the Syrian question is evidently at hand. For me it will be a field even more complicated than that which I have just passed over amidst the whirlwind of revolution, but the interest will be infinitely less.

CHAPTER XXVIII.

1861.

Arrival at Beyrout.—Lord Dufferin.—Visit to Jerusalem.—Sureya Pacha.—Excursion to the Lebanon.—Accident on the Journey.—Fuad Pacha.—Departure of the French Army.—Death of the Sultan.—Great Augmentation of the Fleets of France, Russia, and England.—Leave of Absence from Ill Health.—The Syrian Question Settled.

October 1.—The title-page of this work shews that I proposed to myself the task of submitting to the public an authentic account of such events as I thought might be interesting relative to the rise, progress, and completion of the great Italian Revolution; which fell more immediately under my own observation. That task having been fulfilled, I will now pass rapidly over the events which have occurred during the last six months, whilst I have commanded the N or Second Division of the Fleet in the extreme eastern sea of the Mediterranean.

I arrived at Beyrout on the 10th of April, and immediately placed myself in communication with Lord Dufferin, Her Majesty's Commissioner for the settlement of the affairs of the Lebanon, from whom I learnt that the labours of the Commission would not be completed for several weeks.

The French army of seven thousand men were at this time in possession of a few strategic points between the coast and Damascus, and, in conjunction with the Turkish forces, kept the peace of the country. The French and Russian squadrons had not yet arrived.

Having announced to Lord Dufferin my intention of proceeding forthwith to Jerusalem if he saw no official objection, I received in reply an opinion favourable to the undertaking. I therefore sailed immediately for Jaffa, and on the 16th started for the Holy City, in company with Mr. Finn, Her Majesty's Consul, Mrs. Finn, Captain Farquhar, and a party of wardroom and gunroom officers, numbering from twenty-five to thirty persons.

No British admiral had ever visited Jerusalem before, and as I considered the opportunity should not be lost of showing ourselves in some state to the Turkish authorities and to the inhabitants, I gave directions that uniforms should be carried up and always worn within the city walls.

Three miles outside the gate of Hebron I was met by a cavalry guard of honour, sent by the Pacha to escort me into the city, and on my alighting at the hotel on Mount Zion, sentries were posted at the door of my apartments, and dragomans and cavasses appointed for my service.

On the following day I paid a state visit to Sureya Pacha, the Governor of the province, with the whole of the officers in attendance; and as our large cavalcade, all mounted and in uniform, passed through the crowded streets, the greatest respect and good-will was shown towards us by the population—Jew, Mussulman, and Christian. The Pacha, who is a well-bred and good-looking young man, received us with much courtesy. He knew mine was in all respects a friendly visit, and he was, therefore, really glad to see us.

He did not fail to impress upon me how sensibly he felt the friendly sentiments of England towards the Sublime Porte, and how excellent were his relations with Mr. Finn; and he took pride to himself for the effective protection he had afforded to the Christian community of his districts during the terrible massacres in Syria.

His Excellency returned my visit the next day in great state, and issued the necessary firman granting permission for the English officers to enter the sacred precincts of the Mosque of Omar and site of the Temple.

Of the city of Jerusalem I will only say that its general appearance and the activity of the inhabitants far exceeded any ideas I had previously formed. All the great religious denominations—Jews, Greeks, Latins, Armenians, and Protestants—are in earnest at their work; but the orthodox Greek Church, under the protectorate of Russia, is master of the position. That colossal Power has lately acquired a spacious territory on the high ground close to the Hebron or Jaffa gate, which completely commands the ancient Jewish capital, and on which gigantic works are already commenced, destined to be the envy of the Latins and the dread of the Turks.

On the 23rd I returned to Jaffa, sleeping one night on the road, and performing the whole journey on horseback in fourteen hours, under a burning sun and sirocco wind.

On the 27th of April I sailed from Jaffa with the intention of calling in at Kaiffa, to pay my respects to Lady Dufferin, who was encamped on Mount Carmel; but as I was approaching the anchorage the *Hannibal* was disabled as a steamer by the breaking of the way-shaft of the air-pump, and I made sail for Beyrout to make good the defect.

On the 3rd of May Lord Dufferin came on board the *Hannibal*, and was saluted on leaving the ship with fifteen guns, as Royal Commissioner.

On the 7th I accepted an invitation from his Lordship to accompany him into the mountains of Lebanon, to visit a few of the chief settlements of the Druses and Christians. The party consisted of the Royal Commissioner, Mr. Wood, Consul-General at Tunis, Mr. Rogers, Consul at Damascus, Doctor Pincoffs, and Mr. Kennedy. Starting early in the morning, we reached Deir-el-Kamar after a ride of seven hours, and visited the court-yard, where six hundred Christians had been massacred last year by the Druses. From thence we journeyed to the Palace of Bteddin, built by the renowned Emir Bashir, and now garrisoned by French troops. At six in the evening we brought up for the night at the modern Palace of Moctarah, the princely residence of the imprisoned Druse chieftain, Said Bek Jumbat, now occupied by an Ottoman force under Omer Pacha, who gave us a real welcome and a fair dinner.

In the forenoon of the following day we set out for the Christian village of Gessin. At a narrow pass on the summit of one of the highest ranges of the mountains, my horse and the one on which Doctor Pincoffs was mounted engaged in furious combat, which terminated by my receiving a serious kick on my left knee, which obliged me to return at once to Moctarah. Doctor Pincoffs dressed my wound with much skill, and brought me safely the next evening to Lord Dufferin's house at Beyrout, where I received every attention, and in a fortnight was able to walk.

On the 11th Lord Dufferin and suite and Lady Dufferin embarked on board the *Melpomene*, Captain Ewart, for Constantinople; the Commissioners of France, Austria, Russia, and Prussia having sailed on the preceding day for the same destination in a French steamer of war. His Lordship, with much consideration, placed the spacious house which he had occupied at my disposal, and at the end of the month

I took up my quarters permanently on shore, where I was joined by Colonel Fraser, an energetic officer employed on special service by Her Majesty's Government.

On the 22nd I paid an official visit to Fuad Pacha, who informed me that he had a well-disciplined army of twenty thousand men under his orders, and that after the departure of the European force he hoped to be able to keep the country quiet. He spoke French with fluency, and seemed to be quite the man for the crisis which was at hand.

On the 29th and 30th of May, the French fleet, under the command of my old acquaintance at Naples, Vice-Admiral de Tinan, arrived; Rear-Admiral Paris being the second in command.

The French ships had performed the same feat of passing Malta unobserved as had been previously done in the year 1859, when bound up the Adriatic. One division, skirting the shores of Sicily, took the northern route, touching at Marmorice for water and coals; the other, keeping well to the southward of the Island, called at Alexandria; and the whole of the vessels, screw and paddle, twenty-two in number, reached Beyrout on the appointed day of rendezvous and only nine days from Toulon. The transports immediately commenced receiving the troops, and the whole of them had embarked and sailed to the westward on the 8th of June, three days after the date arranged at the Convention of Paris.

On the day after the departure of the French army two Turkish soldiers of the garrison of Deir-el-Kamar suddenly overpowered a young Maronite girl, as she was drawing water from a fountain in a secluded spot, and effected her ruin. The men were discovered, tried by court-martial, convicted, and immediately shot by order of Fuad Pacha. This is probably the first instance in Mahomedan history of such prompt retribution for the committal of a crime of that nature against a Christian woman.

On the 1st of July we heard of the death of the Sultan, and that his brother Abdul Azzis, aged 31, had ascended the throne. In Turkey, the Sultan is supposed never to die. There are no public ceremonials of grief. An hour after the intelligence arrived from Constantinople the forts and ships saluted in honour of the new sovereign. During the months of July and August, the English, French, Russian, and Turkish squadrons had been greatly augmented. The *Bretagne, Algesiras, Redoubtable, Eylau, Impérial,* and *Fontenoy,* ships of the line, with five smaller steam-ships of war, were under the orders of Vice-Admiral de Tinan. The *Grand Admiral, Mouramez, Gromaboi, Oleg,* all remarkably fine screw frigates, the former carrying 71 guns, and two small vessels, were under the Russian Rear-Admiral, Shestakoff, an officer universally respected, and with whom I had maintained the most friendly relations. The *Cadia,* ship of the line, and three frigates and corvettes, under the Turkish Admiral, Mustapha Pacha.

The squadron under my own command had also been increased to six sail of the line, two frigates, and two despatch gun-vessels, and comprised the following ships, the excess of number being reliefs:—The *Hannibal, Renown, Queen, Agamemnon, Orion, Algiers, Cæsar, Mars*, ships of the line, with the frigates and smaller vessels, *Melpomene, Terrible, Racoon, Amphion, Greyhound, Alacrity, Foxhound, Lapwing*, and *Firefly*. Never, at any period of her history, had Beyrout or the coast of Syria witnessed so imposing a naval force, or the Christian inhabitants of all denominations been so sure of effective succour in case of need.

Daoùd Pacha, an Armenian Catholic Christian, married to an English lady, had assumed the government of the Lebanon, and had taken up his residence at Deir-el-Kamar. He speaks English well, and was hopeful of success in his mission of keeping the peace between Druse and Maronite.

Having visited in my flag-ship the principal ports on the coast of Syria: Jaffa, Kaiffa, Tyre, Sidon, Tripoli, Latakia, Ayas, and Alexandretta, in the Gulf of Scanderoon, and also Larnaka, in the Island of Cyprus, I returned to Beyrout at the end of September. For the last six weeks my health had been gradually failing, from low fever and general debility, and coming so immediately after the attack of small-pox contracted at Naples, I found myself compelled to apply to the Commander-in-chief for permission to quit the station.

Vice-Admiral Sir William Martin, with great kindness, took upon himself the responsibility of granting me authority to proceed to Corfu, and their lordships were subsequently good enough to accord me two months' leave of absence to enable me to go forward to England.

The Syrian question was now definitively settled, and its happy solution is mainly traceable to the untiring energy, tact, and ability of the British Commissioner, Lord Dufferin. The French and Russian squadrons were to leave the coast in ten days, and only a few of the smaller English ships of war would remain to give support to Her Majesty's Consul General, Mr. Moore, and confidence to the British residents.

During the five months passed on the coast, I had despatched the whole of the vessels under my command in rotation to the roadstead of Jaffa, in order to give the captains and officers an opportunity of visiting Jerusalem. Upwards of three hundred officers of all ranks availed themselves of this happy chance. To them it was a great recreation, and to me a satisfaction, inasmuch as I knew the appearance of the British uniform in the Holy City was welcomed by the people, and gave a wholesome influence to consular authority.

On the 30th of September I sailed for Malta, leaving Captain Mason, of the *Cœsar*, in command of the station. As the *Hannibal* steamed between the columns of the fleet, the rigging of each ship was manned, with the intention of bidding me farewell by a salute from the lungs of three thousand seamen; but as I greatly objected to the compliment, I hoisted the letters D. G. P. at the peak, which being interpreted signifies "Annul cheering."

I took leave of Admiral de Tinan on the previous day. We had been associated together during the progress and completion of the Italian Revolution, and during the progress and completion of the Syrian complications. He had had an opportunity of closely scrutinizing ten out of the fifteen sail of the line of which the English Mediterranean fleet was at one time composed, and I had the same means of judging of an equal number of French ships which passed under my own review. The result of my observations, after eight months of conjunction, will be given in the following short chapter.

CHAPTER XXIX.

1861.

Efficiency of the French Navy.—Comparison with English Ships and Seamen.—Serious Illness.—Return to England.

FROM the general acquirements of the officers, the uniformity of the system of discipline, and the perfection of detail in every branch of organization, it may be broadly admitted that the French navy ranks in efficiency amongst the first of the maritime Powers of the world.

The ships are well-built and carefully finished in the minutest details of shipwright and joiners' work, but the strength of the frame and scantling are inferior to the English. This fact I had ascertained during visits which I made to the arsenals of Cherbourg, Brest, L'Orient, Rochefort, and Toulon some years ago, and has been confirmed by information subsequently received.

The form of the stern and counter give great protection to the rudder, a very small part of the head of which is seen above water, and this part is encased in iron; whilst the narrowness of the aperture for the reception of the propeller, which is double-bladed, and in most cases a fixture, affords stability to the after-part of the vessel. This principle of construction undoubtedly gives the French ships of the line advantages over those of other nations in the grand essential of security to the rudder. It may be said, on the other hand, that the screw being a fixture must impede the sailing qualities. This, to a certain extent, is true, though, from the form of the blades of the double screw, and their little hold on the water, it does not appear to be material; and even were it so, the speed under sail alone is of no moment when placed in comparison with so vital a point as the protection of the steering apparatus.

The fine Russian frigates, the sailing and steaming qualities of which are admirable, expose an area of rudder projecting above the water-line that would insure its destruction in the event of being struck by raking or even by broadside shot; and the English ships, though in a smaller degree, have the same manifest defect.

The similarity of build in the French ships, and their stability or steadiness in a seaway, is remarkable. During the westerly gales experienced in the open roadstead off Beyrout, which brought in a heavy swell, the ships of the French fleet were comparatively steady, rolling four or five degrees each way, whilst many of the English vessels rolled from sixteen to twenty degrees. The *Renown* and *Agamemnon* were, however, exceptions; and I do not think there is a ship of her class in the navy of any other nation equal in all respects to the first-named vessel; with her may also be named the *Donegal*, the late *Conqueror*, *Gibraltar*, and *Duncan*.

The steam department and machinery in the French ships of war are now in a fair state of efficiency. The engines are constructed in France, but are not equal in manufacture to those made in England or in America.

Rear-Admiral Paris, the second in command of the French fleet, who is one of the first steam officers of their navy, spent several hours in the engine-room of the *Hannibal* and other English ships of the line, and, speaking English well, astonished the chief engineers by his knowledge of every branch of their profession, both theoretical and practical. Indeed, he seemed to take so deep an interest in the minutest details of our steam machinery, and made himself personally so agreeable to our engineer officers, that I proposed they should pay a return visit to the engine-rooms of the French ships, which many of them did; and the report which I received confirmed the statement of their own officers, that neither the workmanship nor the general arrangements were equal to those fitted in the English ships.

Of the iron-clad ships of the French Imperial Navy I can give no report. I did not fall in with any of them during my service in the Mediterranean, and I wish only to write of that which I have seen and known from personal observation and practical experience. The mere repetition of second-hand remarks or conjectural suppositions can have no practical value, whilst a simple declaration of well-ascertained facts, if it lead to no good result, may be deemed worthy of consideration.

The boats in the French ships, from the first launch to the dingy, demand special notice for their serviceable qualities and excellent fittings. They are all rigged on an uniform plan, namely the dipping lug. The fore and main dip, the mizen is standing. The masts are short, and the yards long, the great advantage being that in any weather they can handle these spars with the greatest ease, whilst the usual rig of an English man-of-war's boat is so unwieldy that in the large boats with the least motion the masts are difficult to manage.

I know it will be advanced, in opposition to this statement, that the rig of the boats of a British ship of war is dependent on the guns they have to carry, and that, as long as the armament is made the paramount consideration, the rig must be more or less sacrificed; but, it must be remembered, the large French boats are also fitted to carry a gun, and the object of these remarks is to call attention more especially to their superiority in workmanship and general equipment.

With the single exception of the launches, which are heavy and unwieldy, the French boats are, in my opinion, better adapted for general service than the English boats, and the fittings in *all* are certainly superior. Under all circumstances, I regret to say, they appeared to have the advantage, in pulling and sailing, over the boats of the English vessels; and I have seen them beat off to their ships, both at Naples and at Beyrout, in weather which our pinnaces and barges could not possibly face.

The duty on board a French ship of war is now carried on in perfect silence, and scarcely any sound is heard but the perpetual whistle of the boatswain and his mates, the latter of whom are more numerous than with us. The chief petty officers, under the head of "*quartiers maîtres*" and "*premiers maîtres,*" of every department, are in fact the leading men, and are practically responsible for the correct and rapid performance of every manœuvre. They appear to be a first-class body of men, and have great advantages offered to retain them in the service. These leading men are decidedly superior to our petty officers, so far as self-respect and discipline are concerned. They keep entirely separate from the crew, who treat them with almost as much respect as they do their officers.

It is not, however, to be expected that this same deference can be exacted from the English seamen. The innate difference of the habits, and the education of the men, forbid it; but there can be no reason why the position and character of the petty officer should not be elevated, and the same respect paid to him by the seamen as by the private soldier to the non-commissioned officer. In late years there has certainly been an improvement in this branch of what the French term "l'organisation du personnel;" but there is still room for a better system as regards the status of the working petty officer and the police force of the ship.

During the year 1860, on the coast of Italy, the French fleet divided their general exercise in equal proportions between making and shortening sail, shifting spars, and other duties of that nature, and the general exercise at great guns; but this year on the coast of Syria the exercise aloft was curtailed, and the general gunnery practice proportionately extended. This change took place from having at last made the discovery that perfection in gunnery was of far more importance than swiftness in the evolution of shifting topsail yards or crossing royal yards from top-gallant masts on deck, the former of which manœuvres, by their harbour appliances and long lifts and braces, was usually enacted in twelve or thirteen minutes, and the latter in a minute and a half; a performance which, though interesting to watch, yet, as it did not involve any question of real seamanship, I considered by no means desirable to imitate.

I observed a marked improvement in the French

gunnery exercise in the second year of the meeting of the two squadrons. The men worked the guns in real good form, and the rapidity with which they moved them from extreme train to the right to extreme train to the left by the tackles alone, without the aid of handspikes, could not be surpassed. The system of trained gunners is carried to the highest point in the French navy. They are termed "*matelots cannoniers brevetés,*" and though divided into three classes, each man is in reality capable of undertaking the duties of *chef de pièce,* or captain of the gun, and three of these men are always apportioned to each gun. The exercise is conducted by the tap of the drum, which is found to answer well, both in calling attention to the drill and in the execution of the work. Of the state of efficiency of their target practice I am unable to speak. The French Admiral never gave us an opportunity of witnessing it, as he invariably sent his ships to sea for the purpose of firing with the great guns at a mark. Their rifle practice, from the picked body of men taught the exercise at the port of L'Orient, under officers instructed at Vincennes, and of whom I have already spoken as the *Marins Fusiliers,* was good both at the short, medium, and long range.

Nine or ten thousand French seamen having been constantly under my review for so long a period, it may be expected that I should say a few words respecting their condition. They are wiry, active, and easily amenable both to instruction and discipline; but they are a less muscular, and certainly a smaller race than the seamen of the British Islands, and are not so cleanly either in their persons or in their dress.

I do not now speak of their appearance at muster on Sundays or holidays, but when in their ordinary working dress, both on board and in the boats. On this particular head, I have been surprised that more pains has not been taken with a view to improvement, for the ships are beautifully clean in every part, and the boats are perfection. The costume of the French sailor is an exact copy of ours in every respect, but they cannot successfully imitate the style of the hat, the cut of the trousers, or the gait of the real seaman.

They are not volunteers, but are drawn by ballot, and are obliged to serve for seven years, after which period they are free, and can demand their discharge. Very few of these conscripts voluntarily remain, and when their time of service has expired on a distant station, this regulation causes great embarrassment to the captain and officers. Generally speaking, they dislike the service, and consequently rarely make the Imperial Navy their profession from choice.

It is strange to observe the difference, when evening has set in, between the habits of the seamen of the two nations. In the English ships the ports are left open, each mess is lighted up, singing is heard, and dancing and merriment go forward till the time for piping-down at the hour of half-past nine. In the French ships all is gloomy darkness; the ports are all closed, not a lantern is visible, nor is the sound of amusement heard. Their day's work is over, the air of night is supposed to be deleterious, and they rest from their labour. Yet the reason of this difference is obvious; the lower deck of the English ship of war is the home of the seaman; the lower deck of the French ship of the line is at the best a temporary barracks. The former has voluntarily chosen the Royal Navy as a profession for life, the latter is earnestly looking forward to the day of his release.

Comment on the above facts is unnecessary. In the two principal elements of naval greatness, the manufacture of the motive power, and the physical capabilities of the crews, there can be no doubt as to where the superiority rests.

Why, then, should there be inferiority on minor, yet still important, heads? This is a natural demand; but it is beyond my province to make a reply.

The admirals, captains, and other officers in active service afloat in the French navy are all comparatively young in their respective ranks. A vice-admiral is placed in retirement at *sixty-five* years of age, and a rear-admiral at *sixty-two*: the captains and junior officers following the same law on a graduated scale, by which means a steady flow of promotion is certain through every grade.

The compulsory removal from the active list at a fixed age is considered one of the main elements for securing advancement in the profession, and it is rigidly enforced to a day by the Minister of Marine.

This system, where existing interests are fairly respected, is highly conducive to the efficiency of the service, but it could never give general satisfaction to the officers of the British navy, nor could it be justly carried out unless flag-officers, captains, commanders, and lieutenants were all made impartially subject to the regulations of the scheme.

I hold it then to be advisable for the well-being and content of the Royal Navy, that some statesmanlike measure, having for its base the principle of retirement from active service afloat at a fixed age, in all ranks, should be introduced by those having authority in these matters; and the sooner this long-pending and irritating question is settled the more acceptable it will be to the Service at large.

On the 7th of October the *Hannibal* anchored in the grand harbour of Malta, when, acting under the advice of Doctor Webb, senior surgeon of the ship, I availed myself of the leave of absence granted by the

Lords Commissioners of the Admiralty, and proceeded to Marseilles in the Peninsular mail steam-packet *Sultan*, and, passing through France, reached London on the 28th of the same month.

The state of my health, from the effect of Syrian Fever, was at this period alarming, and had it not been for the unremitting attention of my secretary, who accompanied me to England, I could not have performed the journey without great increase of danger.

Finding myself at the close of the year still unfit for active service, I sent in my resignation to the Admiralty, which was accepted by their Lordships. The *Hannibal*, at the same date, had arrived at Portsmouth from the Mediterranean, and was immediately paid off. The ship had been two years and eight months in commission. She had carried my flag in the Straits of Gibraltar at the termination of the Spanish-Morocco war; off Naples at the termination of the Italian war, and at Beyrout at the termination of the Syrian difficulties. These were the three absorbing foreign questions of the years 1859, 1860, and 1861, and since their solution complete calm has reigned in the Mediterranean.

I am glad of the opportunity, before closing my journal, of publicly recording my sense of the unremitting exertions exhibited on all occasions by Captain Farquhar for the benefit of the service; and to the officers of the ship in general I feel indebted for their uniform support and strict attention to their duty.

To the captains in command of those ships which formed the second division of the fleet, and who at various periods were under my immediate orders, I also bid farewell, with every wish for their future prosperity, and with many thanks for the valuable assistance which they at all times afforded me with such hearty good-will.

THE END.